# UNCONTROLLABLE

*The Nature of Grace — Book 2*

**by S.R. Johannes**

*Coleman & Stott*

Uncontrollable: The Nature of Grace series, Book 2
Copyright © S.R. Johannes, 2012
www.srjohannes.com

This book is a work of fiction. Names, characters, places, and incidents are products of the author's imagination or are used fictitiously.

*Cover model: Leilani Jade Flannagin*
Cover photograph/copyright by Vania Stoyanova VLC Photo © 2012
Design and typography by GraphicCat.com

ISBN: 978-0-9847991-4-5

*Dedication*

*To my husband and soul mate,*
*who always believed I could create beautiful things.*

# Praises for Series

"Grace is a spunky, independent nature girl who doesn't need a boy to save her. With wilderness survival, a juicy love triangle, and more twists and turns than a roller coaster, this fast-paced novel had me holding my breath until the very last page—and still begging for more!"
**-Kimberly Derting, author of *The Body Finder* series**

"This thrilling story is a dramatic entanglement of mystery, deception, and teen romance. The action flows like a brisk mountain stream interspersed with rapids, holding suspense to the last page."
**- Kirkus Reviews**

"Johannes has done a marvelous job of creating a suspense-filled mystery with surprises that keep you guessing all the way to the end. *Untraceable* is a thoroughly engrossing and riveting page-turner."
**- IndieReader**

"*Untraceable* takes readers on a thrill-ride through a beautiful forest full of dangerous creatures. Grace deals with more than her fair share of tensions and surprises as she works to uncover the mystery behind her father's disappearance." **- Confessions of a Bookaholic**

"It was high-speed, non-stop action/thriller. Any book that has you biting your nails in the first two pages is a definite winner for me."
**- Reading Teen**

"A thrilling murder mystery set deep in the heart of North Carolina's Smoky Mountains, *Untraceable* is a suspenseful page-turner loaded with plot twists, action, and a swoon-worthy romance." **- Mundie Moms**

"Can I just say this book left me going O.M.GAHH! Where to start? *Untraceable* is a non-stop thrilling ride! You have mystery, blurred lines of who is good and who is bad, animals, totally guy hotness *with accent*

...You have a steamy love triangle and one Kick-Butt, do things for herself, strong-willed girl that is Grace. - **SupaGurlBooks**

This book was abso-bloody-lutely amazing and like nothing I've read before. - **Step into Fiction (a.k.a. Fictional Distraction)**

"This book made me feel so many different emotions in a short amount of time. S.R. Johannes definitely made it impossible for me not to love Grace's story. I can't even explain how much I enjoyed reading *Untraceable*. It captivated me until the very end, and I cannot wait to read the next book." - **The Readiacs**

"Chilling, shocking, and horrifying are the three words that come to mind when Grace finally gets to the bottom of what's going on with her dad's disappearance. Some mystery novels are amazing with the build-up of clues and suspense, only to falter anti-climatically in the revelation. *Untraceable* has no such problem." -**Refracted Light Reviews**

"*Untraceable* has a great ending. I enjoyed the book but loved the ending." - **I'm a Reader, Not a Writer**

"Overall, an amazing thrill-ride with real, three-dimensional characters that will have you sitting on the edge of your seat to find out what happens next." - **YA Bound**

"I don't know where to start or how to describe this book. It has a mixture of everything from mystery, to investigation, to romance, to murder making this book a fantastic read. Grace reminds me a lot of Veronica Mars, who will stop at nothing to learn the real truth behind her father's disappearance." - **Once Upon a Twilight**

A fast-paced thriller, full of interesting characters, and a never ending supply of unexpected turns. As Grace's investigation pulls her deeper in to a much larger web of lies and corruption, the intensity rises and just when you (and Grace) think you have it all figured out, Bam! you get side-swiped with a new twist. - **Teens Read and Write**

# Preface

*Until one has loved an animal, a part of one's soul remains unawakened.*

*H*ello...

The word flashes on my computer screen in time to the seconds ticking away on Mom's old clock. *Hello. Hello. Hello.* I stare at it as if I've never seen it before.

Stupid spammers. When will they realize pop-ups never work? No, I don't need a date nor do I want to give you any money for your imaginary hardships. And if I did, I certainly would not send money to an online creepy person.

Ignoring the message, I close the window and finish reading the news article on the Red Wolf Recovery Program.

> **Another Endangered Red Wolf Found Dead on Conservation Land**
>
> Agent Sweeney of the U.S. Fish and Wildlife Service was quoted as saying, "At this time, we think the deaths were due to natural causes or possibly some kind of accident. I assure you, if I find out this was intentional, I will arrest whoever is responsible for these acts against nature and against wolves."

1

I sit back and sigh, still staring at the type on the screen. Four wolves dead. Two found by me; the other two located by the second team. All in different locations.

At first glance, it appears to be natural causes, yet Agent Sweeney seems to think otherwise. Even though there's absolutely no proof, could he be right? After all, being a USFWS agent has blessed him with killer instincts. Then again, why would anyone harm these gorgeous creatures on purpose? And more importantly, who?

Al Smith's sneering face flickers across my mind, and scenes play out in my head. How the poacher attacked me. How his knife gleamed in the dim light. And that awful moment when he shattered my family forever. I hear myself gasp, and my chest tightens as I remember how Dad saved my life.

And lost his own.

I shake the haunting images from my brain before they consume me again. If I let myself slide down that path to despair, I'm afraid I'll never find my way back. Refocusing, I enter the rest of my observation notes from my field research into the database. My fingers skip over the keys so fast they leave behind a trail of typos.

Agent Sweeney is going to freak out when he sees my latest project entry. Because this time, the wolf I'm documenting – or the *Rufus canus* as Dad would call it – was alive!

I scan through my scribble-scrabble to ensure I've logged in all the necessary stats on what I observed:

*Healthy male, about seventy pounds, approximately twenty-six inches at the shoulder and four feet long from nose to tail. Presumed to be the alpha male.*

I note the unique markings:

*Four white paws and white circles around both of his eyes (kind of like a mask).*

In the Extra Findings section, I jot down the name I awarded him: *Bandit.*

Not many people would find that part very interesting, and it's hardly scientific. But it's a way for me to remember the wolf in case I ever see him again – should I be so lucky.

When I get to the Location field, I stop and stare at the coordinates I logged, indicating the exact place where I saw the wolf pack.

If Sweeney is right and someone is hurting these animals on purpose, maybe I shouldn't enter this part. I skip over the fields and submit my report, knowing I can always add in extra data later.

Just then, another message pops up on my screen.

*I see you...*

I shake my head in disgust. Stupid online pervs. It's the one thing I hate most about using computers – creepy lurkers and cyberbullies. At least when weirdoes troll around my woods, their tracks give them away. I see them, and they don't even know I'm there. Online, freaks can hide anywhere – behind pixels, on social networks, or as characters in video games.

They're practically untraceable.

I quickly type *jerk,* and punch the ENTER key with my index finger – just to make a point – before closing the window again. A few seconds later, a single word fills my screen in extra-large font.

*...Grace*

I freeze. It's as if this person can see me through the thin screen. I don't dare move, suddenly feeling totally exposed like a naked mole rat trapped in the bright morning sun. My breath catches in my throat, and I slam the laptop shut – as if that makes everything go away.

I push back from the table and sit still. No matter how hard I try to control my thoughts, a bad feeling churns in my belly. I glance around the room lit only by a dim lamp and wish Mom was back from her trip to Asheville.

Most kids my age would love having a parent MIA. Not me. Not now. Having my grandmother Birdee here is nice, but deep down I just want Mom. After all, it's only been a few months since Al attacked me; a measly one hundred and twenty-one days since I saw Mo, my first love, for the very last time. Not to mention, I'm still reeling from the loss of Dad.

It's something I'm still not sure I can ever get over. The guilt hangs on me like Mom's homemade quilt, cloaking me in shame and sadness. I sigh and wipe my eyes when I realize I'm crying again.

Maybe I'm being paranoid. Understandable after everything that's happened. I glance out the window past the snow-covered driveway. Through the fogged panes, I scan the spindly trees for any sign of movement. The wind moans through the mountainous winter scene. It's just as deserted as always. No doubt about it, I'm alone.

I stare back at the screen and frown. Why am I letting some backwoods redneck who's long gone by now and some crazy cyber creep freak me out? They're not worth my energy or time.

*Come on, Grace, shake it off.*

I roll my neck to try and release the tension. Maybe Mom can snap me out of this funk.

I pick up my cell phone and notice the missed calls. My hands tremble as I dial, causing me to punch in a few wrong numbers. After a couple failed attempts, the phone starts to ring. I tap my fingers as I wait for someone to answer.

Finally, a gruff voice pops into my ear. "Hello?"

"It's me," I say. "I saw you called."

"Thought we could talk. Don't like the way we left things."

I clear my throat and peer out the window again. It'd be nice not to be alone tonight. "Sure."

Wyn's voice seeps through the line. "Give me twenty minutes."

I peek one more time through the flimsy fabric and scan the white world surrounding me. "I'll be there in ten."

Before he can argue, I hang up and exhale a breath of relief at the possibility of company.

Just as I'm about to close the drapes, something catches my eye. A tiny movement most people wouldn't notice hidden among the dark shadows. I squint, trying to make out what it is through the falling snow. A faint red glow bobs in the black night like a lightning bug that's been set on fire.

Only this is no flaming insect.

It's the burning ember of someone's cigarette.

A swirling wind sweeps through the naked trees, stripped of their spring leaves. Snowflakes bounce in the breeze and dance in front of the house, blurring my view.

I rub my eyes and peek again. The red light is gone.

I sigh a breath of relief. Maybe I'm seeing things. Maybe my brain's playing tricks on me. Maybe I'm going crazy again.

That's when I notice a large silhouette slinking from shadow to shadow up the long driveway.

This can only be one person.

Al.

My mind races, and my heart hammers inside my chest. My hands shake, and my eyes dart around the room, looking for someplace safe to hide. I can't stay here; I have to leave. If Al catches me this time, he'll surely kill me. I'll have a much better chance of escaping if I'm outdoors.

Better a moving turkey than a sitting duck.

I snatch my white jacket off the hatrack and strap my hunting knife to my belt. I yank on my coat and backpack, all while keeping my eye on the silhouette creeping closer and closer. Then slowly and quietly, I inch backward down the hallway, keeping my eyes on the front of the house. When my body presses against the back door, I freeze.

The shadowy figure walks up the front steps. Since the outside bulb is broken, I can't make out any features, but the build is large. It's got to be Al. The doorknob rattles, and I hold my breath, praying the lock will hold. We never used to bolt our doors, but that was before Captain Carl ruined my town, and crazy Al managed to escape the law.

The handle jiggles again as it's tested. Hopefully, it will hold off Al long enough for me to get a head start. I quietly open the back door and step onto the icy deck. The frigid air pricks my face like little needles and rushes down into my lungs. I gasp loudly as my body adjusts to the extreme drop in temperature. I pull the fake fur hood around my face and inch down the steps.

A sliver of light from the living room window provides me just enough visibility to see my dad's snowmobile sitting against the house, covered in a tarp. It'd be much faster to jump on that and go, but the noise would definitely give me away. My chance of escape is better if I sneak off quietly without being detected and get a head start.

Just as I'm about to bolt across the yard and into the safe arms of the pitch-black woods, I spot a large shadow lingering, pressed against the side of the house. The hair on my neck stands on end, and without any hesitation, I sprint down the steep hill.

The icy wind tears down my throat. It's as if I've swallowed thousands of sharp, tiny icicles all at once. Huge, white clouds of breath are like beacons in the black night, giving away my position. Heavy footsteps crunch behind me through the new snow, growing closer with every step.

I focus on the woods ahead, not daring to look back for fear of who I'll see. If I can make it into the forest, Al will never find me. I know how to hide without a trace, and my white jacket blends nicely into the snowy backdrop.

Feeling confident, I push forward. Huge snowflakes freeze my eyeballs, making them water. No matter how sluggish and heavy I feel in the thick snow, I call on every muscle to hop over the high drifts.

Behind me, the footsteps get faster and louder. Al's gaining on me. Getting so close, I can practically sense him right behind me.

I dig my boots into the soft, powdery snow and force myself to speed up, half expecting a hand to grab my hood at any second. Tears spring into my eyes, and I resort to something I seem to be doing a lot of lately – praying. *Please, God. Not again.*

When I finally reach the edge of the forest, I veer off the straight path and zigzag into the thick trees. My legs are moving so fast, my foot clips a log, and I tumble face-first into a snowy drift. Without missing a beat, I scramble across the ground on all fours.

Labored breathing grows louder behind me as someone grabs hold of my ankle and yanks me backward. I try to scream, but the piercing air has frozen my lungs. I grasp at anything – roots, branches, bushes – to keep from being dragged away from the safety of the woods.

For a few seconds, I flail around crazily, expending all my energy trying to get away. Being facedown is the worst fighting position, especially for a girl. So I quickly flip over onto my back and swing my free leg, hoping to kick the crap out of a kneecap or land a lucky groin shot.

I hear myself scream, "Help!"

My attacker pounces on top of me, knocking out my breath. A large hand covers my mouth, blocking air from entering or escaping.

I buck wildly and throw up my legs, hoping to encircle a neck, but the dead weight on my chest combined with the lack of chilled oxygen is too much. My body slows down, and my vision blurs.

At this point, my only chance is to stay alert and be smart, catch my attacker totally off guard. I have to rein in my emotions and find the element of surprise if I want to stay alive.

Against all my survival instincts, I suddenly stop fighting. My body goes limp, and all the tension leaves my limbs. I keep my eyes closed and flop to one side, pretending to pass out.

I lie still and wait to make my move.

But for now, I'm trapped.

*A week earlier*

# Survival Skill #1

*In the wilderness, you are only as good as your weakest link (or links), which can be the difference between life and death.*

There's only one thing worse than sitting in class next to my ex-boyfriend Wyn after he's been ignoring me for more than a hundred days. Watching Skyler Trapp cling to him like moss to a moist rock.

I keep my eyes on my own paper but overhear her whisper in his ear. "Are we going out Friday night?"

Wyn smirks. It's the same look I used to be familiar with before he shut me out. The silly, lopsided grin where his mouth turns up on one side, like he knows a secret and he isn't sharing.

"Sure. Why not?" He answers her without turning around, probably to avoid me.

If he faced her, he'd be forced to notice me sitting behind Skyler in the usual alphabetical order. Then he'd have to admit I still exist.

I answer his question silently to myself, *I can think of many reasons.*

As I stare at the back of his head, my frustration mounts. I don't know why Wyn's silent treatment still bothers me. After all, he's been this way for three months – ever since summer, when I uncovered a horrible town secret. The day I proved Skyler's dad, Captain Carl, wasn't the police chief everyone thought he was.

Unfortunately, Carl and several people in our town died that day, and a few others went to jail. Not that prison terms could give me the closure I need. Justice will never be served for everything that happened to me. Nothing could replace what I lost.

But somehow, after all that mess, I've become the one everyone seems to blame, making me not so popular in this crappy town. What no one wants to remember is that Mom and I lost just as much as anyone, if not more.

Skyler says something in front of me and giggles. The noise sends a river of rage pounding through me. If it weren't for her influencing him, Wyn might have already forgiven me for lying to him. But I know she doesn't want that. In any normal situation, I might confront her. But seeing as I'm responsible for her dad's death, I don't blame her for hating me.

Even if Carl was a bad guy, he still was her father.

Now I'm left wishing my last name started with an *A* or *B* instead of a *W*, so I could sit on the other side of the room, away from lovebirds Stevens and Thomas.

As the teacher passes out our homework assignment, I rest my head on my hands, pinching back tears. As much as I want to hate Wyn for being such a jerk, I can't help but miss him. I try to pretend the whole situation doesn't bother me, but to be honest, I'd give anything to go back to any random day last year. Before Mo said he loved me. Before Wyn and I were dating. A day when my dad was still alive. That's the last time I remember being a whole person, without a broken heart and home.

Suddenly my frustration turns to sadness. I struggle to swallow my rising emotions, but the tears climb up anyway. I pinch my eyes closed. Biology 301 is not the place to cry, and I don't want to give Wyn or Skyler the satisfaction.

Just as I'm about to lose it, a door slams at the front of the room, causing my head to snap up. I quickly wipe my eyes before anyone notices my mini-meltdown.

When I spot Agent Sweeney, my body stiffens and all my muscles tense up. He spots me and nods before I can look away. The knot in my esophagus unravels, and all the moisture in my mouth dissipates like water being poured over hot sand.

I force my head to nod back in recognition, wondering what this visit is all about. I haven't seen Sweeney in weeks, not since the never-ending depositions and trial. He's never been to my school. *So why's he here?*

My body relaxes, and a smile teases my face. Maybe he's finally found Al? I sit up straighter with renewed hope and wait.

My teacher, Ms. Cox, clears her throat and smiles at everyone in the room. "Class, listen up. This is Agent Sweeney. He's with the U.S. Fish and Wildlife Service."

A few of the kids obviously recognize his face or his name from the papers, because they all turn around and gawk at me. I let my long, dark hair shield my face and pretend not to notice Skyler's famous "eat crap and die one hundred times over" look. I can practically hear her thoughts as sharp daggers shoot from her bright blue eyes. *Daddy killer.*

My teacher claps to take everyone's attention off me. "Class, listen up. Agent Sweeney is here with what I call an amazing *opportunity* for you to take advantage of."

I quietly exhale, realizing he's not at school for me. However, any *opportunity* to a teacher is either a scholastic trap to a kid or a death sentence to a grade. It's like when Mom says I have an *opportunity* to clean my room, or I should *take advantage* of hauling out the trash. It's usually a clue to head for the hills.

Agent Sweeney removes his signature navy-blue blazer, revealing a white USFWS shirt and jeans. He sits on top of Ms. Cox's desk, and she frowns at the sudden attack on her esteemed pile of education. She discretely slides the graded papers out from under his left buttock. I can't help but hide a smile with one hand.

"As Laura mentioned, I'm Agent Sweeney." Ms. Cox blushes when she hears her first name.

I must admit, Agent Sweeney seems to have a way with the ladies. I guess I can see why, brown-eyed, animal-loving, nature-agents with guns can be hot. I can relate. I can't help but miss Mo.

Sweeney glances around the room slowly, as if he's waiting for us to recite his name in unison like a class of four-year-olds.

He motions to our teacher. "Laura and I have been discussing a special project."

A short kid in my class named Seth whispers, "I bet they've been working on a special project together."

His buddies laugh as I roll my eyes, wondering why boys only have one thing on their minds. I start doodling on my paper while I process the word *special*. This project is only getting worse. *Taking advantage of special opportunities* is not something I'm interested in, thank you very much.

Ms. Cox nods. "I think this project is very timely for this class, especially considering the sensitive topics we are studying."

This time, Seth blurts out his bad joke for everyone to hear. "You mean *sex*?"

The class breaks into laughter as Ms. Cox stares down Seth with her "I'm not joking, I'll give you an *F*" face. He quickly submits and mumbles, "I meant *prokaryotic* sex. Geez."

She frowns. "Of course you did. Seth, see me after class."

Agent Sweeney can't help but smile. "As interesting as *that* sounds, this project is about something much bigger. Much more important."

He stands up and shoves his hands into the pockets of his jeans and plasters a serious look on his face. It's the same one I've seen in court a hundred times. He clears his throat and stares straight at me.

"The U.S. Fish and Wildlife Service is attempting to recover wolves that were reintroduced into this area last summer. With the winter getting worse, we need to ensure their safety. And we want your help."

I stop drawing and drop my pen. A buzz starts to rumble throughout the room.

Ms. Cox puts her finger to her mouth like we are toddlers. "Listen up, or you'll miss something important."

Agent Sweeney walks back to the desk and sits on top of Ms. Cox's flowery nameplate. She stiffens but doesn't attempt to move anything. Though knowing her OCD tendencies, I'm pretty sure she's totally freaking out on the inside.

He clasps his hands together. "Now, the exciting part is we are looking for six students to help us with this project. It will consist of some fieldwork, in which you will locate the wolves for data collection. This will help us decide if we need to extract them before the bad winter sets in."

He holds up his hands. "Before you say anything, let me explain exactly what the study will entail. You will be trained to help us with our field research by tracking and studying the packs' behavior. If you are lucky enough to find their dens, you will be responsible for carefully documenting all of their behavior, from their hunting patterns to pack dynamics to mating."

A few boys giggle in the back as Skyler holds up her hand. "So this will be an outdoor project?"

Agent Sweeney smirks. "Yes. That's usually where wolves prefer to hang out."

The class cracks up. Skyler's face turns pink, but she holds up her hand again. "So… when you say *field* study, do you mean out in the actual woods or at the reserve?"

Everyone snickers again, and Agent Sweeney gives a short answer. "In the grand outdoors."

"But it's winter." Skyler pulls her hair to one side and nervously plucks at her split ends. No doubt a fry job from her dye job.

Agent Sweeney raises his eyebrows. "Yes, well, unfortunately for us, wolves love the cold. I won't lie to you. This study will not be easy work. This is definitely a job for people who prefer the outdoors and are good with details. It will also be over winter break so you won't get to relax much."

Ms. Cox interjects quickly before my classmates start a ruckus at the thought of no vacay, "That's why I'm giving extra credit. The six people chosen will receive an *A* just for participating and doing what is required. This will replace your midterm exam; therefore, you won't have to take one. That's worth forty percent of your grade."

A few kids cheer, while a few others shake their heads, obviously still not up for the challenge of remaking *Dances with Wolves*, not to mention braving the coldest winter in North Carolina history. This is the first year we've had a snowy Thanksgiving. Of course, Mom and I don't celebrate, so it didn't matter to us. But I hear the wild turkeys weren't especially happy. Now it's early December, and we've already had flurries and freezing temperatures. Weather we usually don't see until late January.

Ms. Cox glances around the room. "First, let's get a show of hands from the students who are interested, then we can figure out how to choose who gets the honors."

Without even hesitating, my hand shoots up first. Dad's face flashes in my mind, which makes me smile. He was always the first person to volunteer for stuff like this, so he would want me to step up. This way I can continue some of his work, even if it's just logging numbers. Not to mention, hanging out in the woods with a *Rufus canus* is much better than sitting in class watching my ex-boyfriend wear his fancy new coat named Skyler Stevens.

Agent Sweeney points to me. "Thank you, Grace."

Wyn spins around and stares at me for the first time in months. A confused look is plastered on his perfectly shaved face. I smile quickly, but he abruptly looks away. A few seconds later, his hand slowly rises into the air like it's being pulled up by a helium balloon.

Agent Sweeney points at him. "Wyn."

I almost laugh out loud, but my brain settles on absolute confusion instead. Why in the world would Wyn volunteer to go outside in the snow when he could hide inside and play house with Skyler? Not only does he hate the outdoors, but it's not like his grades need any boosters. For me, this project is the only shot I have at earning a *B*.

A few other kids raise their hands. The obnoxious kid Seth, a new girl in town named Madison, and a huge black dude in the back, who goes by the name of Big Mike. The five of us all look around to see what other sucker will sign up for the *special opportunity*.

Ms. Cox waits a few more seconds. "To be honest, I'm surprised there are not more people interested in this rare opportunity, which will now be fifty percent of your grade."

I smile and look around at all the kids hesitating.

Ms. Cox crosses her arms over her chest. "I need one more."

Skyler stares at Wyn with a huge scowl on her face. No doubt she's peeved he volunteered without consulting her highness first. She glances at me and then again at him. Finally, her manicured hand sprouts into the air.

Ms. Cox smiles and points back in our direction. "Great. Thank you, Ms. Stevens."

Skyler forces out a smile as Ms. Cox continues with the assignments.

She points to the left side of the room. "Seth, you lead Team One with Madison and Michael." Then she points to our side of the room. "Grace, Wyn, and Skyler, you can make up Team Two." Then she glares at the rest of the class. "The rest of you will have a pop quiz tomorrow for not even pretending to be interested."

The class groans in unison as the bell rings. I watch Wyn pick up Skyler's flowery backpack and toss it over her shoulder as he walks her out.

Instead of getting up, I drop my head into my hands, cradling my brain as it starts to pound.

Just my luck to be on a team with Backwoods Barbie and Camping Ken.

# Survival Skill #2

*A hiker should always listen to the warnings of the birds, as they can provide warnings of predators.*

T here was one major thing I didn't consider when I volunteered for the Red Wolf Project: Mom.

No matter how excited I am or how I explain this to her, she's going to totally freak when I tell her I'll be hanging out in the woods again. Winter or not.

On the way home, I struggle to keep my motorcycle steady in the slushy snow. Almost time to let ole Luci hibernate for the winter. Even with her chains, her tires (or her age) are no match for the nasty weather we're having this year.

As I fishtail down the road to my house, my stomach churns with nerves. Not because I almost crash twice, but because I wonder if Mom's going to try and stop me from doing this project. The last few months, she's kept me from the woods, and I've let her.

But I can't ignore the forest forever. This project is the first thing I've been excited about in a long time. And I think it's time to get my waders back in the river as Dad would say. This could be a first step in getting a lost piece of me back.

After turning down my driveway, I slide to a stop. An old, beat-up truck is parked next to Dad's antique red one. An old birdcage sprinkled with snow sits in the back bed.

I pounce off my bike and race inside still wearing my helmet. I burst through the door and yell, "Mom! Mom!"

She comes barreling around the corner with an apron tied around her waist and a hot mitt on one hand. "What! What!"

I push up the fogged shield so she can see my face and lower my voice. "Is that Birdee's truck outside?"

She gasps and places one hand on her chest as if she's about to have a heart attack. "Jesus, Grace, you scared the crap outta me. Thought something happened."

I pull my helmet off and shake out my damp hair. "No, I'm fine."

When I give her a hug, I can feel her heart pounding in her chest.

"Sorry. I didn't mean to frighten you. I was just excited." I search the next room. "So? What's she doing here anyway?"

Mom blows a wisp of brown hair off her face. Small patches of flour dust her cheek, telling me she's trying to cook again.

"We can talk about that over dinner." I raise my eyebrows as she points to the stove. "Macaroni casserole."

"Hm. Can't wait." I wink at her and walk through the living room. "Where is she?"

"Where do you think?" Mom wipes her hands on a dish towel. "She's out back. Talking to her *friends*."

I toss my stuff onto the chair and head out the back door. I creep down the steps and through the yard, careful not to make a sound. Birdee gets real cranky when someone interrupts her conversations. At the tree line, I scan the overgrown woods until I spot the familiar straw hat and white hair bobbing above the bushes.

As soon as I see Birdee, Dad pops into my head. He loved his mother more than anything. Mom says Birdee and Dad are the only two people made from the same mold; only he was obsessed with bears and Birdee's bonkers for birds (or *Aves* as she calls them).

After Dad's funeral, Birdee was so upset about his death, she traipsed off to Africa on a bird-watching excursion for a few months. We hadn't heard from her all that time.

I tiptoe toward her, remembering all the times Dad and I would try our darndest to sneak up on her. We loved scaring her. It was so fun to hear her squeal and then cuss up a storm. Sometimes she wouldn't talk to us for hours.

I'm sure our laughing prevented her pride from fully recovering.

I take a small step forward and scan the path in front of me. It won't be easy to sneak around with the snow covering every dead branch just waiting to snap. But that wouldn't have stopped Dad from trying. He would've seen it as a wilderness challenge.

I move forward along the sparse trail, careful to avoid any patches of ice and piles of dead branches partially buried under the snow's weight. As I inch closer, I get the urge to giggle, thinking about how Dad always tried to push me off balance, hoping I'd make the first noise so Birdee would hear me instead of him. I was his unwilling and always-gullible decoy.

Just as I sneak up, a gray bird flies over me and squawks before landing on Birdee's shoulder. "Intruder alert," he shrieks.

I yell, "Petey!"

Birdee cackles with her bird. "Ha! I taught him that." She hands her African gray parrot a sunflower seed. He takes the morsel in his foot and nibbles on it. Birdee pets his feathered head. "Good Petey."

"So you have him covering your back now?" I ask.

Birdee spins around with a pair of green camouflage binoculars swinging from her neck. The second she spots me, she smiles the exact replica of Dad's silly grin, dimples and all. Her algae-green eyes fix on me for a second. She smiles and feeds Petey another seed.

"You wish! I heard you – along with every bird within a hundred yards - ten minutes ago when you opened that squeaky back door of yours. How many times did I tell your Daddy to get that damn thing fixed? At least a hundred. Never did listen to me."

I lump forms in my throat at how easy she's able to throw around Dad's name.

She walks over to me, the whole time scanning the trees for birds. In the frame of her aging face, I can see the picture of a young woman who used to help her father – my great grandpa - tend the farm from dawn until dusk. Now her tanned wrinkles tally up all the years of hard work. She holds out her arms but remains in place.

"Long time no see," I say.

Her eyes moisten slightly. "Hey, Chicken."

I jog over and hug her. Tight. She wraps her arms around me like a bat's wings. "You know I hate when you call me that."

"Hell, you're a teen. You're supposed to hate everything. What's one more thing gonna matter?"

She squeezes me extra hard and a little longer than her standard thirty second embrace. Birdee and I say a lot in that one hug. Things we can't say out loud. Things we don't want to say. *How are you? I'm sad. I miss Dad. This sucks. How will I live without him? We will never be the same, but we'll try to move on. For him.*

Eventually, she pushes me back with both arms. "I would ask how you are, but I can already see you're way too skinny. Like no chicken I ever raised. Has Mary not been feeding you? Maybe I need to teach her a thing or two about being in the kitchen."

I look down at my thin legs and notice how my jeans are baggier than a few months ago. "Excuse me! I'm eating."

"Eating what? Grass? You're a omnivore not a herbivore."
She studies me and pats both my cheeks with her wrinkled

hands. "Well, don't worry, Chicken. Birdee's here to fatten you up for the winter."

"I'm not a bear. I don't need to hibernate."

She taps her lips. "Hm. How about a date then? No self-respecting boy likes a bony girl. No matter what those damn magazines say. I'm sure Wyn likes a little meat on his girls."

I gasp. "Birdee!"

She laughs and acts innocent. "What?"

I squint my eyes, and it dawns on me that Birdee knows nothing of what's happened in my life outside of Dad. She doesn't know about Tommy's betrayal, that I fell in love with Mo only to lose him shortly after, and she obviously doesn't know Wyn's MIA. She'd probably chase him down and beat him with a stick.

I suddenly feel like I don't know her like I used to – the woman who sat with me every night after Dad died and stroked my hair until I went to sleep, the woman who always stuffed me with MoonPies whenever Mom and Dad went out of town together, the woman who still smacks my hand when I don't put my napkin in my lap. I make a mental note to fill her in later.

I clear my throat of all the feelings swirling around. "Why are you here?"

Birdee straightens up and gives me an indignant look. "Excuse me? What, I can't come and visit my only granddaughter? Besides it's my birthday." She leans in and whispers, "I'm going to be sixty, you know."

I cackle. "Ha! You wish. You've been seventy for like *five* years now."

She grins, and her eyes twinkle. "Have I? Well, damn. Guess I was lying then. *This* is the year I really turn seventy."

"Mm-hm. If you say so."

To be honest, I don't have a clue how old Birdee is, and I'm guessing I never will. Though I'm pretty sure she didn't have Dad when she was ten.

A bird chirps in the distance, and Birdee spins around. She grips her binoculars up and jams them up against her eyes. She pivots as she scans the trees like she's on some spy mission on a stakeout.

"Oh, Lordy, did you hear that, Petey?"

A few other birds join in the chorus, mimicking the same call. I stand quietly behind her and relax, feeling better. Even though everything around me is different, Birdee hasn't changed one bit. It's the one thing about death that's been the hardest for me, how much people change.

Either they aren't the same as they were before, or they don't act the same around me now. The looks of pity, the awkward silences, the cut-off sentences when they think they've said something wrong. That kind of strangeness forces relationships to shift, making it hard to continue being around people. The weirdness is then followed by the pain of knowing you're losing more people than you ever expected.

Even if they aren't dead, they have kinda become dead to me.

Tommy pops into my head, and my spirits sag, remembering how close we used to be. And now, after growing up with him in my life, in a matter of three short months it's like we're merely acquaintances whose only conversation is about the weather.

Yet, no matter what happens, Birdee is always Birdee – same jeans, same old cowboy boots, same haggard straw hat. Dad always called her the same tough old bird. It's hard to believe she still finds the strength to laugh as much as she always has after losing her husband many years back and then Dad this year.

I, on the other hand, can't seem to remember the last time I really laughed. The gut-wrenching kind that leaves your stomach aching. I think I might have smiled last week for the first time, but I'm not entirely sure it was totally intentional.

In the distance, the bird sounds off another distress call. Birdee cocks her head with her ear pointing up and listens. When the bird tweets again, she nods as if it's talking to her. "Well, butter my butt and call me a biscuit." She peers in her binoculars and then quickly pulls her eyes away. "No, it's can't be."

I stare up at the tree. "What is it?"

She looks again and beams when she hears the squawk. I swear she clicks her heels like Dorothy in *The Wizard of Oz*. "Ha! I do believe we have a Carolina Parakeet here." She does a little jig. "Ohhhh, this is so exciting."

"You're crazy." I laugh and grab the binoculars. "Let me see."

Birdee points to the bright spot of green and orange standing out against the brown branches.

"Carolina Parakeets have serious distress calls that can be heard up to two miles away. Some thought they were extinct. Though others have said that bird smugglers may still bring them in and out of the country. Someone must've let this little guy loose."

I pass back her equipment. "You don't need another looney bird in the house."

I point to Petey, who nips at my finger. He meows when I pull away, "Come here, kitty kitty kitty."

I shake my head and glance at Birdee who is smirking. "You are sick to teach him that."

She giggles as she jots some scribbles in her little notebook covered in colorful birds. She hollers up at the trees. "Come on, Big Guy, gotta make it harder than that if you want to trick me!" Then she mutters under her breath, "You old coot.

My mind is just as good as ever. I know every bird in this dang state, extinct, endangered, or stuffed."

Petey repeats after her in his own high-pitched parrot voice, "Old coot."

I laugh out loud. "So you and Petey are challenging God now?"

She winks and strokes the gray bird's head. "Gotta keep the dialogue open so Big Guy don't forget about me. Just in case."

My smile drops at the same time as my stomach. "Why? Is something wrong?" I step back even though my legs quake beneath me. "Is that why you're here?" I can barely get the words out, so I whisper, "You're...you're dying?"

Birdee laughs out loud and picks up her rifle, slinging the strap over her shoulder. "Jesus, child. Don't get all crazy on me. I'm as healthy as Shoney's veggie plate."

She wraps her arm around my shoulders and squeezes me with every step as we head up the path toward home.

"I ain't going nowhere, Chicken. You hear me? I'm right here. So stop trying to kill me off. Besides, I ain't got no money." She winks. "That you know of. Though I could leave you Petey."

Petey falls over on his side and squawks, "I'm dead."

As Birdie talks to her bird, I sigh out loud and push down the frantic feelings that rose so quickly, so unexpectedly. I can't lose someone else. Not now. Dad's death almost did me in, and I'm not sure I'll ever be okay again. Birdee is all I have left of him.

Petey gets another seed from her palm as she rambles on. "Petey's too young to lose me now. He's only fifty. When your daddy gave him to me, he failed to mention I have to live to be more than a hundred to take care of my fine feathered friend. No pressure or anything."

"You love your feathered friend," Petey says and bobs his head up and down.

My dad found Petey in a trailer after he busted some guy for hunting deer off-season. Later, they found out the man was also importing animals. Dad confiscated all his animals and eventually gave Petey to my grandmother. Now they're inseparable.

She kisses his head as I shake mine, sucking on the fingertip he practically bit off. "You'd better live that long, because I'm not taking the little nipper."

Petey squawks, "You don't want to ruffle my feathers."

I eye Birdee. "You have waaaaay too much time on your hands. You've taught him to be the only bird in the world that speaks in complete sentences."

She beams proudly as if watching her baby walk for the first time. "That's right. He's smarter than half the fools in this state."

"That's not saying much." I fling my arm around her tiny waist as we head toward the house. "I love you, Birdee."

She hugs me back. "I love you too, Chicken."

Petey bounces up and down. "I love chicken."

We both laugh, and Birdee pinches my waist. "Now let's get some meat on those bones."

ℭଷ

Birdee doesn't stop talking through the entire meal.

As I scarf down Dad's favorite dinner – meatloaf and macaroni casserole with a buttery side of Brussels sprouts – I can't help but notice how quiet Mom's been the whole night. Every time I look at her, she avoids meeting my eyes, and I think I know why.

Even though Birdee's visit brightens things up around here, like a breeze blowing through a boarded-up home, she can't help but remind Mom and me of Dad. Birdee's got the same dimpled smile, the same obnoxious laugh, and the same quirky mannerisms – the way she piles her food into little separate piles and goes from one pile to the next, the way she scrapes her fork across the plate after each bite, and the way she wipes her mouth with her napkin using both hands. Those are just a few of the thousands of things they do alike. She is so much like Dad, it makes me more aware of the fact that he isn't here.

Birdee rambles on in the background about the Carolina Parakeet she spotted. How they were thought to be poisonous because they ate toxic seeds. I glance over at Mom. This time, she smiles weakly and reaches over to squeeze my hand. She knows what I'm thinking, too.

Birdee reaches over and slaps my hand. "Napkin, Chicken."

I shove the cloth into my lap as she clinks a glass with her knife. "Hello? Attention, peanut gallery? Why am I the only one talking? You know it's not polite to let the guest carry the whole conversation. Too much pressure for one old lady."

I smile. "We were waiting on you to pause. Maybe use a period at the end of a sentence for a change."

Birdee eyes me and then addresses my mother. "Girl's getting too smart. Just like her Daddy."

The D-word hits me hard, almost knocking the breath out of me. I even hear myself gasp for air out loud. I suddenly realize I'll never call out for my daddy again, and tears spring to my eyes.

For a few seconds, no one says a word. We all grasp for a filler-sentence or maybe linking sentences that can take us from the topic of Dad's death quickly to another subject, like the bad weather. It doesn't matter, any subject will do. Suddenly my mind goes blank. No topics scroll through my head. It's just a black screen with a big picture of Dad's face plastered in the middle. Everyone looks at each other – Birdee to Mom, Mom to me, Mom to Birdee, Birdee to me. Birdee places her napkin on the table and sits back in her chair. "Well. We're going to have to get used to talking about Joe at some point." Her voice cracks a little when she says Dad's name, and she pauses as if collecting herself. "We can't all hide from his name forever, and he wouldn't want us to crumble every time he pops up in the conversation. And the good Lord knows Joe wouldn't want to be forgotten. Not even for a second."

A tear trickles down my Mom's cheek. She quickly wipes it away as if that means it never fell and struggles to find words. "It's just, we don't like to talk about it. I guess it hurts too much."

Birdee shakes her head, and her blue eyes water. The way they glisten reminds me of Bear Creek, and all the times Dad and I fished there together in the bright sunlight. I can't help but get choked up when I see her face. I've never seen her cry. Not even at the funeral.

She swallows and speaks softly. "Mary, honey, maybe you two have been trying to forget him. To make it easier. Not me. I *need* to remember him. It's the only way I can get through each day. The more I forget, the harder it is."

I glance back and forth between them, tears clouding my vision. Mom and I talked about Dad a little in the beginning, but at some point after the memorial service and after Birdee left, he fell out of the conversation. I guess it was easier that way, but now I realize Birdee is right. We can't forget Dad just because it hurts to remember.

I half-laugh and half-cry. "Boy, Dad would love us arguing over him right now."

Birdee cups Mom's hand. "Yes, he did love being the center of a conversation, even though he always pretended like he didn't need to be."

27

Mom nods. "That is so true."

Birdee pats my head. "Chicken, it's okay to be sad. All of us." She reassures Mom. "It just means we're feeling something, girls. Better to feel pain then nothing at all. When we feel nothing, that means we're dead, too."

Mom laughs while crying. "Yes. Joe always used to say that. You're right, Birdee, we'll do better. Won't we, honey?"

Birdee squeezes Mom's hand again. Mom reaches over and clutches onto mine. For a short second, we all three sit in a semi-circle holding hands around the table in silence. The bond of that moment somehow heals a small sliver of the scar running through my heart.

A few seconds later, Birdee snatches her hand back. "Well, that's enough *Days of Our Lives* for one day. Chicken, tell me, how's school going? And don't just say 'fine,' because I want deets."

"Good." I smile and rip off a piece of bread. Popping the warm dough into my mouth, I try to act natural as I dive into the wolf project. "Today I got chosen for a special project. The USFWS is doing a new study on the red wolves, and they need some students to help gather data in the field."

Birdee claps. "Well, good for you! Your daddy would be so proud."

Mom jerks her head in my direction. "What kind of data?"

I pause for a second, trying to think of a way to make this project sound as low-risk as possible. "You know, when they eat, when they sleep – just everyday behavior stuff."

Before Birdee can say anything, Mom pipes in again. "When you say *field*, do you mean you're going out into the woods? Or is this at an animal reserve of some sort?"

"There is a reserve." I keep my head down and nod as if the question doesn't matter. I tell a small white lie to ease her anxiety. "So probably both."

Mom doesn't bite. Instead, she pushes back her chair and stands, collecting dishes. As she walks into the kitchen, she simply says one word, "No."

It takes me a second to process and react. "No? Wait! Mom, please. I have to do this. Ms. Cox is giving extra credit, and I need to make up for all the days I missed this quarter because of the trial."

I jump up and follow her into the kitchen with another dirty plate. "Besides, I already said yes. I can't back out now. They already assigned teams."

Mom shakes her head and starts scrubbing so hard, I swear she's trying to scrape the flowery design off the plate. Her voice is flat. "I said no. It's too dangerous being out in the woods again. Alone. Never mind it's going to be a nasty winter." She shakes her head. "No way. Not a chance in Hades, Grace."

I try to keep my voice flat. "I'll be careful, I promise. I won't be by myself. I have a whole team, and Agent Sweeney is in charge."

She crosses her arms. "Sweeney? Has he found—"? She stops.

I know what she's going to say, so I hit the concern head-on, hoping to make her feel better about the project. Show her I'm not scared so she doesn't have to be. "Al? No, I don't think so."

She jerks back, surprised. "You don't *think* so? Uh, that's not good enough."

I can't help but think of Al, and his horrible attacks on my family and me. But I pretend not to be that concerned for Mom's sake. "You know he's long gone. Agent Sweeney said he'd be dumb to come back here."

Mom scoffs. "Well, from what I know, he was–."

Birdee cuts in. "A few feathers short of a duck?"

I can't help but smile at Birdie's way of putting things, but Mom's not amused. "Yes, but don't start with me, Birdee. This is not a funny one-liner." Mom tries to escape the small kitchen.

Birdee stands firm in the doorway, blocking her exit. "Mary, I think you should let her go. Grace needs this. She can't live in fear forever, and we can't protect her forever."

Mom faces her and narrows her eyes. "Stay out of this. I mean it."

I expect Birdee to get louder, but instead she softens her voice and puts her hand on Mom's shoulder. "Honey, what happened to Joe happened. We can't go back and change any of that. And as much as we'd all like to control this grand universe and everyone in it, we can't prevent anything bad from happening to anyone. We can't keep Grace in a bubble for the rest of her life." She points to the ceiling. "Besides, the Big Man's in charge. Not you or I. Control is only an illusion."

Mom shakes her head as tears break through their barrier and stream down her cheeks, smudging her makeup. Even though she's upset, her voice still comes out strong and solid. "Birdee, you can't come in after a few months and philosophize this away and expect everything to be okay! You haven't been here. You don't know what it's been like without Joe around. You left us, remember?"

I stand trembling, waiting for Birdee's response. Looking between the two people I love most.

Birdee frowns and stands her ground. "You listen here, Mary Wells. Joe was my only son, and I'm hurting just as much as you are. I raised that boy on my own after his daddy died, so don't you dare lecture me about pain."

Her face remains stoic, but I recognize the strain in her voice. Birdee pauses to collect herself. "Just because Joe died, doesn't mean we all have to stop livin'. We need to go on. For him."

Mom tosses the dishrag on the counter in defeat. "That's fine, but I'm leaving town. This is not a good time."

"There never is," Birdee answers.

I stare at Mom. "Wait. You're leaving town? When? Why?"

Mom collapses against the counter. "Jim, I mean Dr. Head, wants me to work for him full time. But to do that, I have to go to Asheville for a training seminar on medical filing and insurance stuff. I'll be back right before Christmas."

I add the time up in my head. "But that's a few weeks away. That's way too long."

Mom rubs my arm. "I know it's not the perfect time, but this is a chance for me to get outta that diner and work a full-time job during the day while you're at school. That way I can be home with you more at night and on weekends."

Birdee steps up and squeezes my shoulder. "Now, Chicken. Don't get your boy shorts in a twist. That's why I'm here." She nods to my mom. "And I'll watch her closer than I do my own Petey."

At the sound of his name, Petey squawks from the corner. "I'm watching you."

Mom and I can't help but smirk.

Birdee calls to him over her shoulder, "Mind your own business, Petey. No one needs a dodo's opinion."

Mom glances between Birdee and Petey, as if not wanting to interrupt an important conversation. Eventually she sighs, the universal sign of defeat. "You promise you'll keep tabs on her?" Birdee nods, then Mom stares at me. "And you'll be extra careful?"

I hold up three fingers, a habit left over from being a Girl Scout years ago. "I promise."

Petey pipes in, "*I promise.*"

Mom grins and strokes his little head. "Fine."

31

I run over and hug her. "Thanks, Mom. I swear I'll be fine."

"You'd better."

Birdee hugs us both. "Don't worry. We all will be."

# Survival Skill #3

*Survivor's guilt may cause you to alienate friends and family, which may lead to isolation, loneliness, and denial.*

Sometimes I think the whole town hates me.

All 4,097 of them.

I haven't been into town in a while. I even quit working at Tommy's store to avoid all the stares and comments. Tommy too.

Mom's taken the most heat. Working at the diner, she's forced to put up with the looks and the whispers. Somehow everyone – even the tourists – seems to know or has heard about our town and Dad's case. If Mom had more money, we probably would've moved, but for now we're stuck here. I'm sure that's why she's trying this new job with Dr. Head. To get away from everything I've been avoiding for months.

Today I'm forced to endure the haters, as the temporary space of Agent Sweeney's USFWS office just happens to be in Carl's old building. Right in the middle of town. Walking down the sidewalk, I keep my eyes on my feet as I pass by Mr. Field's old boarded-up general store. When I reach the post office, the new postman, who replaced Louie when he was convicted, doesn't even acknowledge my existence. I pick up speed and notice another store newly boarded up. And it's right next door to *Tommy's Fishing Shack*.

At least his place is still open – for now.

I shield my eyes with both mittened hands and press my face against the frosted window. Tommy is at the register counting money before he opens for the day. The store appears to be exactly the same as it was on my last day working. Not that it would be different in just a few months. But since everything else in my world has changed, I assumed this place would've too.

As I watch Tommy work, the muffled sounds of Native American music float through the store. What once seemed like home to me now feels strange and unfamiliar. I almost knock on the window to get his attention, but I stop myself.

Even though none of what happened with Dad or Carl was really Tommy's fault, I can't help but wonder if things would have been different had he just been honest with me from the beginning. His betrayal still lingers, and no matter how hard I try to let it go – how much I want to let it go – something deep inside me can't seem to find a way.

Mom says it will take time; I'm just not sure how much.

Before I can leave, Tommy spots me in the window and waves from the other side. I force out a smile. He quickly grabs his carved-wood cane and hobbles to the door as fast as he can. Because he got shot saving me, they say he'll never walk the same again.

To be honest, nothing will ever be the same since the poaching ring was uncovered. Not the town. Not Tommy. And certainly not me.

Tommy pulls open the glass door. "Hey, Elu! *To hi tsu?*"

I immediately soften at the nickname he's had for me since I was little. I spin around, but refrain from answering him in Cherokee. It doesn't feel right. We don't speak the same language anymore.

I try to sound happy and lighthearted, "Hi, Tommy."

We exchange a quick, awkward hug. The kind where there's a tiny space between you, keeping you apart. Space that's filled with something you can't control. Space that feels larger than it really is. Space you both pretend isn't there.

I stare at the cane propping him up and can't help feeling a pang of guilt for not being able to forgive him the way I probably should. Maybe I shouldn't be so hard on him. He took a bullet for me. So did Mo, only Mo wasn't as lucky as Tommy. After all, Tommy's experienced loss too, lost his wife, lost my Dad, and lost his nephew, Chief Reed. Even though Reed was in cahoots with Carl, his death caused Tommy to be ostracized from his own reservation. The one his ancestors started.

I force out words. "How are you?"

He holds the door with his hand. "Oh, you know, can't complain. Same ole, same ole."

His voice is tight, almost making me wish I hadn't stopped. He scans the street.

"What are you doing here?" he asks, but he says it like, *Why are you here, because we all know no one likes you and therefore you are in danger of being stoned by a crazy backwoods mob?*

I point down to Carl's old place. "I signed up with the USFWS for a conservation program on red wolves at school. Today is Agent Sweeney's big kickoff."

Tommy frowns. "Does your Mom know about this?"

I stiffen. "Of course." I can't help but feel a pang of anger. Who is he to question me? I try to shake it off. "Mom's doing some training out of town for a couple weeks, so Birdee's staying with me."

Wrinkles form around his mouth, telling me he's gone from frowning to smiling. His eyes light up. "Ahhhh! Well, then, I'm not worried about you. I know what kind of damage that woman can do if someone messes with her kin. Seen it myself."

His chuckle softens me a bit, and for a split second, things feel slightly normal again. Our eyes lock, and so many things pass between us, things still unspoken. Things we will never speak of again. And unfortunately, things we can never forget.

35

A slew of emotions spin around us – regret, pain, respect, betrayal, gratitude, love, and maybe, somewhere deep down, a speck of forgiveness.

Tommy's eyes get a little watery, and he hugs me hard. My body remains as straight as a board. I can't seem to relax around him anymore. He senses it and starts to pull away. "Well, you'd better go, Elu. Let's plan on meeting for lunch soon."

I squeeze him quickly. Just long enough to tell him I'll always love him even if it doesn't seem like it. That I forgive him; I just can't forget. I wonder if he hears my thoughts.

I manage to say, "Sure," knowing that meal will probably never happen.

He adjusts his old fishing cap. "You still got that hunting knife I gave you?"

I can't help but try to slice through this hard loaf of awkward. "Nope, gave it away." At first he looks pained, so I smirk to let him know I'm kidding. "Of course I have it."

He appears relieved. Then his face turns serious. He glances around the town before his eyes land on mine. "Good. Make sure to carry it with you. Always."

No matter what, Tommy can't help but watch out for me. It's in his blood.

"I will."

He stares at me a little too long. As if he's about to say something I'm not ready to hear.

To lighten the moment, I point to his shorts and fishing boots. "You know it's winter, right?"

He looks down and then waves me off. "Shoot, my people have seen much colder than this."

I smile. "Yeah, well it's your *old legs* I'm worried about. Now you'd better get back inside before you freeze to death."

He chuckles. "Alright. You stay out of trouble, Elu. For once."

"Always," I say, waving goodbye and walking away.

Before I turn the corner, I look back and see Tommy standing there, watching me. I wave one more time and grin all the way to the USFWS office. It doesn't matter if it's ninety degrees and sunny or twenty degrees and gloomy, Tommy still wears shorts, a fishing vest, and that silly hat with all his lures hanging off the brim.

That's probably the one thing that will never change.

☙

I study my feet until they automatically stop in front of Carl's old office. I suck in a breath before looking up at the ancient door with the same cracked windowpane. Some of the letters in Carl Stevens' name are still stuck to the glass, forming a chilling message.

_A_L' S _ _ EVEN_.

Just seeing the letters of Al's name makes me nauseous.

A loud voice calls out behind me. "Gracie! Wait up."

I turn and see Les shuffling across the street in his nasty hiking boots. I'm still amazed they've lasted this long. Almost makes me want to send a letter to the manufacturer, informing them of the small miracle. Maybe Les would get a free pair. One can only hope.

"Hey, Les." I wait at the door as he hobbles over.

Even though my dad's old partner and best friend seems to have lost a few pounds, he grunts as he struggles to move.

As soon as Les reaches the building, he hugs me, squishing me into his round belly. I squeeze him back, thankful he wasn't killed along with Carl. I still feel bad for thinking he was involved, but Les always says we should let bygones be gone.

He scoops his finger in his cheek and removes a wad of tobacco from the side of his mouth. He plops it into a cup. "I've been worried about you and your momma. Haven't seen you around much since –."

I cut him off, not wanting to hear the rest, and motion to a group of kids pointing at me. "Yeah. Well, I'm not too popular around these parts."

He frowns and waves off the teenage gawkers. "Hey! Take a picture. It'll last longer."

I can't help but laugh at how immature he sounds, even though he's a wildlife ranger practically Dad's age. The small mob from school walks off.

Les removes his hat and scratches his the sparse sprigs of reddish hair on his head. "Gotta stick up for your own." He looks up at the building we're standing in front of and spits onto the ground. "What are you doing at this place? Doesn't seem like your kind of hangout."

I avoid looking at the door. "I'm working with Agent Sweeney."

"Ahhhh, the wolf thing. Shoulda known you'd be involved." He pulls his hat back on and rubs his gray-and-orange goatee. "Your daddy would be proud."

I nod and drop my head. "I know."

"Well, let's not keep them waiting."

"Wait, you're on this project too?" I feel a bit relieved knowing I'll have one person on my side.

He fights with his shirt, trying to force the ends to stay in his belt. "My territory. I'll be getting updates, but I certainly won't be traipsin' around with you kiddos in the winter wonderland." He grabs the door handle and motions to me. "Ladies first."

I bow slightly. "Thank you, kind sir."

Smiling, he spits one more time and opens the door.

The familiar bell that always announced Carl's visitors sends a chill down my spine. Everything about that day comes flooding back.

It takes everything I have to walk inside.

# Survival Skill #4

*Hike leaders are responsible for the safety and enjoyment of the group; therefore, it is important to choose them wisely.*

ℐ stop for a second, and Les cups my shoulder. "It's okay, Gracie. He can't hurt you anymore."

I can't help but cringe every time he uses Dad's nickname for me. He's the only one besides Dad who calls me Gracie. I force myself to take a step into Carl's space. I glance around and remember the last time I was here. Sneaking behind Bernice's back to crack Carl's records on my Dad's case. I wonder what happened to her when this place closed down.

Luckily, the space looks completely different. Agent Sweeney has gutted the interior and had it totally redone. The internal walls have been blown out, and the old, musty furniture replaced with new, leather-smelling ones. Now the place is pretty much an open room with a few desks off to one side and a large meeting area on the other.

I approach the rows of chairs bordered by bookshelves. A screen hangs in the front, telling me we're about to get some kind of presentation. Old maps hang alongside bulletin boards filled with pinned notes, and the walls are decorated with mounted fish marked with species labels. Over by the window, there's a long, thin table of tagged items, probably confiscated from poachers. I scan the items: furs, guns, and other hunter paraphernalia.

And this is probably just from last weekend.

Agent Sweeney stands at the front of the room, chatting with Les and two other people I don't recognize. Every now and then, Les' big laugh fills the room. The other kids from my class are already sitting in their seats. On the Team One side, Big Mike, the top-rated Right Guard at my high school, is crammed into a chair that's one-third his size. I'm a bit surprised he gave up his Saturday jolt of testosterone at practice to be stuffed in here. Then again, who wants to practice in the cold besides our practice-day-and-night-in-rain-or-snow Coach Gary?

Seth, the shortest soccer player at school who suffers from a serious case of Napoleon Complex (a.k.a. SMS for small man syndrome) is sitting opposite Mike. Seth's small feet are propped up on the chair in front of him. Bright red hair pokes out from underneath his floppy knit cap, reminding me of how my Raggedy Ann doll looked after my dog Bear got a hold of her head. Madison, the new braniac from New York, is sitting quietly, reading some nonfiction book titled *The Return of the Wolves*. She's already updating her database of factoids. The girl probably knows more about everything than Google does.

She glances back at me and smiles. I grin briefly and beeline to my team's side where Wyn and Skyler are already in a PDA marathon. When he kisses her, I cringe. Gross. I squeeze down an aisle and sit a couple rows behind them, close enough to look like a team player but far enough to prevent hurling from all the cooing sounds. The mere sight of them is bad enough.

Wyn glances over and nods. I guess it's a step up. He's at least acknowledging I take up space in this world. Yet, I can't help but be completely peeved. After years of being friends, sharing secrets, and beating him in rock, paper, scissors, all I get is one stupid nod? Like he's some librarian approving my membership or a grocery clerk scanning my frequent-shopper card.

I ignore his nonverbal greeting and look away. I mean, why should I nod back? What does that even mean? Yes? Yes to what? Yes, you abandoned a friendship because of a fake doll. Or yes, you turned your back on me when I needed you the most because your bruised male ego got in the way?

Agent Sweeney walks to the front and leans against a desk. "Well, kids, thanks for coming out on a cold day. Everyone still excited about the project?"

We look at each other and nod while Big Mike raises his large, mitt-sized hand. "Feeling good over here, Boss."

Agent Sweeney claps once and points to Big Mike. "Glad to hear it. I think you'll enjoy being part of such an important project."

He points to an old man standing off to one side in haggard pants and a shirt. If I didn't know better, I would have thought he was homeless. "I want to introduce you to a couple people involved in the project. This is Jerry Porter. He's a retired professor from N.C. State, where he taught in the Forestry and Wildlife department.

"He's also one of the nation's best trackers and has spent a lot of time studying wolves out West as well as here. He's working with the Red Wolf Coalition in this monumental task of researching the behaviors and patterns of the red wolf. We want to be sure there's an adult in the field at all times to ensure safety, so he'll be your guide and go-to person. If you need anything, he's the expert."

Everyone clap as Porter waves. The guy's got to be at least Birdee's age. His thick, white mustache and green suspenders make him look more like an old Grizzly Adams than a wolf lover/retired professor with an advanced degree.

Agent Sweeney motions to Les. "Of course, you all know Les. He'll be looped in since this is his territory."

Les smiles with tobacco-stained teeth. "Howdy."

A pretty blonde lady, who looks very natural in her wrinkle-free cargo pants and red zipped fleece with not a fuzz ball out of place, steps forward. "I'm Katie Reynolds. District Conservationist."

Agent Sweeney nods. "Katie, I mean Ms. Reynolds, is a conservationist in the state, meaning she works to protect our natural resources and the environment. She's also on the board of the Wolf Coalition."

Katie smiles, showing a perfect row of teeth. "You can call me Katie. I just want to thank you all for volunteering on this important project. If you need anything, just ask, and I'll make sure you get it." She smiles at me specifically. "It's nice to see the girls represented in this program as well. I look to you ladies to keep the boys in line."

Madison and I nod. If this lady can work a bunch of stiff politicians and state officials, then Madison and I can lead a hike.

While hopefully Skyler takes one.

Agent Sweeney nods to Porter. "Jerry, why don't you kick things off?"

Porter pushes away from the wall with one foot and walks forward. "Sure thing."

All six of us watch closely, our heads swinging with him as he begins pacing the room.

"As you may or may not know, USFWS has been working to reintroduce the red wolves back into North Carolina for the last several years. Last summer, we released two functioning packs into the surrounding area. With the harsh weather coming, we want to check on them before the mountain becomes impassable. So you guys will be charged with finding the packs and tracking their progress."

Skyler pipes up. "Why a bunch of kids?"

Katie sits on the desk. "Unfortunately, we only have so many volunteers, so we need extra hands on deck. We thought it would be a great experience for students to get extra credit while learning about these wonderful animals our state is struggling to protect."

"And why now?" Skyler says. "Can't it wait until spring?"

Katie shakes her head. "As far as timing, I think we've explained that the winter is supposed to get worse after the holidays. We want to check on our wolves before deciding if we need to extract them. This will be their first winter outside the reserve. Not to mention a bad one."

Seth raises his hand. "Why do wolves need to be reintroduced in the first place?"

Porter presses down his mustache with two fingers. "Good question. Anyone want to take a stab?"

Madison closes her book and raises her hand. "The red wolf is one of the most endangered species in the nation. Not to be confused with its cousin, the *Canis lupus* or gray wolf that lives out West. The red wolf population was pretty much demolished in the 1960s."

Even Porter looks amazed as Katie claps. "Excellent research, Madison."

Madison beams as Agent Sweeney adds, "In 1980, the last seventeen red wolves were rescued and placed into a captivity breeding program. The USFWS declared the red wolf extinct in the wild and started what is now known as the Reintroduction Program in North Carolina's Alligator River National Wildlife Refuge."

I sit still, soaking in the information, processing everything. I had no idea these creatures were practically extinct. I guess I hear so much about gray wolves, I never think about the red ones. Sadness fills my chest, wondering if Dad knew how close these gorgeous animals were to being nonexistent right here in our very own state.

Skyler raises her nail file in the air as if it's a sword. "If the weather is too bad for wolves, isn't it too bad for us?"

I try not to exhale my exasperation at Skyler's attempts to avoid going outside for a nature project.

Agent Sweeney folds his arms across his chest. "Now is the time before it gets really bad."

Everyone's hands go up at once.

Porter holds up both of his. "I put together a slide show for you. Maybe that will answer more of your questions."

Katie dims the lights as Porter fiddles with a laptop. For being an old man, he seems to know his way around computers. Birdee's idea of "booting up" means getting her shoes on for a bird-watching hike. He picks up the remote and begins clicking through slides of red wolves – a mom playing with her pups, a male dragging in a kill.

As he flips through the pictures, he spews out facts like an online encyclopedia. "Today, there are about 100 wolves roaming this state. About forty of them were released."

Madison pulls her nose from her book. "Wait. Did you say only 100? In more than thirty years? I thought it was more."

The shadow of Katie speaks up from the back of the room. "Sad, isn't it? There are only 100 in the wild, but we still have 200 healthy wolves in captivity."

Porter continues on to the next slide. "Unfortunately, our roaming populations suffer more. It appears to be hard to keep them alive in the wild due to many factors."

He flips through a few pictures showing dead wolves, one on the road obviously hit by a car, and another clearly shot. I notice Madison cringe as Skyler covers her eyes, looking through the slits between her fingers. "The top two causes of red wolf losses are either gunshots or disappearances. And to be frank, those are what keep the red wolf from making a solid comeback here. Of the first group released, the Red Wolf Recovery Program lost radio contact with six wolves, four males and two females, all from the same pack. A devastating loss."

I think for a second about the information he's dumped on us, and a question pops into my head. "When you say 'lost radio contact,' do you mean hunters killed them and then hid them? Or that you just can't find them?"

From the side, Agent Sweeney looks back at me and adjusts his hat. He nods slowly as if he approves of my question. What's with all the nodding today?

Porter shrugs and pops his suspenders. "We don't exactly know. Maybe hunters mistake them for coyotes and shoot them, and they panic because these animals are still designated as endangered. So they hide them. Or maybe our tracking systems have failed in some way. Or it could be the wolves died of natural causes, and we just didn't find out where. This is what we hope to uncover. Whatever it is, these deaths take a toll on the population as well as the success of the breeding program as a whole. Many packs and pairs are affected by these deaths."

Porter pauses and flips through a few more photos. "For this project, we will be observing two different packs and documenting their behaviors: feeding, mating, and hunting."

Skyler passes along a red wolf pamphlet that was handed out at the start of the session. "Do they bite?"

Seth laughs out loud, only it's more of a snort mixed with a howl. "Noooo, Skyler. They'll just lick you to death. They're *wolves*. What do you think?"

Wyn immediately comes to Skyler's defense, like the noble guy he's always been. All mouth and no trousers. "Hey, chill out, Seth. She was just asking."

"Whatever, lover boy," Seth says. "It was a dumb question."

Wyn stands. "You want to say that to my face?"

Seth looks confused. "I just did."

Madison interrupts in a sweet voice. "I don't think it's a dumb question. On average, animal attacks account for more than 100 human deaths per year. Of course, that includes pet bites and bee stings."

Seth snaps at her, "Shut up, Madison. We don't need your useless factoids."

Madison looks like she's about to cry.

Big Mike stands beside her and towers over Seth. He pokes Seth in the chest. "Dude, don't speak to the ladies that way, or you'll have to deal with me."

Seth holds up both hands and cowers. "We're cool, Big Mike. Chill out."

Katie steps to the front. "Let's keep the testosterone in check, boys. It's not going to get you anywhere. With the wolves or the ladies."

All of us girls snicker as Big Mike squeezes back into his chair. "Sorry, Miss Reynolds. I mean Katie."

Seth pouts as Wyn sits back down.

Meanwhile, Skyler is still fuming. "Like Seth has any chance at getting a lady."

Seth's face turns as red as Birdee's beets. I can't help but laugh at how fast Skyler put Seth in his place.

Skyler glances up at Porter with big, innocent eyes. "As I was saying before about bites. I just meant if the wolves are coming from captivity, do they still bite, or are they used to people being around? That's all."

Porter sits in a chair and crosses one foot over his knee. He hooks his thumbs through his suspenders. "Well, even though they're bred in captivity, we try our best to give them a wild environment. We minimize contact, provide them with live prey, and let them roam freely within their fenced-in areas."

I take notes and can't help but smirk at the words roam freely and fenced being used in the same sentence. These wolves are about as wild as a bird in a cage or a betta fish in a bowl.

"Skyler, if we thought this project was dangerous, we certainly wouldn't use students." He looks over at Madison. "But to clear up any concern, there's only been one red wolf attack on a human in more than 200 years."

Big Mike adds in a low, baritone voice. "That we know of."

I get a glimpse of Skyler's face, and she looks terrified. Wyn has his arm draped over her shoulders, comforting her. She shouldn't feel too safe. I happen to know there's no way Wyn would stand up to a wolf, no matter how perfect Skyler is. I know from personal experience he's petrified of anything that has more than two legs. I can only assume wolves are not at the top of his "Favorite Animal" list.

Agent Sweeney stands up with two new North Face backpacks. "Let's go ahead and get started. We can talk more later if you still have questions. Tomorrow is our first day in the field, so we have a lot to cover. We'll go over first aid, data collection, and then review basic winter survival skills. Each team will get a first aid kit and a pack of supplies." He faces the left side of the room. "Who's going to be the leader for Team One?"

Napoleon jumps up. "I'll do it." Seth grabs one backpack and holds it over his head like he's the winner of some survival show. Big Mike folds his arms over his chest like he's a bouncer. Seth cowers slightly. "Come on, Big Mike, you can be my wing man."

Madison whispers to me, "Did you know guys shorter than five-foot-five are fifty percent more likely to have serious envy problems than guys taller than six feet tall?" She drops her head toward Seth. "Explains everything."

I smile as she bursts into a fit of giggles.

Agent Sweeney eyes Wyn, Skyler, and me. "And Team Two? Who's the lucky winner?"

Skyler glances back at me and then elbows Wyn in the ribs and whines, "Wyyynnnn."

He winces at the jab and speaks up. "I guess I'll do it since I'm the only man on the team."

I can't help but burst out laughing and address him for the first time in months. "Oh pu-lease. You can't lead a male *solo,* let alone a whole team of girls."

Wyn spins around and speaks to me. "Oh, yeah? Watch me."

I look at Sweeney. "You can't be serious."

"Simmer down, Grace. He spoke up first," Agent Sweeney says.

I shoot him a look that says, *don't you dare let him be the leader, or you'll get us all killed,* but Sweeney shrugs. Though I bet he's smirking on the inside.

"Not my problem, Grace. You guys work it out."

He tosses the second backpack. Wyn misses, and the pack goes crashing to the floor.

I rub my temples. If Skyler's looks don't kill me, Wyn surely will.

# Survival Skill #5

*Before you head out on a hike, make yourself familiar with the wildlife in the area to avoid animal encounters.*

Before Mom leaves for Asheville, she stops in my room and sits on the edge of my bed. Her face is pinched with concern.

"You sure about this wolf thing?" she asks.

I roll over and face her, the pillow squished between my legs. "Mom, stop. I'll be fine."

She strokes my hair. "I just don't want anything to happen to you."

"You and me both." I sit up and look at her with confidence, even though my tummy is tied in knots. The thought of heading back into those woods for the first time since everything happened makes me ill. So I lie. "I'll be fine. I promise. I *need* to do this."

She nods as if she understands, but her eyes do not agree with me. "I trust you, but be sure to check in with Birdee. If I hear of you not telling her when and where and why or what, I'm coming back immediately."

"Uh-oh. Wouldn't want that." I smile and rub my eyes, still half asleep. "Hey, goes for you too, ya know."

My stomach feels emptier than usual, and the truth is, I don't want Mom to go away any more than she wants me to hike. I've already lost Dad, so the thought of anything happening to her overwhelms me sometimes. Probably exactly how she feels about me.

I keep my concerns to myself, because I know she needs to do this training in order to get out of that crappy diner. And if she gets the slightest hint I'm not okay with it, she'll cancel everything. Frankly, though, it'll be nice to have her home more once she's done.

"Deal. I'll check in too." She leans over and hugs me. "I'll miss you."

We hold each other for a second. I've learned the hard way, you always hug someone as if it's the last time. It's hard to believe a few short months ago we were so mad at each other and so hurt, we could barely breathe in the same room without fighting. Now our relationship is better than ever. Kinda sad it takes death to bring two people together.

She tilts her head and releases her infamous sigh. "You sure you're going to be okay?"

I groan and fall back on the bed. "Mooom, please. I'll be fine. I'm actually excited to get back out there again. Really." I glance out my window at the white-capped mountains looming in the distance, anticipating our overdue reunion. "It's been too long."

"Okay." She cups both my shoulders as tears form in her eyes. "I'm sorry I have to go, especially right now."

I nod. "Just promise me when you start working for Dr. Head, we can bring back the return of family dinners and weekly movie night."

She holds out her pinky. "I pinky promise."

I can't help but smile at the fact that she'll always see me as being six. I curl my pinky around hers. "Now I feel much better."

"Maybe if we're lucky, he'll give you some free sessions so you can visit him again. If you need to."

I groan. "Can't wait."

She laughs and rubs my cheek. "He's not so bad." I see something in her smile that I can't quite place. Before I can narrow it down, she changes the subject. "I'll be back before you know it. It'll be nice having Birdee here for Christmas since…"

Her mention of the dreaded C-word sends my head spinning. I think about Dad chopping down our Christmas tree. He was the only one who put up the lights outside and carved the turkey. Who's going to do that now? Me? Birdee? Les? So many holiday tasks to reassign. They may seem small, but those little things are what made our family Christmas so special.

I bite the inside of my cheek and swallow the sadness stuck in my throat. I wish we'd skip Christmas this year. It'll never be the same as before, so why even try? Why pretend when we could just sleep the whole day away for another year?

Because Birdee – Ms. Let's Be As Tacky As We Can - would never go for that. She celebrates Groundhog Day so why would I think she'd skip Christmas?

Mom grabs her purse. "Okay. Well I better go. No use dillydallying anymore. I'll call you as soon as I get to Asheville."

I lift the pink cell phone she got me after Dad died. "I'll text you."

She smiles. "I'll try to figure out how to text back. Still getting the hang of it."

I take her overnight bag down the stairs. As Birdee walks Mom to Dad's truck, I stand in the window, afraid to say a final goodbye. I remember the last time I saw Dad, the smile on his face when he walked down the driveway, the double-toot of his horn as he drove away. On that clear morning, I never imagined it'd be the last time I'd hear his voice.

As Mom pulls away, she honks her horn twice. Even when her truck disappears down the road, I linger in the window. I can't help but feel sad and wonder in the back of my mind if that was the last time I'll ever see her.

Birdee walks in the front door and shakes the snow off her straw hat. She makes a "brrrr" sound and hangs up her peacoat. She notices me still standing there and cups my shoulders.

"You don't want her to leave, do you?"

I shake my head and try to hold back my tears along with the deep-seated fear of losing another person important to me.

Birdee hugs me from behind and rests her chin on my shoulder. Her breath tickles my ear. "You know, you're just as worried about her as she is about you."

I turn around and bury my head in my grandmother's flannel shirt. She strokes my hair as I take in a whiff of her familiar flowery scent mixed with burning wood, obviously from tending to the fireplace.

I mumble, "I'm scared."

She strokes my hair. "And well you should be." She pushes me away and yells, "because when the cat is away…"

I force out a smile at the old phrase we used to always say every time my parents left on a trip. "The mice shall play," I finish.

She claps. "That-a girl! What should we do first? Eat breakfast for dinner or dessert for brunch? So many choices."

I shake my head. "Easy. My answer is always dessert."

"Ha! Your father and I always used to eat dessert for breakfast when his daddy would go on trips." Birdee grabs my hand and escorts me to the kitchen table. She ushers me into a chair and bangs around. "Wait until you see what old Birdee has prepared for you."

"Let me guess… MoonPies." I rub my hands together. You can never eat enough MoonPies. "And it'd better *not* be the mini kind."

Birdee opens a cupboard. "Ta-da!"

At some point in the middle of the night, she cleared all the cans and homemade jars of jelly and replaced them with boxes of different flavored MoonPies.

"Luckily your mother didn't see all this redecorating. So what's your poison?"

I eye the treats. "Hmm. Tough one. I'll take a vanilla double-decker, please."

"Coming right up." Birdee bows before disappearing.

A few second later, she comes back with two plates from Mom's best china, the ones we only use at holidays. It's the set that's missing a plate because Dad tried to spin it on his knife. I grin, remembering the look on his face when it crashed to the floor and how Mom reprimanded him. My smile quickly slips down. Just in time, Birdee slides a plate of MoonPies in front of me. Food therapy.

"Nothing but the best for you, my dear."

We both pick up the snack and clink them together like glasses at a celebratory toast.

I holler out, "Cheers! To MoonPies."

And Birdee follows up with the famous tagline, "They're out of this world."

I bite into my double-decker. Dad used to always say, *when you're down, MoonPies make your spirit soar.* He'd never allow me to mope during MoonPie time; and if I did, he'd withhold the spongy treats like food from a jailbird until I smiled. I stay true to his strict rule and force myself to enjoy the yummy snack.

Birdee talks with her mouth full of a mint chocolate MoonPie. "So, today the big day?"

I nod and lick marshmallow off my finger. "Mm hmm."

She eyes me. "Nervous?"

I stop mid-bite. If it were Mom, she'd wait for my response. Then if I told her I was scared, she'd use my temporary weakness to talk me out of going so she could

53

keep me home safe and sound. Not only does Mom try to protect me from danger, but she also tries to shield me from my own fears.

I decide to be honest with Birdee because I know I can. "Yes."

Birdee takes another bite. "Good. Nerves keep you on your toes."

"That's your pep talk?"

She wipes a marshmallow chunk off the corner of her mouth. "There can be no courage without fear?"

I look at her.

She chews for a few seconds before asking what sounds like another nonchalant question. "Got your knife?"

I look in her eyes. That question is more up Birdee's alley. "Always."

Her face turns serious. "You listen here, Chicken. Don't be afraid to use it if you have to. On *anyone*."

I try hard to swallow, but even the soft graham cracker crust seems to stick in my throat. "Why? Do you think… anyone will?"

Birdee reaches over and grasps my hand, looking me in the eyes. "No, I don't. Sweeney would never put you in danger. I believe that. If he thought there was even the slightest chance that maniac was here, you bet your sweet donkey, he'd never let you go. But it never hurts to be safe. And you need to know that you can take care of yourself."

I nod and study her face to see if she's really telling the truth, or if she's trying not to scare me. She goes back to chewing as if we just discussed the weather.

Then, Birdee takes another bite without looking at me. "Not to mention, I wouldn't let you go if I thought you were in danger either. Maybe I'm naïve but I do believe one thing, we all have to get back out there or the bad guys win."

"I know."

We eat our third MoonPie in silence. I'm not sure if it's because she's afraid to say anything, or if it's because she's thinking of eating a fourth snack. When I glance over, I happen to catch a hint of something in her expression. I can't tell if it's fear or uncertainty, like maybe she's unsure of what she's saying. Or she's not 100 percent confident in my decision. Then again, maybe she's a little scared.

Maybe I should be, too.

ɞ

At the station, Agent Sweeney spends some time reviewing the basics. In a nutshell, his wisdom is pretty much this: stay together, stay on the path, and stay warm. Not woodland science, if you ask me. Yet Wyn and Skyler hang on to every word as if it's a new revelation, making me even more concerned about my team.

Skyler raises her hand when he pauses for a mini-second. "Do you think we'll see any other wild animals?"

Porter stands up. "You could see cougars, bears—"

"Cougars and wolves and bears, oh my!" Seth blurts out in a high voice and dances around. Big Mike laughs his baritone, belly laugh while Madison shakes her head in disgust.

I can't help but add fuel to the fire. "And don't forget those wild turkeys."

Skyler shoots me one of her mean looks. I'm starting to think those are the only ones she has – besides googly eyes of course.

I shrug. "What? Turkeys can be very dangerous. Don't underestimate them. Especially this time of year. And trust me, if they see you with a pocketknife, they will not hesitate to attack and defend themselves against the Christmas tradition." I cover my mouth to hide a pending smile.

Skyler scoffs. "Ha. Ha. Very funny."

Agent Sweeney shakes his head. "I'd never know you were all on the same team here."

Wyn speaks up, "Okay, so we know the basics. But what exactly are we looking for when we get out there? How do we know when we're close?"

Porter sits on the desk and removes his Indiana Jones-style hat. "Wolves keep to themselves. They are very shy and try to stay hidden. So they're very hard to track." A pair of paw prints pops up on the screen. "Of course, you can look for their tracks in the snow. Listen for howls. Or…"

Seth jumps up behind Skyler and screams, "Find bloody carcasses of their half-eaten prey!"

Skyler screams and then cringes away from him. "Ew."

As always, Wyn comes to the rescue. "Cut it out, Seth. Jesus, get a life."

"Me?" Seth frowns. "In case you didn't realize, white knights in shining armor with small *swords* are not cool anymore."

Madison and I groan at the start of another Battle of the Egos.

"Neither are *jerks*," Wyn snaps back.

Agent Sweeney stands up to intervene again, but this time Katie cuts him off. "Guys, the childish banter is getting old. This is a serious project, and I need you to focus and treat it as such. Or you're out. I'm sure Ms. Cox would agree."

Seth salutes Katie and Wyn mumbles an apology. She smiles. "Porter, you were saying?"

Porter props his boot on one knee. "Not to refuel a dying fire, but in actuality, Seth is right."

Seth gives Wyn an "I told you so" look as the professor explains. "Feeding signs are a good indicator a wolf pack is nearby." He pulls out his smartphone and shows us a picture. "This is a wolf den I came across once. You can see they drag most of their kills to the same place. Except for the occasional snack."

Skyler whines and covers her eyes. "This is so gross."

"Circle of life, baby." Seth blurts out as Wyn shoots him another look.

Porter advances to another picture. "And this is a picture of wolf scat."

"Of what?" Wyn leans forward.

"You would probably know it as wolf *poop*." I inform my leader.

"Gnarly." Seth pushes into Madison to get a better look at the hairy mound. "How do you know that's not from Bigfoot?"

Skyler looks petrified but tries to smile. "Bigfoot? Yeah, right." She studies Porter as if waiting for him to confirm there is no Sasquatch in the area.

I play along just to freak her out. "Never know. That guy in Shelby says he saw one cross the road. Right in front of him. Didn't even yield to oncoming traffic. Pedestrian violation if you ask me."

Maybe that will get her off this team, so I can focus on the seriousness of the project. As opposed to Lessons from Country Mouse to City Mouse.

Skyler frowns. "We didn't."

Wyn waves us all to be quiet. "Shut up, you guys. There's no Bigfoot, Sky. Can you be serious for once? This is a matter of life and death."

I roll my eyes.

Call the CDC, because we now know Skyler's drama is highly contagious.

Porter flips through a few more slides of old dens, more tracks, and clumps of hair left stuck to branches.

"Again, this is an organized tracking effort. Most of the wolves are tagged, and we know where they are within a mile radius. However, it's always good to know the signs. You never know if a tag has malfunctioned, or how the weather will affect the equipment. We just need to find the wolves, observe them from a distance, and mark down everything we see. Very simple. The weather will be our biggest hurdle at this point."

He holds up the backpacks we were given yesterday. "Don't forget. You have everything you need for basic winter survival and tracking."

Agent Sweeney hands out a list of the bag contents. "Make sure you designate someone to conduct bag checks each time you leave. You may need to restock your supplies."

Wyn assigns that duty to me with another lame nod. This time, I nod back, a little more dramatically followed by an obnoxious salute.

I skim the checklist. It mainly lists the basics needed for a one- or two-day hike: flashlight, knives, compass, maps, and safety items. Plus a few luxuries like hand and feet warmers, extra matches, a fold-down survival shovel, and even a small sterno to heat food or water.

Porter walks around the room as Big Mike and I double-check the team packs. "You have some tracking tools in there. In addition to the observation folder and data sheets, there's a tape measure, trail markers, orange surveyor tape, and a disposable camera for documenting."

Agent Sweeney continues. "We will be monitoring you at all times. There's a tracking device on each pack. Porter will give each team a map of their assigned areas to search. The locations are not as far out as you would think. He'll be going back and forth between the two teams to ensure safety, so you shouldn't be more than a mile or two away from each other.

"Each team will have a radio, though sometimes the signal is a little testy this time of year. According to the weather check, today should be cold but sunny, so we don't expect anything out of the ordinary. But as most of you know, the weather up there can be unpredictable, especially this time of year, so if you see any signs it's worsening, head back immediately the same way you hiked in."

Porter helps me reload the pack. "And don't forget to stick to the map. Following those trails will ensure we know where you are at all times in case we need to extract you."

The way he keeps saying extract makes me feel like a black head.

He continues, "These paths were chosen for a reason. They are the most passable and have been identified as the safest routes. Only fools stray."

I look around the room, not feeling very confident no fools exist in this bunch.

Agent Sweeney takes off his baseball cap and rubs something off the brim. "Any questions?"

"Yeah." I raise my hand. "When do we start?"

# Survival Skill #6

*When hiking in the winter, there are four basic wilderness survival priorities: shelter, fire, water, and food (in that order).*

There's only one thing worse than being in the woods with a boy who hates me as much as he hates foliage – spending time with Malibu Barbie Goes Camping, a girl whose only experience with nature is killing two silk plants and watering a cactus.

Skyler pulls her pink coat tighter and repeats herself for the umpteenth time. "I still don't understand why we have to do this in winter and on our vacation!"

*Well, maybe you shouldn't have volunteered,* I think to myself. I try hard to ignore her never-ending complaints, but after listening to her squeal at every bug and mud puddle for two hours, I'm about at my breaking point.

"It's so cold." Her high-pitched voice rings in my ears. "How much colder do you think it will get?"

Following behind them, I roll my eyes and can't resist mumbling under my breath, "Not cold enough."

"I'll keep you warm." Wyn hugs her and rubs her arms to warm her up.

I'm praying Skyler's breaking point is nearing with every step, because I could do this assignment much faster if I was on my own. I watch her and Wyn walk in front of me, all cuddled up like they're window-shopping in an outdoor mall. I can't help but miss him and how he used to take care of me, or how he'd try anyway.

No matter how much I don't want to envy them, they make me think of Mo. Our last night together at his camp, cooking and kissing; our day in the stream, fishing and laughing. The way he always called me Blossom, the same way Wyn calls her Sky. But mostly, I miss the way Mo wouldn't let me pull away from him when I was scared. God, I miss him so much. It's bad enough he's not here, but it's definitely not fair I'm forced to watch Wyn and Skyler fall in love.

Their happiness rubs salt in the gaping hole Mo's death left in my heart. For a long time, I thought he might still be alive, but as the days pass, that hope becomes a crazy dream.

After watching them a few more minutes, I fall back a few steps from the happy couple. Serious trackers don't giggle. And just a wild guess, but I'm pretty sure trackers don't find any tracks on each other's face or lips.

As I trudge along, my eyes scan the snow-covered path for prints of any kind. When I spot a pile of animal scat frozen in the snow, I can't resist calling out to our designated documenter.

"Ohhh, Skyyy-ler. I think I found something you should note in the log."

It takes a few seconds for her and Wyn to sludge their way back through the snow. I try not to laugh as they both bend over, inspecting the *poop*-cicle.

I rub my gloves together to warm my hands and watch Skyler wrinkle her nose. "How do we know it's wolf poop?"

I mumble with a smirk on my face, "Oh, it's not. Wolf scat is much hairier than that. That's just deer poop. Thought you might want to see the difference. Up close and personal. For the sake of research."

Skyler shoots to her feet. "What's your problem?"

Instead of saying what I want to say, which is YOU, I act totally innocent. "What do you mean?"

"Don't play dumb, Grace," she growls.

"Wouldn't dream of it, *Sky*. That's your area of expertise."

"Oh really?" She steps closer, giving me a whiff of her perfume.

Who wears Chanel No. 5 in the woods? I glance at Wyn, who's now staring off into the trees, avoiding the conflict.

I point to Romeo. "Besides, he should know wolf scat from deer scat. Don't you think, Wyn? After all, you are the *leader* of the team."

He frowns and steps between us like we're having a playground duel. "Take it easy, ladies."

Skyler eyes him. "Why are you sticking up for her?"

He faces her and turns his back on me. "I'm not, but you girls bickering out here is not going to get us any warmer."

I nod. "He's right. Wyn knows all the answers out here. Don't you, Wyn?"

He tosses me a sharp glance. Not one hint of a smile, which is rare for Wyn, since he has a hard time being serious at a funeral. "Cut it out, Grace."

Him saying my name totally catches me off guard. I bet I even stumble back a step or two, like he's kicked me in the chest. It's the first time he's addressed me as a real person since that day at the station when he told me he'd never speak to me again. And I believed him.

I didn't realize how much I missed hearing him say my name until now.

I swallow the lump in my throat and try not to soften at his imaginary blow. "So you *do* remember my name."

The smile I long to see never comes. Instead he looks away, as if he's stared at the sun too long. "Maybe we should stop and build a fire."

I let my voice show the irritation. "Are you serious? It's only noon. This is the warmest part of the day."

Wyn hugs Skyler, and his voice sounds strange, like his mouth is stiff from being half-frozen. "She's cold."

I snap back before I can stop myself. "Because it's *winter.*" Then I mumble again. "You guys should have thought of that before you decided to play Tarzan and Jane. Maybe she should just go *home.*"

Skyler puts her fuzzy white mittens on her hips, and I can't tell if her cheeks are pink with cold or anger. "Oh! You'd like that, wouldn't you?" She mouths *Graceless* behind his back, so he doesn't hear or see.

I ignore her and study a few broken branches. "Let's just say I wouldn't object."

She hops over to me in her furry, non-hiking boots like some snow bunny. I can't hide my smile when I realize they're already completely ruined, and it's only Day One. Maybe she'll bow out due to a lack of inappropriate footwear, suffer from a little frostbite on her probably perfectly painted toes. Not anything to take off an appendage, but maybe enough to get her out of my face.

She leans in close. "You just want Wyn alone so you can have him to yourself."

I laugh out loud before she can even add a period to her ridiculous sentence. "Ha! Like he's any better. I'd rather do this alone. Without the catalog couple. By myself."

"Well, that can certainly be arranged," Skyler shouts back. Her voice echoes through the trees.

I scoff. "Should I be so lucky."

Wyn gets between us and grabs Skyler's hand. "Ladies, this isn't helping. Let's just stop fighting and gather some wood so we can warm up. Make a plan." He looks at Skyler. "Deal?"

She smiles up at him. "Sure, Wyn."

He glances at me.

I notice his hand in hers and push away any sadness. Instead, I stand at attention and salute the so-called leader. "Yes, *sir!*"

Without responding, he frowns and marches off into the woods. As he walks away, I notice the seat of his pants are slightly damp, and I can only assume his butt is freezing cold. I cheer on the inside. Serves him right. Should have worn some real clothes. His Old Navy coat and Levis aren't going to keep him warm, and I'm pretty sure the wolves won't be that impressed either. Maybe he should have referenced the "What to Wear" checklist like I told him.

Skyler hops back and forth to keep warm like she's in some kind of line dance at Bronco's Bar and Grill on a Saturday night. I clear an area for the fire and form a circle with some large stones.

"Grab those little sticks and break them up."

She snaps back. "Do it yourself."

I stand and face her. "Look, I'm trying to help."

She glares at me and pulls her fake fur hat down over her ears. Her nose is red, and her eyes are watering, a true contrast to her voice, which is sharp and cutting. "Yeah? Well, you've done enough already."

Her words cut me deep, and the semi-permanent lump in my throat swells. It's the first time I've realized that Skyler holds me solely responsible for her dad's death. Maybe she'd feel differently if she knew how much I miss Carl, too. Well, the old Carl anyway. Sometimes, I lie in bed at night and remember his laugh, they way he helped Dad build a tree fort for Skyler and me when we were barely in elementary school. How the four of us used to go snowmobiling in the winters. Contrary to what everyone thinks, I loved Carl like he was part of my family.

I try hard to swallow back the untapped emotions from the past few months. "Skyler, you're not the only person who lost someone, you know." My voice comes out scratchy, like it's been pushed through the splintered wall of hurt and guilt I've stacked around me.

The look coming from her bright blue eyes shocks me. It's pure hate. Not a "we are not from the same crowd in school" hate, but a real, deep down to the core hatred. And as much as I don't like Skyler and how much she's changed from the days when we used to catch tadpoles in the stream together, I've never hated her.

She takes a breath and forces words out through her clenched teeth. "Yeah, but I didn't *kill* yours."

My body heats up in anger at her horrible comment. Instead of lashing out, I force myself to turn away. I can't face her anymore without showing her my weakness, my guilt. And no matter what I want to say or do, it won't heal the damage that's been done. Skyler will never forgive me and neither will Wyn. I suddenly feel very alone.

As I resume gathering sticks, tears fill my eyes. I suddenly feel like crying for Carl, Dad, Mo, and my dog Bear; for losing Tommy and Wyn; for everything I did to let them walk away. A tear trails down my cheek. I hear Skyler sniff behind me. This time, I don't turn around for fear she might be crying too.

A few minutes later, Wyn breaks the awkwardness by crashing back into the clearing, carrying a few logs. He drops them in the circle. So much for tracking quietly.

I dry both eyes with my shirtsleeve and drop a few more sticks onto the pile. He takes out a flint and steel from our survival pack and beds down to light the pile of tinder just like Agent Sweeney taught us. Only Wyn doesn't know matches are in the kit, too.

"Wyn…"

He keeps using the flint. "Grace, let me handle this. For once."

I bite my tongue and wait. Little sparks shoot out, but nothing catches fire. If he'd just listen to me, I could help him. But I'm not going to say any more until he asks. Or begs. Let him be the self-appointed leader who chooses fashion over function if he wants. He can figure it out by himself. Or better yet, let Skyler help him light his fire.

After a few tries, he glances up at me. "I could use some help here."

I look around. "Wait, are you talking to me?"

"Come on. Give me a break."

As a brisk wind comes through the clearing, I pull the hood over my head and zip up. "Thought you wanted to handle this."

He stands and faces me. For a split second, our eyes lock. I see his face soften. "If you think you can do better, be my guest."

I smile. Wyn challenging me to build a fire is like me challenging the sun to shine. "Fine. Step aside and learn."

I pull a box of matches from my pocket and strike one until flames dance off the red tip. I quickly light the tinder and smile. "There. I think those made it much easier. Don't you?"

Wyn frowns and shoves his hands into his jacket pockets. "Very funny. You could have told me about those."

"I tried." I shrug. "But you wanted to *lead*. And, you're the boss."

He tosses me the backpack. "Not anymore."

Wyn walks away dejected, and I immediately feel bad for embarrassing him. But as soon as I stand to apologize, Skyler is already at his side, hooking her arm through his. They both sit down together to get warm, and she whispers sweet nothings in his ear.

There's no way Wyn and I will ever patch things up as long as she's standing between us. And I'm pretty sure there's no way she'll get out of my way so we can. Feeling like the third wheel, I decide to search for more signs of the pack we're supposed to be tracking. I move in a circular path around the fire, venturing farther and farther away from the makeshift campsite. Finally, I come upon a print.

Only this is no wolf.

My heart starts to race as I skim the trees, looking for something. Or someone. I check my radio to see if Porter's called and is on his way. Nothing. I don't want to yell, so instead I whistle to get Wyn's attention. When he looks up, I motion him over. He reluctantly leaves Skyler's clutches and makes his way through the trees.

"What is it this time? Something else I'm doing wrong you want to show me?"

I point down at the print. "Look."

He studies the marking and shrugs. "Yeah, so?"

I put my finger to my lips and my mouth turns dry. "Shhhh." I point down to an indention in the snow. "It's fresh because of the snow melting around the edges."

He looks down and then back at me. "And I care about this because why?"

A branch cracks in the distance.

I whisper. "Because we're not alone."

# Survival Skill #7

*A track in the snow may look different after the warm sun has enlarged and distorted it.*

ꟼ realize I've been out here for a couple hours and not once have I thought of Al.

Until now.

I stare at the print a little longer and make out the edges. I think back to the bootprint pictures I gave Mama Sue to use for tracking down the owner, but I can't seem to remember the details. Did Al wear a size 10 or 11?

A scuffling of leaves catches my attention, and I immediately crouch down.

Wyn squats next to me and touches my shoulder. "You okay?"

I flinch and stare into the wall of trees drooping with melting snow, looking for anything out of place. As the wind blows, it loosens the powder and sends it tumbling to the ground, making the air a fuzzy white. My head snaps to the right when my peripheral vision catches movement.

A dark silhouette weaves through the woods, hidden in the shadows created by the thick, white blanket of the treetops sheltering us. I can't help but think of Mo, remembering the first time I saw him slinking around Bear Creek. I squint as snowflakes land on my eyelashes, making my eyes water.

I hear myself take a breath, a small gasp no one would hear but me. Could this be Mo? It's been three months and still no sign he's alive. There's barely any sign he ever was. Agent Sweeney won't say anything about knowing Mo whenever I inquire, but I'll never forget what he said when I brought in the papers Mo left me. He snatched them up without any explanation and gave me his "condolences," said he was "sorry for my losses." Not loss. *Losses.* More than one. And I'm pretty sure he doesn't count Carl. He could've only meant two people, Dad and Mo, which means even he thinks Mo is dead.

I snap out of my thoughts and watch the figure move closer. But when the shadow is only a few yards away, I immediately know it's not Mo. I know Mo's walk, the way he sways and swings one arm more than the other. Then it hits me – this shadow is much larger.

The hairs on my neck stand, and I hear myself whisper, "Al."

Just then, Porter steps out of the trees with snow on his hat. He stops and stares in the direction we're facing. "See a ghost or something?"

Wyn screams like a little girl. "Jesus!"

I jolt back to life but stay squatted because my legs are shaking. "Ah, sorry. We were wondering who you were."

Porter takes off his hat and hits it against his leg to shake off any dirt or debris. "Who else would you be expecting?"

I mutter, still staring into the forest, "No one special." Bummed he's not Mo, but relieved he's not Al.

I pull my eyes away from the woods and turn around. Still can't help feeling as if Mo and Al are out there somewhere. Crazy. That would mean one was coming back from the dead, and the other was coming back for revenge.

"Radio wasn't working or I'd have called." He slings the hat back on his head and rubs his hands together. "So... taking a break?"

Skyler is still sitting by the fire, looking like a blob of fluffy cotton candy in her white and pink furry get up. "It was cold."

She was obviously completely unaware of what happened in the last five minutes – my moment of hope followed by a moment of fear.

Porter nods a little longer than necessary. "Yep, and it will get colder. A bad front's coming in a couple of days." He grabs a handful of snow and throws in on the fire. The flames hiss in anger. He stomps out the embers and claps his gloved hands together. "Time to find the wolves before it gets dark. You guys are close. Transmitters show them within a half mile."

"Let's go then." I sling the backpack over my shoulder.

Porter smoothes his graying mustache down with two fingers. "New leadership?"

I smile. "Let's just say there was a *coup d'état*."

Wyn frowns. "Very funny."

Porter tucks his lumberjack shirt into his snow pants and zips his coat. "Fine, then. Half a mile to the north. Grace, why don't you lead the way?"

I can't help but smile. Finally someone smart.

The four of us hike in a single-file line up a thin path bordered by two-foot embankments. One step to either side, and we'd be in snow up to our knees. No one says a word. Well, except for Skyler, who is still grumbling several. Luckily with two people between us, I can't hear much, which allows me to finally relish in my surroundings.

The mountain sounds are different in winter than in summer – not as much twittering or skittering. Just the wind whistling through the thinning trees, the sparkling snow crunching under my feet, and the faint song from a family of nuthatches perched high in a tree. The smooth, untouched snow hides the land's blemishes and gives the impression we're walking amongst the clouds.

As we move up the mountain, I can feel the temperature change. Soon my nose is numb and running, and a chill skitters down my spine. My breath comes out in puffs as I cut through the untouched trail for everyone behind me. It's difficult, and I can already feel my thighs throbbing. But I'm not about to give Wyn the last laugh by quitting or taking a break.

I forge ahead and talk over my shoulder to Porter, who's close behind. "How long have you been tracking wolves?"

He huffs as he answers. "More than forty years. Used to live out in Montana. Friends owned a cattle ranch there and used to complain of wolves getting their sheep. I used to volunteer to relocate the wolves. Course those were gray wolves. Not red ones."

"Aren't they pretty similar?"

I move aside a branch and hold it so it doesn't slap him in the face. He nods his appreciation.

"Gray wolves are much larger and live in packs of up to thirty; whereas, red wolves are usually found in packs of ten. Gray wolves also tend to be much more aggressive than red wolves, who tend to be much harder to spot."

I keep moving up the mountain. "Have you ever been to North Carolina before now?"

"My wife died here."

"Oh! I'm sorry."

Porter pauses for a second. "Me too."

I take a few more steps and decide to change the conversation quickly. I don't want to start sharing our stories of death. Not right now. "Do you think the reintroduction will work?"

His breath is a little labored as he answers. "Depends on if we can keep them away from poachers and cars. Keep track of them to be sure they stay healthy." Porter drops his voice to a whisper and points up the mountain. "One of the pack's main dens should be just over that ridge."

I keep walking along the path until I start to see small wolf prints in the snow. Only one set. They lead up the mountain. I kneel down to touch them. Next to them is what looks like more shoe prints.

I hear myself whisper, "You been up here today?"

Porter almost slams into me from behind. "No, why?"

A chill skitters down my back. Without answering, I mutter under my breath. "Oh, no."

Before Porter can ask any questions, I take off up the hill, kicking my feet out to the sides over the high snow. My pack weighs me down and my legs resist, but I push on through the thick ground cover.

Porter calls after me. "Wait!"

But I don't stop. To be honest, I don't know why I'm running, but my gut tells me something isn't right.

Both prints head off on the same path, as if one is tracking the other. I veer right and sludge through the snow until I come upon the source. A red wolf is lying in the snow.

*Please, God. No.*

As the rest of my team crashes through the trees behind me, I move quickly around to one side, keeping my distance. Hoping. Praying that this animal is merely hurt but still alive. As soon as I see his eyes, any hope I had is crushed. I cover my mouth as Porter comes into view. He throws down his pack and yells when he sees the wolf lying still.

"Damn it!"

Wyn calls out. "What's wrong? Is it dead?"

I nod without looking at him, and Skyler wails. Wyn hugs her as she buries her face into his shirt, crying. To be honest, I feel like crying, too, but I don't. Instead, I reach over and touch the beautiful creature. My fingers slide through his thick, reddish fur.

Porter kneels down, inspecting the dead animal, cussing under his breath.

My lip quivers when I talk. "What happened?"

He lifts up the wolf's head with his hand. "I can't tell."

I stare at the animal. His soft fur quivers in the light breeze, and my stomach churns in distaste.

Porter takes off his hat as if paying his respects. "There's no blood." He looks around the area and points to a slew of other prints. "Looks like the pack was here. Maybe he was sick. They left him when they heard you crashing about."

He frowns at me.

"Sorry. I couldn't help myself." I stand and move back to give him room so he can inspect the animal more. "Do you think it was an accident?"

"Probably natural causes."

I look back the way we came. "I saw footprints back there. Maybe a poacher?"

Porter sits back on his heels and shakes his head. "Doesn't look like it."

"But how do you know?"

He narrows his eyes. "Because I've been doing this for decades."

"Yes, but…"

"And you've been doing this a few minutes." He stands and softens his voice. "Look, I know this is hard. Seeing your first dead one always is. But this is why we're out here."

"To find them dead?"

He unzips his pack and takes out some tracking supplies. "No, to find out why they can't survive. So we can help them live." He starts marking the trail and noting coordinates. "Look, why don't you go rest? I'll take care of this. You've been through enough."

My head feel fuzzy, so I lean against a tree to steady myself.

Wyn appears next to me and cups my elbow. "You okay?"

I look up into his eyes, and my body starts to tremble. I try a couple times to speak, but my mouth is so dry. It's like I haven't had water in days or like I've been drinking sand. His expression changes and he puts both hands on my shoulders.

It's more than the wolf.

It's the death. Seeing it and being around it again.

"You're cold. You're shaking." Wyn takes off his coat and wraps it over my shoulders.

I flinch at his touch and look up into his eyes. "I'm fine."

I can feel Skyler's eyes bearing into my skull, but I don't dare look. No use seeing another dagger shoot from her eyes. She calls out. "Wyn?"

But Wyn doesn't budge. He just stands there staring at me, like he's frozen in the snow. Flakes land on his eyelashes, but he doesn't blink. It's the first time we've stood face to face since that day at the station. Even though it was months ago, I remember it like it was yesterday. The things he said, the look of disappointment on his face. Even though I'm still mad at how he's treated me, I realize how much I miss my best friend. In this one moment, it's like nothing has ever changed between us. It's as if we only paused for a few months and now someone has pressed Play again.

I hear Skyler again. "Wyn?"

He snaps to life and immediately drops his hands. "Huh? Oh, sorry."

"It's okay."

"You alright?"

I smile. "Always."

He spins around and heads off toward Skyler, probably to do some serious damage control.

I move next to Porter, who is standing with his hands on both hips, staring at the dead animal.

"Damn shame. Definitely not good for the project."

I look from the animal to Porter. "But you said this happens."

He rubs his neck. "It does, but that doesn't mean we like it. It's another sign telling us maybe wolves aren't meant to be out here anymore."

"But they are. They have to be." My sadness flips into anger. These creatures deserve to be out here more than any of us do.

Porter leans over the wolf and removes the transmitter from its neck. He reads the number aloud. "M79. Looks like one of the smaller males." He wipes his face with a rag. "This won't be too detrimental for the pack."

I wait for him to say more, but he goes quiet. "So does that mean they'll be okay?"

He looks into my eyes. "Let's hope so."

Wyn breaks our gaze. "What do we do now?"

Porter points off into the trees. "We have to carry him out."

Skyler groans behind us and mumbles. "Great."

Without being asked, I find two long, thick branches. Wyn and I drag them over next to the wolf. I take out the tarp and rope to make a stretcher.

Skyler covers her mouth as we load up the wolf, but I see her gag. "Can't we just leave it? I mean, it's dead."

No smart comment comes from me. I don't have the energy to answer or argue. My voice is weighed down by my heavy heart. I didn't expect this at all, or I might not have volunteered.

A person can only take so much death.

Porter drags the animal onto the tarp. "No way. We need it for research. If we leave the body out here, no telling what could get it." He covers the body and claps his hands together, wiping off the snow. "Wyn, you grab one side, and I'll get the other. Grace, you lead us out."

The four of us set off back down the way we came. The light flurry has already covered our tracks. No one says anything the whole hike back, not even Skyler.

But my head is buzzing.

I can't help but wonder what happened to that wolf.

# Survival Skill #8

*The rapport with other hikers is critical to making decisions in the wild.*

"Maybe you should bow out of this thing?"

Agent Sweeney sits very still and doesn't take his eyes off me. Even though we've been discussing what happened in the woods, I wasn't expecting this comment to come out of his mouth.

I fiddle with the zipper on my jacket and shake my head. "What? Why?"

He takes in a deep breath and exhales through his nose, causing a slight whistling sound. "You know why."

My heart thumps in my ears. "You think he's back?"

"I didn't say that."

I look him in the eyes and spot it – the concern, the worry. "You don't have to."

He gets up and walks around the room, up and down the aisles, until he sits on the desk. "Look, Grace. I'm not going to lie. I didn't necessarily like it when you volunteered for this project, but who was I to hold you back if you were ready to go into the woods again?"

"I was. I mean, I am."

He shakes his head. "I know, but this changes everything."

I don't want to believe he's right. "Porter says it was natural causes."

Sweeney rubs his hands together as if trying to keep warm. "Doesn't matter."

I pull my long hair back off my face and tug on my turtleneck, suddenly feeling claustrophobic. "Do you think Al is involved?" I cringe when I say the name out loud.

Agent Sweeney removes his baseball cap and scratches his head. "I doubt it. He'd be pretty dumb to show his face here again. He knows he's a wanted man. Not only by me, but by the FBI as well. This has nothing to do with Al. This is because I don't want you to get involved."

"In what? The wolf project?"

He crosses his arms, and I'm suddenly reminded of all the times Carl tried to get me off my Dad's trail. "In anything that's going to upset you."

I shrug, playing off any feelings I have about the dead wolf. "Do I look upset?"

He twirls a pencil between his fingers. "No, but I know you. We've spent a lot of time together the last few months, and you've gone through a really traumatic event. More than one. A dead animal bothers you just as much as a human."

His comment stabs me in the stomach to the point I almost double over. Agent Sweeney obviously notices and shakes his head. "I'm sorry. I shouldn't have that, but you know what I mean."

I nod.

"I know this upsets you. If something… anything is going to impact these wolves, it will hurt you just as much. I don't want you going through anything else. Not now. Not after everything that's happened. Maybe you need to be a regular kid for a while."

I know he's right, but I push back anyway. "Maybe I can't be a regular kid. Look, I'm fine. Really. This project is helping me. It's getting me back into the woods. I need to have something to focus on right now. Please don't take me off this project."

A voice pipes up from the back of the room. "No one's taking anyone off the project. What's going on?" Katie is speaking as she and Porter walk down the aisle. She sits next to me like we're in school together and looks around. "Where is everyone?"

Agent Sweeney drops his writing utensil. "I sent them all home. They were a little shaken."

Porter shoves his hands into his pants pockets. "Why would you do that? We have data to enter into the system."

Agent Sweeney cuts in, "I just don't know if the kids are prepared to see this kind of thing. Watching wolves play is one thing. Finding them dead is another."

Katie speaks up before Porter can answer. "Aren't we overreacting here? I mean, animals die." She folds her arms. "We've got a lot riding on this study, Agent. We can't cancel the research because a wolf dies. This happens in the wild. It's part of the process." She studies me. "I think these kids realize that. Don't you, Grace?"

I try to ignore Agent Sweeney's looks and nod. "Yes."

She smiles at me. "I think men underestimate us girls."

"They do." I smile. Finally someone who gets it.

She faces me and crosses her legs. "None of us should speak for you. You're a strong girl, so you tell me, how do you feel? If you want off the project, we can replace you with another student who might be more equipped to deal with this sort of thing."

I don't want Katie thinking I'm weak. If she can deal with the hassles of conservation every day, I can deal with a project. "I'm *equipped*. Trust me."

Katie looks between Agent Sweeney and me. "Then why are we discussing this? If Grace wants to be involved, why stop her? She's not a baby, and she's probably the best person we have." She winks at me. "Boys and all."

Agent Sweeney interjects. "As much as Grace wants to be involved... she has been through a lot lately, and I'm a little worried about her."

Katie comes to my defense. "Well, I don't think we should talk about her like she's not here." She rests her chin on her hand. "It's your call, Grace, and don't feel pressured either way. No one will hold a decision against you. But I think it's your decision to make."

Any nervousness I might have felt morphs to anger. I stand up. "Thank you, Agent Sweeney, I can handle it. I want to do this project. I *need* to do it."

Katie nods. "Good. Then that settles it. We'll continue the research and Grace remains on the team. We will reevaluate as the project continues. Sound good, Agent?"

Agent Sweeney studies me. "Whatever you say, Katie."

She claps. "Good. We just need to figure out how we proceed."

Porter spreads out a map on the desk. "I say we start out first thing in the morning. The pack has been tracked to this location. Wyn's team can start here and head north." I wince when he says Wyn's team. "And Seth's team can head due east to scout out the other pack."

He glances out the window at the steady stream of flurries. "We want to cover as much ground as we can before the weather turns against us."

ⱌ

After we're done discussing the plan, I leave before Agent Sweeney can corner me again. As soon as I'm outside, I head to the parking lot where I parked my bike. I need to get home before Birdee sends out an APB. The sidewalk is slippery, and the snow is coming down heavier. If it freezes tonight, there's no way Luci will be able to make to drag herself into town in the morning. Antique motorcycles and winter weather don't mix. I just hope I can get home.

As I turn the corner, my hackles rise when I see a figure standing against the wall. Wyn steps into the light. He changed and somehow is even more underdressed for the weather in a corduroy jacket with the hoodie pulled up over his head.

"You alright?" he says.

I grip my chest. "Jesus, Wyn, you scared the crap out of me." I continue through the parking lot toward my motorcycle. "What are you doing here?"

He jogs after me. "I was worried about you. What happened in there?"

I zip my white coat and pull the fake fur hood up to block the wind from my face. "That's none of your business. Why aren't you with Skyler? Doesn't she need comforting from her traumatic day in the woods?"

As he catches up to me, his feet slip on the slushy ice, but he manages to skate until he steadies himself. I can't help but smile under my hood, kinda wishing he'd bust a move in the wet snow. It would be total justice for the way he's treated me.

He tilts his head like a puppy wanting to play. "I take it you're still mad at me?"

I poke him hard in the chest. "Me? Mad? You're kidding, right? You don't talk to me for three friggin' months, and now I'm the *mad* one?"

I stomp through the slush, my hiking boots thumping along the pavement. He grabs my arm to stop me, causing me to slip. We both slide along the ground and hold on to each other until we get our footing.

He looks directly at me. "Look, I'm sorry."

"Sorry?" I can't help but soften at the sad expression on his face. "That's it? Now we're all better? You're acting like you accidentally pushed me down, and I skinned my knee."

He swipes a wet piece of hair off my face. "Fine. Will it make you feel better if I said I was a total jerk and you're the Goddess of Nature?"

I refuse to smile and fold my arms across my chest. "A jerk for what? Oh, you mean for turning your back on me like everyone else in this crappy town has? Or for not being there when I needed you most?"

My voice chokes, and my eyes water. I hope he thinks it's because snow is drifting into them, and not because everything I've held in is about to come pouring out on my best friend.

"Fine. I was a jerk. About everything. I was mad and hurt, but it's not like you're innocent, you know. You lied to me. Way too many times. All I wanted to do was help you, and you played me."

I hang my head, knowing he's right. "I didn't mean to. I just didn't want to hurt you or get you hurt. And in case you didn't notice, it wasn't the best of times for me. I was confused and not in a great place."

His gloved hands grasp mine. "After hearing about you and that other guy, then losing Carl, I got lost too. I'm only human."

I raise my eyebrows. "That's still up for debate."

He cups my face. "I'm serious. No joking. I took all my stuff out on you, and I'm so sorry." He pauses. "You didn't deserve all I dished out, and I wasn't there for you when you needed me most. Especially about your dad. Your poor dad. I'm sorry, Grace."

Without warning, the tears that I wanted to attribute to snowflakes dribble down my cheeks. He wipes one away with his glove.

"I let you down. I wasn't there for you, and I suck."

I sniff so my nose doesn't run. Not cute. "Maybe we both suck a little. I'm sorry, too. I should have trusted you. I just wasn't thinking. I was only focused on one thing. Finding Dad."

Images of that day come trickling in, and all the emotions surge back like a rolling tide. It's as if I'm back in that cave reliving my father's death all over again.

I whisper, "God, I miss him."

Wyn reaches out and touches my shoulder. "Can I hug you, or will you try to beat me up?"

I laugh through a cry. "Try to? You wish."

He pulls me to him and says he's sorry over and over. I bury my face in his jacket, and I smell the mixed scent of his cologne and shower gel. He kisses the top of my head. "You forgive me?"

I mumble a yes and pull back. "But if you turn your back on me again, I'll have to kick your ass."

"What's new?" He winks and motions with his head. "So tell me, what happened back there with Sweeney?"

I shrug. "Nothing much. Agent Sweeney thinks I should drop off the team."

"You can't do that. It's the only reason I joined."

I frown. "Seriously? I was wondering why you did it. You've never volunteered for anything. Especially if it included the outdoors."

He sighs. "When you volunteered, the thought of you hiking around those woods again was too much. Mad or not, I couldn't let you go out there alone. I did that once and look what happened. I almost lost you. If something happened, I'd never forgive myself for not speaking up."

"So you wanted to babysit me?"

"Not babysit. Protect."

My frown flips into a smile, and I laugh. "Protect? You? Be serious. So then, why did Skyler join? Is she *protecting* me, too?"

He hops in place a little from the cold seeping into his crappy outerwear. "I think she was protecting me. I had no clue she'd ever volunteer for this. Honestly, it didn't even cross my mind when I raised my hand. The girl hates to be outside. Even more than I do."

"If it makes you feel any better, she's miserable." I smile, and he holds out his hand to me. "Speaking of which, can we get out of this weather? It's freezing."

"I gotta get home. Birdee's going to be worried."

He drops his head to one side and looks injured. "That's why we have cell phones in these hills. Call her. I'll drive you and Luci home. After we get some hot chocolate and catch up." He holds out his hand.

I slap my hand into it. "You drive a hard bargain, Wynford. Only if you're buying."

Just like that, Wyn and I are friends again, and that's how I know it's a real friendship.

Even when we haven't spoken in months, after only five minutes, one apology, and a couple of bad jokes, it's as if we've never been apart.

# Survival Skill #9

*You must constantly evaluate your situation. Move with a level head and a good idea of what's necessary to get through.*

$\mathcal{L}$ater that night, Birdee and I sit in the living room watching TV.

She's knitting a pillow cover complete with different birds, while I pretend to focus on reading *Hatchet* for the third time. It was my dad's favorite book when he was little, and for some reason, every time I read it, I feel close to him again.

"Why do you like to knit?" I ask as my eyes follow her movement.

"Keeps my hands busy." She holds up her artwork and shuts one eye. "Does anything seem off to you?"

I watch her contorted expression as she inspects every thread. "With you, or the pillow?"

She tosses a different pillow at my head but not before I duck. "Be very careful, Chicken. Or payback is —"

Before she can finish, Petey squawks from his perch. "Hell-o."

We both laugh, and I lean over to point at a colorful bird. "So what's the real story with that bird?" I ask, watching her needle weave in and out of the yarn, creating straight rows.

She holds up the cover and picks at a showing loop. She tucks it in. "Extinct. Well, in the wild anyway. The other day was the first time I've ever seen one."

"They're cute. Tropical."

She weaves the ends to prevent it from unraveling. "Yes. It's the only parrot that's indigenous to our country."

"What happened to them?"

"Thought you'd never ask." Birdee gets up and slides a bird book off the shelf. She flips through it until she finds the page she's looking for and then hands me the open book. "You know the drill. Same problems everywhere. Deforestation. People shooting them. They're very colorful, so easy targets, I guess." She holds up another page. "Even used the feathers in fashion."

I grab the book and stare at the antique picture of a lady wearing a hat adorned with red and yellow feathers. "That's just sad."

"They're very loyal birds. Probably led to its demise. They'd go back for an injured flock member, and that made it easy for farmers to kill whole flocks. Plus, they were thought to be monogamous. So if one died, chances are, so did the mate."

"Aw." I flip the page and study the pictures. "But why would farmers kill them?"

She sits back down and goes back to her knitting. I can't help but notice one thing. The more Birdee concentrates, the more she sticks out her tongue to one side. Just like Dad. "They considered them pests because they ruined farmlands. And they have a very noticeable stress call – a loud, shrilling noise. It's a warning signal that something's wrong. Can't miss it."

I pull up an mp3 file on my laptop and play a sound bite. The noise shrills through the room. Petey imitates the bird call behind me and I cover my ears. "Man that is much louder up close and personal."

"They say you can hear it a couple miles away." Then she points to the TV. "Wait, I want to hear this." She hunts

86

around for the remote in the cushions and turns up the volume.

The newscaster speaks evenly with planned inflection. "As our viewers know, a few months ago, the City of Asheville declared a ban on all commercial building within the Great Smoky Mountain National Park. Though land had been allocated and surveyed, they wanted to put a halt to developing. A team of environmentalists working with the USFWS is trying to introduce endangered animals back into the wild."

The reporter pauses as a prerecorded clip begins to play. "In addition to the Red Wolf Conservation effort, there have even been reports of rare birds living in the area that was originally designated for commercial building."

A picture of a Carolina Parakeet pops up.

I look at Birdee. "You reported it?"

She nods once. "My avian-lover's duty. If they can catch it, they might be able to bring it back into the wild."

"Doesn't it need a mate for that?" I look at Petey.

"Don't look at me." Petey says.

Birdee laughs as the clip plays out. When it's over, a perky lady dressed in bright yellow interjects more information, "One concern for locals is eBuild's scheduled groundbreaking after the holidays on their largest development to date. Of course, the company stands to lose millions if the land is protected. Our own district conservationist heading up the wolf efforts is in the middle of the fight."

The camera pulls back and shows Katie Reynolds dressed in a black cargo and a button-up.

I point to the TV. "Hey! That's the lady who's working on the Red Wolf Conservation project I'm on."

The newscaster addresses Katie. "Miss Reynolds, how do you feel going up against the real estate companies in this area?" She holds the microphone in Katie's face.

Katie Reynolds beams and looks straight into the camera. "We've got wolves in this area that have not been thriving, and we have sightings of a rare bird. These need to be investigated before someone makes a buck."

The newscaster laughs a little. "Have you spoken to any representatives from eBuild? They are not commenting on the story."

Katie laughs. "Do you blame them? We don't want anyone building on any land if it impacts the state's environment in a negative way. The natural resources of this area need to be preserved. Conservation comes first, real estate second. In my mind, you can't have one without thinking of the other."

The reporter nods. "And how do you think eBuild is going to take this?"

"I have no comment about them. My focus is on conservation."

Birdee mutes the T.V. as a commercial for tampons comes on. "Interesting."

"I wonder what eBuild is."

She smiles. "Saw a sign down the street. It's that big developer that's snatching up all the prime real estate in these mountains and building fake cabins. Ruining the Smokies, if you ask me."

"I thought eBuild only built sustainable properties."

Birdee shrugs. "Could've fooled me. They seem to be everywhere there's a tree." She takes a sip of her hot tea and makes an *Aah* sound. "Is that Reynolds lady active in the research project you are on?"

I read the same sentence for a fifth time. "Not really. But after yesterday, I assume she will be."

Birdee stops drinking. "What happened yesterday?"

*Oh crap.* I grab my book and hide behind it, pretending to be immersed in words. If she senses anything wrong, she'll pull me out of those woods faster than Petey can say *seed*.

Birdee peers over my book. "Maybe you didn't hear me. I asked, 'What happened yesterday?'"

I turn the page and keep my eyes down as she hovers over me. "We found a dead wolf. Total bummer."

Her voice doesn't change, but I can feel the heat of her gaze over the pages. "That's awful. What do they think happened?"

I shrug and turn the page again without even reading anything. "Natural causes."

She pauses so long, I almost put the book down to see if she's still in the room.

She grabs my book and closes it. "You were on that page about fifteen minutes ago. You should really make sure you read from front to back."

I squirm in the plushy cushion. "Oh."

She lays my book on the side table. "So? What does Sweeney think? He always has an opinion. And don't lie to me. I can always tell because you never look directly at me when you're lying."

I focus on keeping a stoic face and meet her eyes. "I don't know…exactly."

She studies me for a few seconds and then points. "Nope! You're lying. I can tell by the eyes. Your daddy used to get that same dang look. Shifty eyes followed by biting his lip. How do you plea?"

"The fifth."

"Guilty as hell." She motions me over to her. "'Fess up. You promised to be straight with me."

I walk over and sit down next to her, knowing this is it. When I tell her more, she's sure to pull me off the project. Then I'm back to where I was before this assignment gave me some kind of short-term purpose. The worst is it will leave me with a gap of time right before the holidays, so I can obsess over missing Dad and wait until Mom gets back.

Birdee eggs me on. "So?"

"I told you. We found a dead wolf. But there was no sign of human involvement. That's it."

She presses on. "Do *you* think it was natural causes?"

"I don't know. I'm not the expert. But Porter does because there was no blood."

"But what do you think?"

I shift in my seat and decide not to hold back the truth this time. I can't shut everyone out like last time and Birdee is not one to give up easily on an inquisition. "I think I saw a footprint, but Porter didn't seem alarmed."

She raises one eyebrow. "You think? I know you better than that. You don't think, you *know*."

I massage my head. "I couldn't really tell. You know how it is tracking in the snow. Edges expand in the sun. It can make a deer print look like Bigfoot if it sits undisturbed long enough."

She sits back and remains calm. "What does your gut tell you?"

I chew on my fingernail, feeling as if the FBI is questioning me again. "Someone may have been there, but it doesn't mean it was related. There was no blood, no bullets, no other proof."

She reaches over and picks up the phone. "Mary would want to know about this. I think we should call her."

"No!" I jump to my feet and grab the stretched-out cord. "Birdee, please don't. I don't want to bother her. She'll just worry and that doesn't help anyone. Besides, she needs this job."

She holds out her hand, waiting for me to let go of the cord. "What's the real story?"

"She'll make me quit." I flop down in the seat and blow my bangs away from my eyes. "Birdee, please. I wouldn't stay on if I thought it was dangerous. Trust me. I'm tired of everyone overreacting to every little thing."

"Hmm. A girl after my own heart." She faces me. "But do you blame us, Chicken? We lost your dad and almost lost you. And I know you lost more than most."

I wonder if she's talking about Mo. Maybe Mom told her all the things I couldn't say.

She sits down in her chair and folds her hands in her lap. "Your mama and I can't go through that again. I don't want you to be scared or in danger."

I sigh. "I know, but Reynolds and Porter really think it's nothing to be concerned with. I chose to stay on because I need this, too."

Birdee puts down the phone. "So what do *you* want to do? And don't say *nothin'*, or I'll get your mama back here before you can whistle *Twinkle Twinkle.*"

I think for a second. To be honest I'm conflicted. Part of me does want to give up, walk away from the constant fear. The woods aren't what they used to be for me. I used to go to them when I felt astray; now they remind me of everything I lost. Instead of going there to be alone, now I feel alone there.

I stare at the picture of Dad feeding a small bear from a bottle. I smile at the picture of Simon. Even when all signs pointed to Simon dying, Dad kept him alive. He never gave up on anything he believed in. Even in the end. Even when he probably should have, he always stood his ground. He always did what was right. I want so much for Dad to be proud of me. Unfortunately, Simon was another casualty of the poaching ring. But Dad's work ethic is what is calling me most.

"How about if I continue on the project, and if anything else happens, I'll come to you first?"

Birdee slaps the table with her hand. "Sounds like a very well-thought-out plan. For a hormonal teen." She winks at me.

"So you won't call Mom?"

She studies me for a minute. "Not if you promise to keep me in the loop. If not, I'll have to send Petey out with you for protection."

I eye the bird ruffling his feathers. "I promise."

She strokes my hair. "Then it's a deal."

# Survival Skill #10

*Before snowmobiling, be sure to check out your
protective gear as well as any snowmobile maps to see
what has changed in your area.*

When I wake up the next morning, I can immediately tell
it snowed the night before.

Not only by the freezing temperature in my room due to
an old heater, but also by the thin layer of frost on the
windows. It's as if someone snuck by and breathed on every
window during the night. The thought makes me uneasy.

I waste no time in getting up and throwing on my winter
hiking gear. Then I refill my backpack with all the necessities,
half wondering if the research trip will be cancelled due to
gloomy skies. I kiss Birdee goodbye after she agrees to let me
take Dad's snowmobile into town. After gearing up and
checking the equipment like Dad taught me, I jump on and
head into the forest, down the mountain trail that leads to the
meeting place.

I'm already chilled to the bone, and I've only been riding
fifteen minutes. The fact that it's only December and already
freezing with inches of snow on the ground confirms it's
going to be a nasty winter. Usually there's not enough snow
to support a snowmobile except high on the peaks or in the
dead of winter after a storm, so this is a lucky treat for me.
Freezing or not.

The mountain air stabs little needles into my lips, which are
the only exposed skin available for attack. My breath puffs
out in large clouds, fogging my shield. The only sounds I hear

are the loud rumbling of the motor accompanied by the soft whisper of the wind through my helmet. I keep a lookout for low, dangling branches and hidden rocks in the snow-covered trail. Last thing I need is a crash or injury. As I head uphill, I stand up on the foot steps to get a better view, stopping at the very top. I turn the engine off for a moment and look down on the valley.

Even though it's cloudy, the brightness causes me to shield my eyes, and the snow looks beautiful. Untouched. No footprints, no tracks, no blemishes. Just pure and perfect.

Down below, it's still gray enough for me to see the sparse dots of colored lights marking the holiday season. They're like beacons of hope in a world of gray. But I'm not ready for hope. A coldness permeates the depths of my soul and touches the very center of my bones. The blanketed gray sky feels hollow and damp and hopeless to me.

Behind me, I hear a crash in the woods. Startled, I quickly start the mobile and jerk away just as a deer bounds out of the forest, crosses the path, and disappears on the other side. All in a matter of second. How life can change on a whim.

My heart is still fluttering a few minutes later as I inch down the hillside, avoiding sneaky snowdrifts and hidden crevices.

Even though sometimes the idea of being swallowed by the earth doesn't seem so bad.

∞

Wyn finally shows up unfashionably late, dressed like he's going to the movies. Porter and Agent Sweeney gather us up in a van and drive everyone to the entry point, amid the constant protests, hints, and sighs from Skyler. They seem to be unaware of the weather, approaching this hike like Dad always did. Like it's a nice, winter day for a beautiful, winter walk. After making sure we're geared up and ready to go, they give us our routes. The plan is to hunt the packs from opposite sides, look, and meet up in the middle at designated coordinates. Today, Porter is traveling with Team One first before he meets up with us.

My team heads in first. I let Wyn lead with Skyler bounding close on his heels like a new puppy. I volunteer to bring up the rear as we tramp into the white woods. The crunching of our feet along the path is the only noise besides an occasional bird sounding off a warning of our location. No one talks for the first thirty minutes. Sometimes when it's abnormally quiet, you just follow suit as if silence is a requirement, which I'm thankful for, considering it isn't one of Skyler's strengths.

About a mile in, I notice how quiet she and Wyn are today. They're no longer the cooing doves they've been since we started. I wonder if he told Skyler about our dinner the other night. How we teased, dueled in thumb wars, and avoided drudging up on the sad details we both missed in each other's lives. The good part was that our friendship clicked right back into place as if nothing was ever broken.

I glance around as we hike and breathe out a long exhale. The magic of the woods has returned wrapped up in its brand-new blanket of winter snow. The air smells of wet pine, and the towering white trees add a whole new dimension above. Rhododendrons recently laden with snow droop along the path, exhausted from the extra weight. Green sprouts punch through the fresh snow, trying to escape the smothering load. Scattered light breaks up the shadowy forest refusing to be dimmed by the winter gloom.

About a mile in, we meet up with a small creek. The moving river hops over little waterfalls, carving out tiny ice formations in the frozen snow. Icicles reach down toward the river, hoping to tickle its glassy surface. I stand hypnotized by the roaring sound of the pure spring water somersaulting over the rocks that have been smoothed and rounded by years of erosion and weather.

Wyn calls out from a few yards ahead. "Looks like there's a shortcut."

I yell after him. "I think we should stick to the path."

I trail Skyler and him until they stop. The creek has widened a bit, and the only way to get to the other side is to walk over a tree that's fallen across the freezing water. Unless we go around.

Skyler shakes her head. "No way. I can't walk on that."

Wyn grabs her hand. "Yes, you can. It's only about seven feet across."

For once, I'm on Skyler's side and it sucks. "Wyn, come on. Let's be smart and stick to the plan."

"How is going a mile out of our way smart? I don't want to be out here any longer than I have to." He ignores my warning and faces her. "This will save us tons of time. We'll be able to get warm faster. I still owe you that hot chocolate."

She smiles and bats her eyes like a fake baby doll. "Yeah you do." But then she peers over the side at the small ravine leading into the water. "But what if I slip? That's gotta be like a twenty-foot drop."

Seeing as Skyler knows as much about distance as she does plant species, I can't help but correct her. "More like ten."

Wyn looks at me from the front of the line and frowns. "Yeah, that's not helping, G. Some moral support for your teammate would be nice."

I shrug. "Sorry. I was just clarifying." I reach out and pat her shoulder a little harder than I should. "Come on, Sky, Wyn's right. All you have to do is tightrope seven feet across a six-inch log suspended ten feet over a cold and icy river. And all while wearing fancy boots with pretty pom poms. What are you worried about?"

I glance up at Wyn and smile. "Is that better?"

He ignores me and takes Skyler's hand, leading her to the edge. "Let's just move."

Skyler leans over the edge and mumbles, "Okay, I guess."

Everything in me screams *Bad idea!* "Wyn, please," I say.

He frowns. "Can you just let me lead for once?"

I back down, not wanting to rock the flimsy boat we've just barely pieced back together.

He holds his hands up. "You wait here. I'll go first to be sure it's uber safe."

Uber? Definitely not a Wyn word. I mumble to myself, "The foolish hero's last words." Dad used to always say, *the best way to prove a hero wrong is to let him have his way.*

Wyn hugs Skyler and kisses her forehead, making me want to stick my finger down my throat. Sometimes getting sick is better than feeling sick. Though seconds later, a pang of jealousy washes over me. Mo used to protect me the way Wyn tries to protect Skyler. And I miss it.

Wyn starts to walk across the nature-made bridge. He teeters in the middle from the awkward weight of the backpack and almost falls off.

I stop him. "Wait. Let me hold the pack while you cross, and I'll throw it over to you."

He nods. "Good idea."

He tosses me the pack and easily tightropes across the thin log. I don't realize I'm holding my breath until he reaches the other side. To be honest, I expected him to fall since his shoes have zero traction, which would have given us an excuse to bail on this tricky plan. At this point, I just want us all to get over safely so I can stop kicking myself for giving in to Wyn's wilderness whims.

He hollers out to Skyler. "Your turn. Now just take it slow, and you'll be fine."

Skyler steps forward, one foot in front of the other. She gets about halfway out when her pretty fur boots struggle to grip onto the frosty log. She slips and lands on the tree, clutching the bark as she slides off.

"Help!" she screams.

Instinctively, I lunge forward to try and grab her hand, but she can't hold on long enough. Her fingers slip, and she screams as she drops into the freezing creek. At the bottom, she doesn't move.

Wyn drops to his knees and looks over the side. "Jesus! Skyler! Are you okay?"

I jump off the end of the log and slide down the embankment with Wyn hollering like a banshee across from me. All I'm focused on is getting Skyler out of the creek as soon as possible. In this weather, being wet is the kiss of death. When I reach her, she's cries out in pain. Her right leg is twisted underneath her in an awkward way, and a gash slices across her forehead.

Before I move her, I check in to see how severe her injuries are. "Are you okay?"

She whimpers but somehow still manages to grit out, "I... I don't know."

Wyn comes sliding down the opposite embankment. "Is she okay? Please tell me she's okay."

"She's fine, no thanks to your brilliant idea." I ignore Wyn's questions. "Skyler, I need you to get out of the water and it's going to hurt."

Surprisingly she doesn't argue. But when she tries to stand, she screams. A flock of birds scatters from a nearby tree.

Skyler doesn't move so I grab an arm and quickly yank her up onto the embankment. A primal noise escapes her lips followed by sobs.

"Sorry, but you can't sit in that water." I mutter as I inspect her head. Thankfully, the wound is not too deep.

"Don't worry. You're going to be fine." I pull a bandana out of my bag and wrap it around her head. "Does it hurt?"

She just nods with a quivering lip.

Wyn comes sloshing through the water to Skyler's side.

I look at him and frown. "Jesus, Wyn! Why in the world would you get wet on purpose? Don't you know anything?"

He looks surprised. "What do you mean?"

I point to his shoes. "Your feet are drenched. That's like Rule #1 in Boys Scouts' winter survival."

"How would you know? Aren't you a girl?"

I refrain from mumbling *idiot* under my breath and pull out the first aid kit from the pack as he kneels next to Skyler. By now, she's wailing.

"What's the damage?" he says.

I talk over her sobs and give it to them straight up. "Her leg is obviously broken, but it doesn't seem like she has a concussion or a head injury. We need to move her up to dryer land so I can splint her leg. Then I need to get her warm while you go get help. Because from the looks of it, she won't be able to walk out of here."

Skyler whimpers as Wyn pulls me out of her ear's reach. "Me go? Alone?" He puts both hands on his head. "Are you serious?"

"No, I'm joking." I hit his shoulder. " Of course, I'm serious."

"Why can't I just carry her out? She can't weigh more than 120 pounds."

I rub my temples. "Two miles? In those shoes? You'd never make it. Not to mention, she's wet, and I'm assuming she doesn't have a change of clothes. I need to get her dry and warmed up before hypothermia sets in."

"Holy crap! I thought that only happened on Mount Everest," he says.

Wyn pulls the walkie-talkie out of the backpack and tries to radio for help. The static that answers is quickly drowned out by Skyler's yelps and moans.

I look at the hills stretching up on both sides of us. "We're in a valley. It probably won't work unless you get higher up."

He starts to climb the slippery slope, and I tug on his arm. "Let's just get her situated first. Before she goes into shock."

I face Skyler, who's shivering and pale as the snow. "I need to get you up on flat land so I can support your leg. Then Wyn will go for help. Do you understand?"

She nods through the tears streaming down her face. "Will it hurt?"

I don't even bother to sugarcoat it. "Like you won't believe. But only for a minute. Or two. You can do this."

Wyn and I each grab an arm. "On the count of three. One… two… three!"

Wyn and I heave Skyler off the mud embankment. The horrible sound that comes out of her mouth brings tears to my eyes. I've heard that primal sound once before. The day in the woods when Dad got shot, he made a similar sound. My eyes water at the memory as I help move Skyler up the embankment. She screams the whole way, and I can't stop tears from falling. I hate to see anyone in that amount of pain. Even her.

It seems to take forever until we reach the top. Once we set her down on a bed of pine needles, she stops screaming and sobs hysterically.

Wyn sits next to her and tucks the tarp around her to keep her warm as I get to work.

I take out the scissors and cut her pants up to her thigh. "The blood is from a gash in your thigh, so luckily the wound is closed. No showing bones."

Skyler speaks between sniffs. "Oh, lucky me."

I find two solid branches that are the proper length and cut off any protrusions with my knife. I line the sticks on both sides of her legs, hip to ankle, and use my extra sweatshirt as padding. "Wyn, give me your t-shirt."

He slips his shirt off and hands it to me. "I hope you know this is one of my favorite shirts."

I ignore him and rip it into strips. Then I tie the material tightly around the sticks to stabilize her leg. The whole process takes me about ten minutes.

When I'm done, I sit back. "There! Good as new."

Skyler wipes her face with her mittens and starts to shiver. "Now what?"

"Now we need to find some shelter and warm you up while Wyn goes for help."

A horrified look washes over her face. "You mean, you have to move me again?"

I nod. "Yes, but it shouldn't hurt as bad this time because your leg is supported."

Wyn takes her hand. "I'll help you."

He puts her arm over his neck and lifts. Skyler bites her lips as she stands. I have to hand it to Wyn, he works hard to get her up that hill.

At the top, she collapses, her body shaking uncontrollably. "I… I need to sleep."

"No!" I bark. "You have to stay awake." I quickly pull Wyn aside. "Listen, you need to go get help fast, before it gets dark. Or she could be in serious trouble."

"What about you?"

I scan the woods. "I'll find shelter around here and get a fire going until you bring back help. She can't make the hike, and I need to get her warm immediately."

He glances around the woods. "In case you haven't noticed, I am not a woodsy kind of guy."

101

"You don't have a choice, Mr. Let's Cross the Raging River. So buck up and pull it together."

He glances back at Skyler, who is lying in the snow, eyes closed. He nods slowly as if he's not sure. "Okay. Where do I go?"

I pull a map and compass out of the bag and point to the route. "Just follow this. Stay to the trail. If you head northeast, it will take you to the meeting point."

"Northeast by northwest?"

I scowl. "Very funny. Be serious."

He rolls the map and sticks it in his back pocket. "I got it. Don't worry."

I hand him the radio. "Here. Please don't get lost. She might not make it."

"No pressure." He walks over to Skyler and kneels. "I'll be back. Try not to have too much fun without me on your Girls' Day Away."

She grips onto his hand. "Don't go. Please."

He pats her hand. "This is my fault. I gotta get help, or she'll never let me live it down."

I roll my eyes while I look through the first aid kit for aspirin.

Skyler pulls him closer and hisses in his ear. "I can't stay here. With her. Alone."

"You don't have a choice. You're in bad shape." I notice he looks at me to see if I'm listening, then he lowers his voice. "Give Grace a chance. She might be a pain in the ass sometimes, but she's the best. And she knows what to do. You're safe with her."

Skyler mumbles. "Figures you'd say that."

Wyn kisses her forehead and comes over to me. "You sure you're going to be okay?"

I lean on one leg and cross my arms. "Are *you*? I think you need to worry about getting out of here and bringing back help for her. I can take care of myself."

Wyn salutes me as if he's off to war. "See you later, Miss Independent."

And with that he disappears into the snowy trees.

I glance over at Skyler, who is glaring at me.

It's going to be a long day.

# Survival Skill #11

*Most wild animals do not consider human beings prey and are not likely to attack unless threatened in some way.*

𝒯 he wind outside picks up. "We need to get under some shelter in case the weather gets worse."

Skyler scoffs, "And how do you suggest I do that?"

"I guess I'll have to drag your grumpy butt. So you'd better be nice to me."

Her eyes turn cold. "At least I'm not hitting on someone else's boyfriend."

I drape her arm over my shoulder and laugh as I lift her. "I can only assume you're talking about Wyn. So that's a joke right?"

"Do you deny it?" she says, sounding a lot like Birdee.

Skyler is not very heavy so I take a few easy steps. "What is this, a court of law? I plead the fifth."

"Ha! So you admit it."

I stop and face her, still holding her up. "Let's get something straight. Wyn's been my best friend as long as you've been dyeing your hair. So let's not talk about who stole who from who."

"I think it's *whom.*"

I reposition my arm around her tiny waist and drag her along the path. "I don't care who is whom."

She spouts off in my ear. "You left him. You didn't want him, and then you got another boyfriend. Wyn was fair game.

I didn't steal anything." She stumbles, and I prevent her from tumbling into a slushy spot. She grits her teeth and winces.

I shake my head. "You make it sound like Wyn's prey in some dating challenge. You win, okay? I'm not in the market."

"Like I trust you."

"You'd better since I'm taking care of you." Off to one side, I spot an overhang with a dry spot underneath. "Over here."

Skyler whimpers as we hobble through the snow and into the enclave. I can't imagine how much her leg hurts, yet surprisingly she's not complaining at all. She's different than when Wyn's around. With him, she acts weak and needy. With me, she's cold and stubborn.

Once we get to the overhang, I lower her onto a small boulder and get to work on the dry space. I lay one tarp on the ground and hang one up to keep the wind out. I quickly start collecting branches and logs. Within minutes, I have a fire blazing and a kettle of water on the flames. I sit down and zip up my jacket to keep the chill off my neck.

Skyler shivers. "I'm so cold."

I take out the hand warmers. "Here. You can use these."

"Thanks." She slips them into her dirty mittens, which are now not so fuzzy. Her face is bright red, and her breath seems shallower. Shock and hypothermia do not mix well in this weather.

"Move closer to the fire. You need to keep warm, and you need to stay awake." She yelps as I help her move a few inches closer to the flames. Tears appear in the corner of her eyes. "Sorry, I know that hurts."

"No, you're not."

I ignore her snide comment, because if I don't, I'm going to say something nasty. I'm out in the cold wilderness taking care of her. I could have easily left her alone and trekked home to my warm bed. I'd be there within an hour at most. Instead, I'm stuck taking care of someone who can't stand the sight of me. I stare at the flames flickering against the tarp like it's some kind of shadow-puppet show.

Skyler's voice breaks the silence. "You like him, don't you?"

I sigh. "Do we have to talk about this again?"

"I do, too. You know, he's all I've had since…"

I can only respond with, "I know."

And I do know. She's talking about Carl, and neither of us wants to say his name. "Skyler, I'm sorry. About everything. I just wanted my dad back."

"So you took mine instead." She focuses on the fire.

"This wasn't a barter. I didn't mean for any of this to happen, you know. I had no clue what was going on."

"Doesn't mean I have to forgive you."

"I don't expect you to."

I feel dejected and exhausted from trying to make other people happy. I think about Carl and everything he did to my dad. To Mo. To me. Anger festers inside me, and I want to go off on Skyler–and Wyn, for that matter. How could either one of them turn against me and defend a man who betrayed his family and killed animals for money. Someone who was ultimately responsible for killing people, including my Dad, who never did anything to anyone. As far as I'm concerned, even though it's sad, Carl dying was the only way I could live.

But I hold back. There's been enough hurt. If I have to take an ego hit to help her feel better, so be it. A howl pierces through the wind, and Skyler's head snaps up.

"What was that?"

I poke at the burning embers. "A bear?"

She frowns. "Very funny. That was a wolf."

"They say there are a few up here," I mutter sarcastically.

Wincing, she scoots her back against the rock. "Yeah, but with us. Now."

I pull up my hood and lie back against a log. "They hunt at night, so usually you start to hear them around dusk."

"Thought they didn't like to be seen?" Her eyes shift wildly around the small space. "Will they hunt *us*?"

I smile under my hood. I might not be able to get mad at her about Carl or attack her about her relationship with Wyn, but I can torture her with wolf trivia. "They eat meat. They're not picky."

As if on cue, another wolf howls. This one sounds a bit closer.

She gasps. "What do we do?"

The tension of the day seeps from my bones. "I'd stay quiet if I were you."

Skyler whimpers a little. "I thought Wyn would be back by now. What's taking him so long?"

I sit up and check my watch in the dim light. To be honest, I was expecting Wyn to be back by now, too. I had no intentions of staying out here all night. Especially with Little Red Riding Hood and the Big Bad Wolf. If I'd known it was going to take him this long, I'd have gone instead. I picture Wyn stumbling through snowdrifts in his fancy shoes, possibly lost. I rub my temples. I assumed he'd be able to walk the couple of miles on his own, but maybe I was wrong to send him.

I pull out the radio and speak into it. "Wyn? Anyone out there?"

Once again, nothing but static, which doesn't surprise me. We're in a valley, the weather isn't great, and he's probably out of range by now. I should have made him take the radio. That way if he got lost, he would've had more of a chance to call someone.

"Something wrong?" Skyler says.

I try not to let on that I'm a tad worried. "Nah. Wyn's not the greatest hiker. What would take me two hours takes him too long. The weather isn't great. Maybe he got out, and they decided to wait until morning."

Skyler starts to rock. "Oh my God. You mean we have to stay out here all night? In the dark? With hungry wolves?" Her voice starts to tremble.

I stop playing games and sit next to her. "We'll be fine. Trust me. They know where we are."

I try to comfort her more. Maybe now I'm trying to ease my own rattling nerves as well. I never expected to be out here at night either. Al pops into my head. Suddenly every crack and scuttle has me jumping like a flea.

I try to ease my own mind. "It's just a matter of time before they find us, and we'll be slurping Birdee's potato soup before you know it."

"I hate potatoes."

"Trust me, after being out here too long, you'll love anything they stick in front of you." I drop my head back and stare at the gray sky. As clouds pass over, every now and then the sun peeks through and reassures me I'm not alone.

Another howl breaks the silence, and Skyler scoots closer to me. She whispers as low as she can in her high voice. "What about the wolves?"

I keep my voice down. "Porter said there's never been an attack on humans."

Just as the words leave my lips. A growl sounds off on the other side of the tarp blocking our view. My heart soars into my throat. I know right away it's a wolf, and that he's closer than I want him to be.

Funny. We've spent a couple of days trying to spot these wolves, and they show up *now*? How rude.

Skyler's eyes are as wide as an owl's. I put a finger to my lips so she doesn't say anything. Picking up a large stick, I motion to her head. She immediately rips off the fabric and hands me the bloody bandana. I slowly wrap it around my stick and plunge the end into the fire.

As the torch blazes, I pull back the tarp, keeping it in front of me as a flimsy barrier. At first, I see nothing but a black canvas. Once my eyes adjust, I spot something a few yards away, hidden in the trees. A pair of glowing eyes.

Holding the torch, I pick up a rock and launch it, taking the animal by surprise. The wolf darts away and crashes through the piles of brittle branches scattered along the snowy ground. I scan the woods, swinging my torch from left to right. Wolves never travel alone, so there's bound to be others out there. Waiting.

Just when I'm about to lower my guard, something moves off to my left. I swing the torch toward the shadow. A large wolf slowly appears from the darkness with its teeth showing. I can only assume it's the alpha male, though I'm not sure why it's acting so bold. I guess we're a threat to his pack somehow. Red wolves aren't normally very aggressive unless a litter or den is in danger.

The wolf takes another step forward. I hold the flames out in front of me and wave them in the air while keeping my eye on the trees, looking for more. I can hear Skyler whimpering behind me, which is not helping at all. You can't appear to be prey to any wild animal. They only back off if they think you're a huge threat, not when they know you are a weak meal.

I stand completely still, staring into the wolf's eyes. If I move, he'll charge. Besides the makeshift torch, all I have to defend myself is the knife Tommy gave me. And that's strapped to my hip. I stay behind the tarp for protection in case he attacks.

My hands shake as the wolf takes another step. Skyler shifts behind me and groans again like a wounded animal. The wolf snaps his head in her direction and sniffs the air. I bet he can smell the blood from her leg. Maybe that's what drew him out.

I rattle the tarp to get his attention. He jumps as if startled and then crouches like a tiger, hunching over with his teeth showing. The glow from the fire catches the light of his eyes, making him appear slightly possessed. I focus on breathing steady. He takes another step forward, and I get ready to throw the torch, hoping I can grab my knife in time.

Just then, a gunshot goes off in the air. I jump and spin around as the wolf darts off into the woods. The sound of gunfire triggers a slew of flashbacks to that day in the camp. My whole body freezes and chills race along my spine. I press my back against the mountainside and draw my knife, not knowing what to do. I put my finger to my lips.

A beam of light sweeps the ground and someone calls out. "Grace? You out here?"

I exhale as the adrenaline pumps through me. "Agent Sweeney! Over here!"

Skyler laughs and cries at the same time. "They're here. Oh, thank God."

Agent Sweeney appears from out of the thick woods, resting a large gun on his shoulder. He points the barrel at the tarp. "Love what you've done with the place."

"What took you so long?"

He walks over to Skyler and inspects her leg. She winces at his touch. "Got yourself a mighty nice break there."

She reaches up and hugs his neck. "You came. Thank God. Where's Wyn?"

Agent Sweeney unpacks a few medical supplies from his bag and begins making Skyler a proper splint.

"We found him about a mile off course. He told us what happened. He's back at the office waiting on you guys to make it back safely." Agent Sweeney grips Skyler's shoulder.

"You'll be just fine. We have a chopper waiting for you on the ridge." He pulls out a foldable nylon stretcher. "Grace and I can carry you there. It's not too far."

Skyler hops over to a long stick and picks it up. Leaning on it, she eyes me. "No, thanks. I'll walk."

I frown. Some thanks. Then my spirit sags. To some people, no matter what I do, I will never be able to make up for what I've done.

"Tough girl."

I almost laugh, but hold it in. *Yeah, as tough as snails.*

Agent Sweeney hands Skyler a couple pills and some water. "Take these. They should help you feel better until you get to the hospital."

She focuses on me and for the first time looks worn and sad. "That's okay. I'm used to the pain by now."

# Survival Skill #12

*In a snowy whiteout, try not to move; windblown snow can fill in contours, obscure cairns, and conceal drop-offs.*

The next morning, as soon as Wyn walks into Agent Sweeney's office, I race over to him. "Are you okay? I was worried about you."

He laughs. "Me? I was worried about *you* guys. Didn't think they would get to you in time."

"It was cold, but we were fine."

"I wasn't talking about the cold." He smirks. "Afraid you and Skyler would kill each other if you had to stay the night. Glad to see you made it."

"Ha. I would've won that fight, trust me. Skipper never let Barbie win a round."

Agent Sweeney calls out from the corner. "Yeah. Grace could scare off the wolves and the cold. Can you believe it?"

Wyn stops joking and gives me a quick hug. "I'm sorry I didn't listen to you. We should have stuck to the path."

"I'm always right. When will you learn that?" I pretend punch his jaw. "So. How is Skyler?"

Wyn runs his hands over his head. "She'll be fine. Broke her leg in a couple of places, so it'll be a long recovery. Her mom's peeved with me, though." He shoves his hands inside his coat and shivers a bit. "To be honest, I think Skyler's kind of glad. She's getting tons of attention – which she loves – and it gives her an excuse to be off this project. Seems to be more upset at having to hang up her heels for a while."

I can't help but smile at the strange benefit of a broken bone. "That's awful, I guess."

"She said it, not me." He folds up his collar. "Now, what are we waiting on?"

Porter walks around the corner. "The rest of the team."

Wyn looks confused. "What?"

My mouth drops open. "We're going back out today?"

Agent Sweeney frowns and pulls on a baseball cap. "Against my protests, I must add. It's too cold, but Porter wants to merge the two teams together."

Forget the weather, I'm more concerned about being trapped outdoors with the other team. At least I enjoy Wyn's company. Skyler is easy compared to Seth who's totally obnoxious. I barely know Madison, but from what I do know, she's a bookworm, not a nature girl. And Big Mike is, well, he's just big. I can only imagine how loud he is in the woods. Not conducive for tracking. The wolves will hear us a mile away.

"Does Katie know we're hiking in today?" I ask.

Porter nods. "Yes. But she insisted I go with you."

Wyn looks frustrated, his face all pinched. "Can this not wait until tomorrow?"

"No. Bad storm is coming in a few days. We gotta move now. If anyone wants to back out, they can. No one's forcing you." Porter studies his watch. "They're late."

On cue, Seth and his posse appear around a corner like some street gang. He's in front, and the other two are trailing close behind. "Better late than never. You guys ready to help *my team* find these wolves?"

"Your team?" I ask.

He shrugs and pulls on a knit hat. "Yeah, I assume I'm taking over as leader. I mean, majority rules, right?"

I try not to sound too perturbed. "Wrong. Skill comes first, and you know what ass-u-me means?"

He looks to Agent Sweeney for some backup. "Surely we're not going to have a chick lead us. And Wyn doesn't know a log from a bridge, apparently."

Wyn puffs up. "Watch it, Seth."

Seth laughs. "What are you going to do? Push me in a river? Break my leg maybe?"

Agent Sweeney waits to answer, somewhat amused with the banter.

Meanwhile, my blood boils. "Trust me, Seth. This is not your average Boy Scout expedition with a nature badge waiting at the end. I'm the most qualified here, so I'm leading." I look at Wyn. "We see what happens when we leave it up to the boys."

Instead of being mad at me for ranking on him, he nods. "I'm with Grace. She's the best out of all of us. Though it hurts to admit."

I smile at his support. "Thanks." I grab one of the packs and toss it to Seth. "Don't worry. You can be my *ass,* though. Seems right up your alley. I need someone to carry the bags."

Agent Sweeney chuckles in the corner as he works.

Big Mike laughs out loud and slams Seth on the back. "Looks like you got beat by a girl."

Seth points at me. "Wait a minute, *that's* a girl?" He hands Mike the pack. "Since you think this is so funny, you haul it. You're the strongest… if we're going by skill."

Big Mike shrugs and straps on the backpack, making it look tiny against his muscular physique.

Porter is already standing by the door when Agent Sweeney hands him an extra pack. "Since this is your brilliant idea, I insist you carry another bag of supplies. Just in case."

"Fine by me."

I speak up. "What's the plan?"

Porter smiles and hands me a map that has a path highlighted with coordinates. He studies a beeping electric contraption while he speaks. "The wolf pack has been somewhat stationary. So you should have no problem."

Agent Sweeney crosses his arms. "In case you all didn't hear, Porter's going with you. It was the only way I would allow this again. Les is on high alert in case you need anything, and Katie's ready to pull the plug if anyone else gets hurt."

Wyn raises his hand. "With all due respect, Skyler's accident was my fault. Grace told me not to cross that bridge. I was just trying to get us across faster."

Porter glares at him. "Yes, it is your fault. Not only did you get someone hurt, but your carelessness has also jeopardized the project. If you stick to the plans and routes, we will be fine." He looks at all of us. "Any of you guys mess up again, and you're off the teams. No questions asked and no free grade."

Wyn lowers his head like a beaten down mutt.

I speak up in his defense "There's no need going on about it. Skyler's fine. It was just an accident."

Seth plays with his phone. "A fool's only accident is birth."

"That's stupid." Wyn shakes his head. "What does that even mean?"

"Come on, boys. Cut it out." Agent Sweeney opens the door. "Now all you fools get out of my office. I've had enough of your bickering for one day."

Porter puts on his large hat. "Let's go then. Grace, you lead, and I'll bring up the rear in case we miss anything."

I nod. "*I* won't."

Agent Sweeney drives us up a few miles to the drop off location, and the six of us head into the thick trees. As soon as we're out of Agent Sweeney's sight, Seth jogs past the line like a child running ahead of his parents at an amusement park. He veers left at a fork in the path, and I veer right. I don't think anyone else even saw him. I almost say something, but stop myself. Let him get lost. See if I care. I'm staying on the path this time.

Nothing good happens off trail. And one dumb person can get a whole bunch of smart ones killed out here.

The rest of the group follows me as we walk through a winter wonderland. Frost-covered trees line up against the white sky. The dim light reflects off the icy branches, making it look as if the world around us is sparkling. I've always loved a crisp walk in the winter. Besides the sound of melting ice and footsteps crunching through the crusty snow, the best sound of winter is the sound of silence. The early morning sky acts as a warm backdrop to the chilling landscape. The smell of evergreen in the air gives it a Christmas tone. I even spot the perfect tree Dad would haven chosen for the holiday.

Obviously, Seth isn't as dumb as he looks because he eventually jogs up next to me. "Dude, we're supposed to stay together."

I keep slushing through the snow. "No, you're supposed to stay with me. You were going in the wrong direction."

He jumps in front of me. "I could have gotten lost back there."

I mumble and walk around him. "Somehow, I knew you'd figure it out."

He stops me with his hand and gets in my face. "And what if I didn't? What happened to no man left behind?"

"Doesn't include boys."

Wyn walks up next to me. "Back off, Seth. Why are you always causing trouble?"

Seth gets in his face. "So is this your new girlfriend for the day? Why do you keep crushing on a girl who thinks you're a total loser? You'd think you'd learn. I mean, it's been like ten years already."

Wyn's face turns red, but before he can respond, Madison's whispery voice floats from the back. "Just let it go, Seth, jeez."

When she speaks, Big Mike speeds up and grabs both Wyn and Seth by the back of their jacket collars. "Ladies. Stop bickering, and let's do what we came to do. I'm getting tired of being out here and not seeing squat. I didn't miss football to hike around with a couple of fighting sissies."

I check my compass. "Yeah, and if we keep bickering, every wolf within a five-mile radius is going to hear us coming. Let's keep it down."

Big Mike tugs on the hood of Seth's coat. "You bring up the rear with me so I can keep an eye on you."

I wait until I spot Porter on the trail and then continue on.

Madison walks up next to me and joins my pace. "Seth's not all that bad, you know. His ego gets the best of him."

I hop over a slushy puddle in the trail. "Yeah, I noticed."

"So how long have you lived here? You seem to know your way around."

I keep an eye on my compass. "All my life."

She doesn't miss a beat before she's onto the next question. "Ever seen a bear?"

I smile thinking of Simon. Then I remember how I found him dead due to poachers. My spirit drops as I choke out. "A couple times."

"Whoa!" Madison opens a small book in her hands on red wolves. "Hey, did you know a red wolf can travel up to twenty miles a day and run up to thirty miles an hour?"

I really don't want to talk, but I know Madison is new here and excited, so I play along. "I didn't."

She flips through the book and trips over a root. Stumbling a bit, she catches herself and laughs. "I've never been out hiking like this before. To me, the jungle is New York City."

I can't help but laugh, but I try not to say too much more, hoping not to encourage an ongoing conversation. We need to be quiet if we're ever going to come across a live creature. Let alone the elusive wolf.

"Did you know some red wolves could be up to a hundred pounds? Can you imagine?"

I keep my voice hushed. "I'd like to find out."

She laughs nervously. "Yeah, me too. I guess."

I exhale my frustration. Is she going to talk the whole time? Do these people not take this seriously? I feel like I'm the only one out here who wants to find a wolf. The only one who is here for this project besides Porter.

Madison takes a few steps without reciting any facts. As soon as I hear her take a breath to speak again, I stop and turn to face the group.

"Hey guys, maybe we should split up a little. It looks like we're close to one of the suspected dens. If we come in from two different sides, maybe one of us will be able to spot something if the wolves decide to move."

Porter hikes up behind us. I can understand why he's hanging back so far. Can't take the noise. "Sounds good. We should still be within a mile of each other. Are you guys okay with that?"

Madison tucks her small book away in her jacket pocket. "I thought we were staying together."

"It might be a smarter way to find them," I say.

Porter nods. "It's settled then. Just don't tell Katie, or she'll have my hide. But I trust you guys. I'll take Mike and Madison. Grace, you stick with Seth and Wyn. I think you know these woods almost as good as I do."

Better, actually, but I don't say that out loud. I can't help but be slightly disappointed at getting stuck with Seth. I guess I was being too optimistic thinking Wyn and I could go at it alone. "Okay," I mumble.

Seth claps. "Sounds good to me."

"Great. You guys circle around to the east, and we'll circle around to the west. We'll meet here in one hour." Porter points to the center of our route. "So don't dillydally. Sound good?"

Mike salutes me as the three take off in the opposite direction.

About five minutes into our hike, Seth pipes up. "Smooth move, Grace."

"What do you mean?"

He thumbs over his shoulder. "Getting rid of the baggage back there. I couldn't take Madison's chitchat anymore. Between her 411 and Big Mike's grunting, there was no way we were going to spot any Rufies out here."

I don't bother to correct his scientific reference. Instead, I reorganize. "Seth, since you're so good at pointing out other people's mistakes, why don't you bring up the rear? Trail behind us and make sure we don't miss anything. Be our Porter."

"Yeah. 'Cause you know you will." He jogs back down the track and lingers a few yards behind us.

Wyn files in behind me. "That's only going to keep him busy for, oh, two minutes."

"I'll take whatever I can get."

As we head toward the coordinates mapped out for us, the air turns chillier by the minute. Eventually, I stop and watch a low mist roll through the trees, making it a little tougher to see.

I call back. "Grab a stick for support."

I hear Seth crash off into the trees and crack a branch. *Idiot.*

Wyn snags a small twig from the path, "Why?"

"It helps when things get foggy, so you can keep your bearings." I pick up two long branches and snap them to the

119

perfect length. "Here. Your stick's too short. Needs to be as long as your leg."

He raises his eyebrows. "I'm pretty sure that's something a guy *never* wants to hear."

I smack him upside the head. "Gross."

When I turn back around, I notice the long-distance visibility has gotten worse. Now we can only see about ten or fifteen yards in front of us.

"Looks like Mother Nature is getting grumpy." I call out to Seth. "You okay back there?"

I hear Seth whistle in response and watch as Wyn picks up an even larger stick than mine. He tests it against his leg and tosses the one I chose for him. Guys are so lame. No matter where they are or who they're with, they're always trying to prove something. Must be exhausting carrying around those heavy egos all the time.

"We need to wait for him to catch up," I say.

Seth's hair appears over the white dune. He digs the walking stick into the snow. "Looking nasty out. Maybe we should head back?"

I study my coordinates against the maps. "According to this, the pack should be right on the other side of that ridge. Let's get there, and if they aren't around, we'll head home."

Surprisingly, he agrees. "Sounds good."

The wind picks up as Wyn and I hike up the hill with Seth trailing behind, now trying to make a sling shot out of a vine. I zip my white coat the rest of the way and pull my hood around my face. My cheeks are practically raw from the wind chill. I can't help but feel sorry for Wyn, because he doesn't look the slightest bit warm in his peacoat.

"You okay?" I ask.

He blows into his hands. "Tell me why I signed up for this again? I could be indoors with a nice cup of cocoa, watching a football game."

I smile and hop over a log. "Because you wanted to *protect* me."

"Right."

A gust of wind picks up, and I spot something ahead. I squint through the blowing snow as Wyn runs into me from behind.

He talks a little louder. "I think we should head back. It seems to be getting worse. We don't want to get stuck out here."

Seth catches up. "I say we keep going. Lewis and Clark never stopped on their adventures, and look what they found."

Wyn squinches his face. "And you think that's motivating?"

For some reason, I don't want to go back either, but that would mean I'm agreeing with Seth, which somehow feels wrong. "Guys, let me think."

Seth plops down on a rock. "I need to rest for a second."

I lean into Wyn and keep my voice down. "Wait here with motor mouth. I'll go ahead and check things out, see how it looks. The weather didn't look bad when I checked this morning, so a few more minutes won't hurt us."

"Yeah? Well, does Mr. Snow Miser know that?"

I smile at the holiday movie reference. "I'll be back."

Wyn grabs my sleeve. "Let's stay together."

"Isn't that a song? Seriously, I'm only talking right there. Not miles. You'll be able to see me. If you come, Seth will want to come and I need a break." I pat his shoulder. "Don't worry, I won't leave you. Today." I smile and punch his arm.

He give me a look. "Believe it or not, it's not me I'm worried about."

He sits next to Seth, and I make my way down the trail a few yards.

I squint into the dusty air. Up ahead, a dark mound is lying in the snow. My stomach lurches at the thought of uncovering another dead wolf. I had a feeling this is what I would find when I saw it from the path but was hoping I was wrong. I dig my stick into the snow and push forward to get a closer look. When I get a few feet away, I make out the wolf's features.

"Oh no." I drop to my knees.

He's still alive, barely breathing with his eyes fixed on me. For a second, I'm not sure what to do. I yell back to the group, "Wyn, Seth, come here! I found one!"

I listen for a second but don't hear anything in return. No whistle, no hoot. I don't want to leave the poor wolf alone. I yell for them again but the whipping wind drowns out any noise. I stare down at the red wolf. For some reason, I'm not afraid. I reach over and slowly stroke his head, still on guard, ready for any movement. But the poor thing lies still, with his tongue protruding through his teeth. I run my hand over his ear and down along his neck, the whole time checking him out visually. Once again, I see no sign of what might have caused this. Same as before.

"I'm so sorry."

The wolf whimpers a little and then closes his eyes. I place my hand on his side and feel him take each breath. Soon, they become more and more shallow until finally he exhales one long sigh, and his body goes limp under my touch.

Tear spring to my eyes, leaving wet paths as they stream down my cold face. I shake the wolf a little with my hand, hoping for the best, but he doesn't move.

He's dead.

Part of me wants to scream at the world. Why does everything around me seem to die? Why can't I save one lousy thing in my life?

I stroke the wolf again and stand. No use feeling sorry for myself. The wolf is the one who got the crappy deal. I should go back and tell the guys. Figure out what to do. Porter will want to know about this immediately so he can recover the body.

I mark the area with orange tape and head back. About halfway there, the snow around me starts to swirl, reminding me of something. The time Dad and Les were caught in a total whiteout up here. Dad said it came out of nowhere. That in a matter of seconds, the world around him turned completely white and he'd lost his bearings. Didn't know up from down. In a whiteout up here, hikers have been known to get extremely confused. Some people walk off cliffs. Some disappear into hidden snowdrifts and are never found again.

Alive, anyway.

Wyn and Seth won't know what to do. Suddenly, a huge gust of wind churns up snow, and the air thickens. It's as if someone has dumped a vat of flour on top of my head. My visibility fades, and all I can do is shut my eyes.

"Hang on!" I scream out to my team, hoping they hear, Then I quickly jam my walking stick deep into the thickening snow. Hopefully it will keep me stable enough so I know which way is up when this blows over. The frigid wind picks up and throws spindrift snow into an opaque cloud that reduces my visibility to nothing.

I try to take in a deep breath, but snow fills my lungs. I cough and cover my face with my arm so I don't choke to death or drown my lungs. I've got to get back. As I take another step, the earth collapses under me, and suddenly I'm falling.

Without any warning, I disappear into a sea of white.

ᴄ₰

123

When I'm finally able to focus, I'm not sure where I am or what exactly has happened. Nothing but brightness surrounds me. It takes me a couple of seconds to realize I'm completely buried in snow. Somehow, without knowing I was even moving, I stepped into a deep snowdrift.

I cough to clear my lungs but powdery snow tries to climb down my throat. I wiggle around, but the snow is packed around me. Tight. I can't move my arms and legs enough to dig myself out, and I have no idea how close I am to the surface. It could be a few inches or a few feet. My lungs beg for air, and I start to panic.

Oh my God. I'm buried alive. My worst fear of all.

Freaking out makes it worse, because I'm wasting any oxygen I have left. I focus on relaxing and keep my breathing steady and shallow to conserve air. *Think, Grace.* I quickly go back to that time when Dad rescued a skier who had fallen into a snowdrift. She had survived under the snow for over two hours. Dad said it was because the woman had stayed calm and worked slowly to carve out a small pocket for air until she was rescued.

I can do this. I just have to ward off asphyxiation and hope Wyn saw me go down.

Keeping my breathing steady, I carefully start twisting and moving my head around to carve out some space in front of my mouth. As soon as I have dug out a small pocket with my head, I force myself not to struggle. Some of these snowdrifts can go down deep, and I don't want to slip further. Or I'll never be found again. Not to mention, I could either deplete the air I have left or inhale carbon monoxide. Neither is good.

As I hang there buried in snow, I can't help but wonder if Wyn or Seth will even find me. I don't know if they heard me, let alone knew where I was exactly. And whiteouts can bring in a huge load of snow, making the drift even deeper. Even if Wyn's a couple feet off, he might never know I'm here.

Pressure rises in my chest, but I keep my mouth shut. If my lungs fill with snow, it's similar to drowning. What if I die here and no one ever finds me? I think of Mom. She will go through the same thing she did with Dad when he was missing, and the not knowing is worse than the possible outcomes. I know. And poor Birdee. She will feel guilty for letting me stay on the project. She'll blame herself and so will Mom. Tommy will feel bad for not repairing our friendship. And poor Wyn will never forgive himself and probably marry Skyler because he'll suffer from post traumatic stress.

And it will all be my fault. Once again.

I start to nod off from the lack of oxygen and shake my head to keep myself awake. Forget it. I don't want to be the cause of anyone's pain. My survival instinct takes over, and I cry out, gasping for air, not knowing if anyone is around or if anyone can hear me. My head gets fuzzy, and I start to feel lightheaded as I suck in another short breath. I panic and flip around, begging to break the surface and take in a huge breath.

Finally I stop. How long have I been here? How much oxygen is left before I pass out? My body relaxes and my head spins.

Maybe I'll be happier if I just slip away.

Be with Dad again.

No more pain, no more fear, no more guilt.

I blink, and snow falls onto my cheeks. Even though I know it isn't smart, I start to cry.

I don't want to die.

Suddenly, I think I hear muffled voices above me. I gasp for more air and thrash under the weight of the snow, hoping to somehow bust through the heavy layer of snow and let someone know I'm here. I imagine the snow parting, and the fresh, cold air finding my lungs, allowing me to breathe freely. Allowing me to live.

I gulp in one last breath of air and scream until my oxygen is depleted. Along with any hope of surviving. My lungs convulse, begging for air, and my body cries out in pain. I try not to breathe, but my body forces me to suck in a mouthful of snow.

My air is cut off, and I suddenly feel as if I'm being held under water.

Drowning.

Finally, everything goes dark.

# Survival Skill #13

*Even though the victim may appear alert, symptoms of hypothermia include trembling, loss of coordination, disorientation, and hallucinations.*

Someone screams in my ear, and I feel my body jerking left and right.

"Grace! Grace!"

I feel pounding on my chest and pressure on my mouth. Then more words.

"Damn it, Grace! Come on!"

My eyes flutter open, and I hear myself take in a huge breath as if I've plunged into icy water and finally come up for air after a long dive. I start coughing, as my lungs get greedy, taking in the air they were robbed of for so long. But how long? I hear words and voices around me, but I can't make out what they're saying. Am I dead?

My eyes flutter open. At first, all I see is white and black stripes above me. As my eyes focus, I make out trees backed by a light gray sky. Wyn is kneeling next to me with a horrified expression. His eyes are red and tears are streaming down his face.

Seth slaps his hands on his forehead. "Holy crap. She made it."

Wyn practically falls over me and kisses my face. "Oh, G! Thank God you're okay. "

Seth pulls him off me. "Dude, give her some space. This ain't the time for kissing. She needs air."

Wyn pulls back and lifts my torso off the ground. He hugs me, rocking back and forth. "I thought I lost you. Jesus, I thought you were gone."

I try to speak, but nothing comes. It's like I'm frozen in time. My mouth can't form any words, and my brain seems stuck in the same place. I keep hearing Wyn say a variety of cuss words over and over. Finally my lungs recoup, and I'm able to push out two words.

"I'm okay." My voice sounds raspy and raw. Even to me.

Wyn lowers my head onto his lap and strokes the wet hair away from my face. "Are you okay?"

I manage to smile. "Been better."

"You scared the shit out of me."

I look into his swollen eyes and mumble, "Sorry."

Seth's face pops into my view. He has a big grin. "You look like crap."

"Seth!" Wyn shoves him back. I don't bother to try and answer. To be honest, I can't even if I want to. I'm still having a hard time processing anything.

Seth leans over me again, this time with a huge grin plastered on his freckled face. "Just so you know, I saved you."

Wyn frowns but nods at the same time. "It's true. He did. We heard you calling us and saw you standing. Right there. Then you just disappeared. Seth reacted first. He made it to you in no time flat. We didn't know exactly where you went or how far you fell. We just dug like badgers, praying we were at the right spot."

Wyn gets choked up as he explains.

Seth plops down and rubs his forehead. "Dude, that was a serious rush. I thought you were a total goner. That we'd find you all frozen like Han Solo in *Star Wars*."

Wyn pushes Seth away from me. "This isn't the time for your dumb jokes."

Seth looks all innocent. "What? I'm serious. I don't know how long it takes for someone to freeze. Turn into a block of ice. A human ice cube."

Wyn ignores him and focuses back on me, still lying there. "It felt like forever. Luckily, Seth spotted the fur on your hat, and we just started yanking. I don't know how in the world we were strong enough to pull you out but we did."

Seth nods. "And you were totally blue. Like a freakin' Smurf or something. It was narly."

"Shut your piehole!" Wyn's voice sounds more like a growl.

Seth looks down at me with a sad face. "Sorry, Grace. I'm just all jacked up. I'm really glad you're okay. It would suck to die."

I touch his hand and force out a whisper. "Thank you."

"You're welcome." Seth winks and leans closer. "You know, I gave you mouth-to-mouth."

Wyn tries to grab his jacket hood, but Seth dodges him. "I swear, I'm going to kick your ass."

"Whatever. Like you could." Seth tumbles backward in a somersault and pops up on his knees a safe distance away. He raises his eyebrows in amusement. "You know you owe me, right, Grace? Like a life's debt. That's what happens when someone saves you. Eye for an eye."

I can't help but smile and nod in agreement. "Done."

Seth makes a "call me" sign with his fingers.

Wyn lurches at him again. "Dude, she may have to save you from me."

I can't help but laugh and cough at the same time. My ribs are sore from inhaling so hard. Thoughts are going through my brain, but I still can't seem to form a sentence. It's like the wire between my brain and my mouth has been severed. My teeth start to chatter, and I try to force myself to sit. But my body is heavy like a wet towel, which I know is not a good sign. I try to push up but collapse on my back.

Wyn grabs both arms and pulls me into a sitting position. "Take it easy, G."

Seth looks genuinely worried for the first time. "Dude, she doesn't look so good. Her skin's kinda grayish."

"Don't tell her that. You're supposed to make her feel better."

Seth snaps back. "Well, she ain't going to feel better if she's dead, now is she?"

Small sensations come back to me. A tinkling starts in my toes and works up my legs and into my body then trails down my arms. That's when the pain sets in. Every part of me starts to burn. Like I'm on fire. Any small movement is a jolt of pain.

I try not to move. "I'm cold." My body starts to shiver badly, like I'm having a seizure.

Wyn holds me down. "Jesus. She's going into shock or something."

Seth jumps up and grabs a few things out of the pack for his journey. "I'm gonna go find Porter. They can't be that far from here." Seth leans over me. "Hey. Don't you die on me. I want to be a freakin' hero." He winks and runs off.

"Go. Hurry!" Wyn calls after him. He glances back down at me with a pained look on his face as I shiver uncontrollably in his arms. "G, what do I do? I don't know what to do."

I focus on controlling my words as best as I can. "I… I need to get warm. Hy–po–thermia."

His eyes light up. "Build a fire. Got it." He spends the next five minutes trying to start a fire, but all the wood nearby seems damp from the snow. He looks defeated. "Now what?"

I motion my head to the backpack. "There."

He starts yanking stuff out of it, sifting through the gear. "Here. These will help." He takes off my wet glove and slips his dry ones over my hands. Then he slides the extra hand warmers inside, so they're touching my palms. He shoves a couple into my boots too. The heat feels so good until my hands thaw a little. Then they start to ache.

"The tarp," I whisper.

He flattens out the tarp on the ground, and I crawl onto it to get my butt and legs off the wet snow. I scan the area and try to think about what we can do. There doesn't seem to be any natural covering around. Usually building a snow shelter is best, but they can take forever to dig. I'm still trembling, and it seems to be getting worse, not better. Even with the warmers.

"What do I look like?"

Wyn stares at me. "Beautiful." I look at him blankly until he answers again. "You're pale as hell."

"What about my lips?"

"Perfect." Then he answers again. "Very blue."

I immediately know that moderate hypothermia has already set in. Luckily, I'm still in Stage Two because Stage Three is not good. It's hard to talk through the shivers so I throw out single words, hoping he'll understand. "Shovel."

He grabs the folding shovel from the pile of stuff and opens it, clicking the lock in place. "Bingo. Now what?"

I point to a dead tree stump on the side of the embankment. It's already dug out underneath and just needs to be cleared out more.

"Clear." I stop to catch a breath because it hurts to talk. I hold out my arms.

"Three feet wide. Got it." Wyn takes off his jacket and wraps it around my shoulders before folding the tarp over me. My body tries to get warm, but the air is blowing right through me. And my clothes are still sopping wet from being buried in the snow so long. Once I'm situated, Wyn jumps up and starts digging. Fast. I don't think I've ever seen him work this hard. After what seems like forever, he stops. Sweat is dripping down his face.

"Is that good enough?" he asks.

At this point, I'm shaking uncontrollably. Almost Stage Three, but I still have my wits about me. I focus on the task at hand.

"Yeesss. Vent."

He climbs up on the stump and drives a stick down into the top of the man-made cave. It goes through pretty easily. This might actually work. The wind picks up and swirls some snow. Wyn glances around.

"What else?"

I've never seen him this eager. I smile and hiss two words. "Mountain man."

He gives me a serious look. "Come on. Be real. It's getting darker and colder by the second."

He wraps his arms around his body and hops in place. I remember he doesn't have on his coat. Lucky for him, Old Navy fleeces are warm enough. At that moment, a wolf sounds off in the distance, reminding me of the one I found before the whiteout. I wonder if the wolf died of being cold. I suddenly feel like I want to lie down, sleep, and dream of a warm, cozy place.

I close my eyes as I talk. "How deep?"

Wyn gets on his hands and knees. "About eight feet. It was already hollowed out because of the tree roots."

I nod, still trembling. "Will it hold?"

He pushes down on it. "Seems sturdy enough."

"Line it."

I try to stand so he can get the tarp from under me, but my legs are like noodles and won't hold my weight. Wyn helps me to my feet and props me against the tree. He quickly crawls inside the cave, dragging the tarp behind him. I glance up at the sky. Huge dark clouds are rolling in, and the snowflakes are getting larger. It could dump on us at any minute.

My legs and feet are so cold, my body stings. My mind seems to be getting foggier. I start to lie down in the snow, but Wyn is in front of me in a second. He snaps his fingers in front of my face, causing my eyes to pop open.

"Hey, G. Come on, stay with me. Let's get you inside. It's good enough."

He drapes my arm around his neck and drags me to the opening. My whole body screams out in pain as if my muscles are angry and lashing out. I squat down and force myself to crawl in. Once inside, my body collapses onto the tarp. I already feel much warmer just being out of the wind, but now I just want to sleep. Wyn crawls in behind me and plugs the door with our gear.

"You okay?"

I just lay there shivering. He wraps his arms around me and starts to rub my legs and arms, trying to warm me up. My frozen body barely feels a thing.

"I just want to point out that I'm taking care of you," he says.

I stutter. "Shhhuuuttt uuuppp."

He smiles and continues to massage my limbs.

My mind goes in and out as I step into Stage Three hypothermia. I try to close my eyes, but Wyn shakes me.

"Listen. I don't know much, but you said it's not good to sleep." I nod. He looks helpless and scared. "What can I do?"

I lie still, shivering and chattering my teeth. My thoughts goes in and out. Like I'm here but not really here. Like this is all a bad dream. Foggy and strange. Distant. Like it's not happening to me.

"I'm...so... cold."

"I know." As Wyn pulls layers of clothes off his body, he explains. "I saw in a movie once that a person with

133

hypothermia needs to be skin on skin. It warms the body faster than anything."

Yes. Why didn't I think of that? Because my brain is like a Slushee. Surprised he knows anything about it, I stare as he unbuttons his flannel shirt and slips it off, now wearing only a white t-shirt. He trembles from the cold.

I try to stop him, "W…W…yn." But that's the only word my mouth will form.

He cups my face. "G, you have to get warm. You don't look good."

And I know he's right. It's our last option. To strip down and get warm from direct body heat. I manage to nod and try to take off my coat, but I can't seem to get my fingers to bend.

"I'll do it." He comes over to me and unzips my coat.

I can feel his breath on my forehead as he slides my stiff arms out of the sleeves. I can't help but remember being this close to Mo when we were camping, how I would lie next to him, feeling his warmth from behind. I push Mo out of my mind as Wyn unzips my sweatshirt. I look up at him but his face is serious and pinched as he concentrates on what he's doing.

Saving my life.

I try to help by unbuttoning my shirt, but my fingers won't work together. He cups my hands and blows before rubbing them between his palms. Then he unbuttons my shirt. My vision goes in and out as I feel my shirt slip off me. He lays me on my back and unzips my pants.

Suddenly, I'm back at Mo's camp. His arms wrapping around me as he kisses my neck and shoulders. I remember his lips being so soft and silky. How they would slide over mine like lip gloss.

Wyn's voice brings me back. "Stay with me, Grace."

He works faster now and slips off my cargo pants, leaving me in nothing but my Paul Frank undies and sports bra. He takes off his t-shirt and then slowly lies down next to me, pressing his chest against my back. I shiver violently next to him. Almost convulsing.

He wraps his arms around me and pulls me close. I immediately feel warmer and snuggle into him, pressing my cold body against his warm one. He reaches over me and wraps the tarp around us tight, like a human burrito. His body heat draws me in, and I roll over to face him, letting my body melt.

Soon, I can feel my body thawing. I become crazed for more warmth and slide into him more, getting closer by entwining my legs through his. Soon, my body stops trembling so much, and Wyn rubs my back. His heart beats against my chest as I bury my face in his neck, smelling his aftershave. He rubs my arms and legs, giving me permanent chill bumps.

But it's not enough. My mind goes foggy and once again everything around me blurs.

Suddenly, I'm back in the woods again. With Mo. We're hugging each other but he's asleep next to me. I'm lying still, listening to the night noises, the cicadas and the frogs. But mostly, I'm listening to the rhythm of his breath in my ear as he sleeps under the stars. I can't help but touch his face.

He opens his eyes and tucks my hair behind my ear.

I hear myself whisper, "I miss you."

"I'm here," he says.

He slides on top of me, molding us into one person. My breathing quickens, and I hear myself moan a little when our mouths finally meet. His lips lightly press on mine. His breath fills my mouth, giving me no desire to breathe on my own. My body goes warm inside as his lips glide over mine. I taste almonds and remember what it was like to be with him, why

I've missed him so much. He made me feel so open and so alive.

I open my mouth and wait for his tongue to find its way in. I wrap my arms around his neck, pulling him closer and closer, so we will never be apart again. We are kissing passionately, and his hands are all over me, touching me.

His body presses into mine as we fit perfectly together, piece by piece. He kisses my neck and every space on my shoulders. I want nothing more than to make love to Mo tonight. For the first time in my life to finally be with someone like that.

I start to cry. Mo's back, and I'm finally home again. Where I belong. I open my eyes and search the foggy world for his beautiful face. His smile. His dark-chocolaty eyes.

"I love you." I whisper.

Wyn's face appears in my blurry view, and he kisses me lightly. "I love you too, Grace."

# Survival Skill #14

*If you think you have hypothermia, seek medical help to be checked for frostbite and receive external warming*

ꟓ bolt upright and hit my head on the low, icy ceiling. "Ouch!"

I'm no longer shivering, but my whole body aches and throbs as if someone has thrown me around the small cave. It takes me a minute to remember where I am and what has happened.

I'm out in the wilderness. In a cozy snow cave. I glance to my right and sigh. Only I'm not with Mo; I'm with Wyn. Slivers of memories from the previous night piece together in my mind. The shivering, being so cold, the fever. The kissing. As soon as it all floods back, I glance down at my body, barely wrapped in underwear and a bra. Thank God, I'm still somewhat clothed.

Wyn is sleeping with a slight smile on his lips. He looks much younger than usual. That baby face. At some point in the middle of the night, he'd gotten dressed, leaving me to believe nothing happened. Thank God.

I quickly pull on my pants and shirt. Then I sit there quietly, staring out the hole into the bright sun as everything replays in my head.

What have I done? I hit my palm against my forehead a few times. How could I? Kissing Wyn was a huge mistake, and this time it might cost me my friendship for good. I rub my temples. How am I going to fix this mess? Can I? Will he ever forgive me if I reject him again?

All I remember is being so confused last night, and my head being so mucky. Like a swamp. For a while there, I really thought Mo was with me. That he had come back. My heart grows heavy, remembering how wonderful it felt thinking we were together again. I've tried so hard to block him from my mind, but now I miss him more than ever.

I sigh and glance back at Wyn. Poor guy. He probably thinks I meant all that for him; that I feel that way about him. He doesn't realize how bad the side effects of hypothermia can get. Delirium and hallucinations are quite common. I was not coherent enough to stop it from happening. But he doesn't get that. How am I going to explain this to him? *I kissed you because I thought you were Mo. I only said those things because I was temporarily insane.* Nice, Grace.

Wyn sits up next to me and strokes my hair. "Good morning, beautiful."

In my head, I hear Mo's voice say *Blossom.* I flinch and shake away the thought. I try not to jerk away from Wyn's touch and mumble, "Hey you."

He rubs his eyes. "What's the plan for today?"

I can't even look him in the eye as I start to gather my things. "We have to leave."

He rubs his eyes and tries to smooth down his cockatoo hair. "You sure? Maybe I want to stay."

A chill runs down my back and my hands start to tremble. "I'm not out of the woods yet. I need to get to a hospital."

Suddenly, outside I hear crunching in the snow.

"Someone's here." Wyn's ears perk up. "Betcha it's Porter!"

I almost stick my head out the front door until the sound of whistling fills the air. Al and Carl fill my thoughts. I'll never forget the song they used to whistle in the woods. I still hear it in my sleep sometimes. I grab Wyn's arm and shake my head without saying anything. His eyes grow wide.

I whisper, "Stay quiet."

Even though I know he doesn't understand, he hisses back. "We need help."

I shake my head harder and mouth, *please*.

My whole body starts to shake again. I can't tell if it's the after-effects of hypothermia or the onset of complete terror. The heavy footsteps get closer and closer. I put my finger to my lips and mouth to Wyn again, *trust me*.

He nods once, and we both sit quietly. Neither of us makes a sound as the footsteps walk above us. The weight of the person sends a shower of snow down on our heads. I stare at the ceiling, praying the roof will hold. I hope no one can tell we're hiding down here. Luckily it snowed, so any trace of us would have disappeared in the night.

I think of the wolf and wonder if the person standing above me is connected to its death. Wyn reaches over and grabs my hand. I don't pull away. My heart drums in my chest as the whistling continues. Al's face flashes in my mind. The songs. His sneer. His alcohol breath. His knife. The way he gunned down my Dad right before my eyes.

I bite my lip to prevent me from wailing. I would rather stay here and freeze to death than run into Al ever again.

The person must stand on top of us for a while, because there is no sound. Is he looking for me? Does he know we're here?

A few minutes later, the footsteps start up again and slowly fade into the distance. I let out a long sigh.

Wyn frowns. "You going to tell me what's going on?"

"Porter doesn't whistle."

He looks confused. "Maybe a rescuer does."

I shake my head. "Not like that."

He faces me. "No one else would be out this far. We need to get you help."

"I found a dead wolf. Right before I fell."

He combs his fingers through his hair. "Are you serious?"

"Yes, but this one was alive. I saw him take his last breath. That means someone else might be out here besides us. Someone who isn't supposed to be."

"You think someone is killing the wolves? Because Porter doesn't. Did you find anything different?"

I shrug. "No. Same as before. No marks or evidence of anything. I just don't know what's going on or why someone other than Porter would be out here. And surely they would have been calling my name or something. That person was sneaking, like he was stalking something. Or someone."

Wyn thinks for a second and rubs his five o'clock shadow. "So what... you think that was—"

I place my hand over his mouth before he says Al's name. "I don't want to think. I just want to get out of here and go home. I'm sure Birdee is freaking out right now."

Wyn quickly packs up the rest of our things. As I start to crawl out, he stops me. 'Wait. Let me go first. Just in case."

I nod as he crawls out the door, and for a few minutes, I hold my breath. Wondering. Is there a person still out there? Hiding? Waiting?

Wyn pops his head back in the doorway. "All clear."

I stay where I am. "You sure?"

"Positive. The sun's out too, so let's hurry and hike before it gets bad again."

I slowly inch my way out of the safe space. As soon as my body hits the cold air, I start to shiver again. "I can't get stuck out here for another night."

He holds out his hand to help me up. "Oh I don't know. It wasn't *that* bad."

I make a point not to look at him. I just can't bear to see the satisfied, happy smile on his face, knowing he thinks our relationship has moved to a new level, a level I don't ever imagine for us again. Whether or not Mo is here.

My legs buckle underneath me. "Let me sit here for a second to catch my breath." But really, I'm too petrified to move. I don't know which way that person went, and we could be walking right into him.

Wyn scans the trees. "You rest. I'll do a quick check around."

He walks slowly around the area, in and out of trees. Even though I'm tense waiting for him to return, I lean against the makeshift cave and study the tracks in the snow, heading the opposite way we're going. But there are no markers, which is usually what a search and rescue team does to indicate their trail. What if Wyn is right, and we missed a chance for help? This long hike out is not going to be easy for me.

Just then, I spot something in the frozen snow. At first it appears to be a long leaf or a branch, but when I lean in closer, my breath sticks in my throat. It's a green bandana. My hand trembles as I pick it up. It looks just like the ones Al and his whole posse carried. I gasp for air as my throat closes. My heart stammers in my chest, and my eyes dart around the trees. What if he's watching me, waiting for a moment to strike, like a cobra on a weasel?

Wyn pops out of the trees, startling me. "You ready? I found the way out."

I shove the bandana in my pocket without telling him and keep my eyes on the trees. "Yeah, let's get out of here."

Wyn and I walk down the path. Actually, he walks, I stumble along while he does his best to hold me up. My legs feel like wet noodles, and my lungs feel as if they've been sawed in half. I have to stop every few yards to catch my breath and recharge.

"I don't know if I can do this."

He urges me on. "You don't have a choice. And by the way, since when can't you do something you want to do? Where's that feisty spirit I love about you?"

When he says the L-word, I mumble, feeling somewhat sick to my stomach. "It's frozen."

He supports me as I walk down the path. The icy breeze burns my face and sends me into trembling fits as the wind's cold fingers reach down into my clothes, piercing my layers. I just want to crawl under a blanket and sleep or slide into a hot bath and submerge under water. Never to surface again. I'm not sure how long we walk. I just focus on taking one step at a time.

"I can't feel my toes and fingers."

Wyn checks my watch. "We don't have far to go." He obviously doesn't realize how fast he's walking because he moves ahead some.

I collapse right where I'm standing and gasp, taking in a few deep breaths. "I'm sorry. I need to rest."

"We don't need you getting wet again." He lifts me to my feet.

I shake my head. "I can't walk anymore."

Without saying a word, Wyn places one hand on my back and slides his arm under my legs, scooping me up. "Don't sweat it. I gotcha."

I lay my head on his shoulder and close my eyes. "I didn't know you were strong."

His breath tickles my hair when he talks. "There's a lot you don't know about me."

"Since when?"

"People can change without you even noticing."

I don't say anything else as Wyn carries me the last mile out of the woods. By the time we reach the road, Agent

Sweeney and a crew of people are lined up under a small tent, talking. As soon as they see us, Sweeney rushes to my side.

"Thank God you guys are okay." He takes one look at me and motions to a stretcher. "Jesus, Grace. You look awful."

I mumble, "Gee, thanks."

A stretcher rolls up next to me, and Wyn lays me on it gently before he collapses onto a fold-up chair. The medics lay silver heated blankets over me and tuck them around my body. Like I'm a hot potato wrapped in foil, waiting to cook. The heat permeates me immediately. I'm so relieved to not feel cold anymore. I'm still shivering, but I can feel my body finally thawing.

Wyn leans over me with a blanket over his shoulders and lightly kisses my forehead. "You're going to be okay."

I whisper, "Thanks to you."

He smiles and rubs my cheek. "My pleasure, Little Miss Independent."

# Survival Skill #15

*When surviving a trauma, sometimes to get past it,
you must face the people and places
that remind you of the event and not shy away.*

Even before I'm able to even open my eyes, I hear someone crying.

I peek through my eyelids and see Birdee sitting next to my hospital bed. She is clutching my hand, and her head is rested on my arm. The only other sound is my heart monitor beeping in the background. I attempt to say something, but the inside of my mouth is parched and cracked. I lick my lips, but my tongue feels dry and swollen.

I hear her mumbling, "Please, please, God. Let her be okay."

I clear my throat. "You're praying now? The other day you two were arguing."

Her head pops up. Her eyes are almost swollen shut, and tears are streaking down her cheeks. I immediately feel horrible for putting her through this.

She strokes my head. "Thank God you're okay."

I look around the room. "Is Mom here?"

She shakes her head. "I haven't been able to get a hold of her yet. The storm took down some of the lines, so phones have been out." She starts to cry again and cups my face. "Are you okay? Tell me you're okay. Does anything hurt?"

"Everything hurts." I hold her hand. "I'm fine, though. Really. Wyn took care of me. I got a little cold, but really I'm going to be good as new. No permanent brain damage. At least not anything new."

She forces a smile. "I've been so worried about you. They didn't think you'd make it. The storm came in so fast and so hard. When Agent Sweeney said you two weren't back yet, I just didn't know what to do. Then it got to be nighttime, and I thought for sure you were—"

"Not even close. I'm fine." She nods and wipes her face. I try to make her laugh. "What happened to the Birdee who never worries about anything? Tough as nails? The one allergic to drama."

She remains serious and keeps a straight face. "I guess she left when your father died." She covers her mouth with one hand and shakes her head. "I can't lose you too, Chicken."

Tears fill my eyes thinking of Dad. "Ditto."

Birdee sits on my bed softly. "What happened out there?"

I tell her everything. About separating from the team. About the dead wolf. About the whiteout and falling into a deep snowdrift.

"Wyn stayed with me. I didn't think he had it in him, but I wouldn't be here without him."

She smiles. "Yes, so I gathered. Poor boy's been driving me nuts since you got here. Coming in and out every other minute. Asking me if you've woken up. If you need water. Checking in with the doctors. Damn boy's gone looney over you."

"He's mental alright."

I don't say any more than that to Birdee, but I can't help flashing back to the cave and remembering kissing Wyn. I don't know how I'm going to deal with this. Again.

I quickly change the subject. "The weather came in so fast, we had to build a snow cave and hunker down for the night."

She strokes my hair. "I remember when your Dad used to build those in the backyard every winter. He loved making tunnels and secret dens. Some kids wanted to do sleepovers in tents, but your dad always wanted to sleep outside in his snow caves. In the middle of winter. Crazy kid. Wasn't afraid of anything. Not even Mother Nature herself." She stops and swallows. "Maybe I shouldn't have encouraged him."

I close my eyes, suddenly exhausted again. "Oh, stop feeling sorry for yourself. I'm the one who needs some attention here."

She laughs and in one second, she's back to the same old lady. "You are a little smartass like him, too. I like it." She strokes my hair. "Can I get you anything?"

"Maybe some water?"

She walks over to the sink and pours me a glass. Then she holds it up to my lips. "Drink."

I take a few sips and let it slosh around in my mouth, washing away the dryness. "You are a great nurse. I didn't know you had it in you."

Birdee scoffs. "Ha! Don't get used to it. Tomorrow I'll have you doing chores again. You can only milk this for so long." She looks at me with her green eyes and sighs.

"What?"

"I need to say something, and I know you're going to get mad. But I just gotta say it."

I notice my butt's fallen asleep and try to sit up a little in my bed to change positions. "What is it?"

She adjusts the pillow behind my head and sits down again, this time folding her hands in her lap. Never a good sign. "I want you to quit this project." I open my mouth to protest, but she holds up her hand. "Before you say no, hear me out."

I nod. "Go ahead."

"To be honest, I can't take it. After sitting there all night worried, I can only imagine what your mother went through last summer with you and your dad. I can't do this to her

146

again. She won't make it if anything happens to you, and I promised to take care of you."

"Birdee, I—"

She frowns. "Now I don't want any arguments. I'm older than you, and you have to respect your elders."

I smile. "Since when?"

"Just do it for me. Please."

Just then, someone knocks on the door. Tommy pokes in his head. "Is it okay to come in?"

At first I don't know what to say. He's the last person I would expect to drop by, and I answer with a scratchy voice. "Oh. Hey, Tommy."

He smiles and opens the door. "Birdee! How are you?"

She doesn't give her usual hello. She simply nods, which is not a great sign, and says his name with a flat tone. "Tommy."

Something strange passes between them. Anger. Tension. Which is odd because they've been friends for years. Both Tommy and his wife, Ama, always spent the holidays at our house with Birdee.

She jumps up and heads to the door. "I'll go tell Wyn you're okay. He's been waiting."

I watch the two of them pass each other without saying another word. Birdee is obviously still upset over Dad, even though it wasn't Tommy's fault. There's no one else alive for her to blame. Or me for that matter.

She grabs her hat off the table. "You alright?"

I nod as Tommy bows slightly. "It was good seeing you."

Birdee frowns. "Wish I could say the same." Then she looks at me. "Think about what I said."

I nod. "I will. I promise. We can talk more later."

She puts a stern look on her face. "Nothing to discuss."

She walks out the door without another glance or word for Tommy. He keeps his eyes on the floor until the door clicks shut.

I shift uncomfortably and try to make him feel better, not that I have to, but he looks so sad I can't help but feel sorry for him.

"Don't worry about her. It takes her a while to get over things but she'll come around. Sooner or later." I leave off *never*.

His sad eyes meet mine. "Will you?"

I draw back, slightly caught off guard at his directness. Usually not a strong trait of his. "Uh, what?"

He pulls up a chair and sits, still holding the flowers in his lap. "It's been three months, Elu. I wanted to give you your space, but I'd hoped you'd come around."

I look to see if Birdee is still outside so I can motion her back in. I'm not sure how to handle this exactly. "Tommy, I…"

Tears form in his eyes and fall down his cheeks, reminding me of the old Native Americans in pictures of the past. I've only seen Tommy cry once. And that was when Ama died after he'd tried so hard to help her beat the cancer. He didn't even cry when he was shot. And he didn't attend the funeral. Not because he didn't want to, but because Birdee asked him not to.

He clears his throat. "You see, I love you, and I'm so sorry. About everything."

"Tommy, it's okay…"

He shakes his head. "No, it's not. And don't let me off the hook that easily. I know you and Birdee and your Mom blame me for Joe's death. I would too if I were you. I let you down." Tears stream down his face, and he sobs as he talks. "It was my fault your dad died. I never should have held back anything from you."

I interject. "You were just trying to protect me."

He goes on as if I haven't said anything. "I should have made that call myself instead of anonymously. I should have

148

made sure someone followed up that lead. Shoot, I should've checked out the camp I found myself. Had I done that, Joe would still be alive."

"He was alive." I sit up and touch his hand. "If it wasn't for Al, he'd still be here. It wasn't your fault. I don't blame you. I blame Al and Carl."

He wipes his face with both hands and tucks his long white hair behind his shoulders. "I didn't do everything I could to bring Joe home alive. I sat back and—"

"Sat back? Tommy, you took a bullet for me. You almost died coming to rescue Dad and me from that camp. You did everything you could." Hearing myself defend Tommy out loud makes me realize one thing. I've been blaming the wrong person this whole time. I sigh. "Look, I haven't been all fair to you either. I don't know why I pulled away. I guess I just needed time or space. I was mad and wanted someone to blame. Same with Mom and Birdee. Everyone responsible is either dead or gone."

He takes his hat off his head and sets it on the table. "I shouldn't have let you pull away. I should have let you yell at me. Get it off your chest. I'm too passive, not aggressive enough, or I would have come to talk to you sooner. It was my place to step up and reach out to you, not yours. I'm the adult."

My head is starting to hurt. "Why did you come today?"

He fiddles with the flies hanging from his hat. "When I heard you were missing, I couldn't take it. I realized I might not have another chance. So when Les told me you were found, I raced right over."

"I'm glad you did." I close my eyes for a second. When I open them, he's at my side.

"I've stayed too long. I'll let you rest."

I nod slowly. "But you still owe me lunch."

He smiles. "That sounds fair. I'll call you in a few days when you get well." He walks to the door.

"Hey!" He turns around and faces me, looking much older than I remember. "You going to give me my flowers, or you taking them with you?"

He looks down at the bouquet in his hand and smiles. "I almost forgot."

"Yeah, that's what happens when you get old."

His eyes twinkle. "Ha! I'm young at heart. That's all that matters." He sets the flowers on the side table and leaves again. He stops just before he shuts the door. "*Gv-ge-yu-hi*, Elu."

"*Gv-ge-yu-hi* right back."

When he shuts the door, I lean back and smile. I never stopped loving Tommy. He's been like a grandfather to me my whole life. Through the window, I see him stop and confront Birdee. The man is on a mission.

A few minutes later they hug.

In that moment, I realize it's true.

Out of bad things, good things can come.

# Survival Skill #16

*After any traumatic event, don't make any decisions you may regret later. You never know how your body or mind will respond after a life or death situation.*

Before I open my eyes, I can already sense someone is in the room.

"Hello, Blossom."

I sit up and smile, almost in shock. "Mo?" He leans over and hugs me, but I remain stiff, not sure of what I'm seeing. "Are you really here?"

He smiles that grin I've missed so much. "Abso-blooming-lutely."

I reach out to him. "Come here. Tell me I'm not dreaming."

He leans over and whispers in my ear. "Grace, wake up."

It takes a second for my eyes to eyes flutter open, and I see Wyn.

He looks concerned. "Hey. You okay?"

I search the room before answering. "Wyn?"

"Expecting someone else?" He smiles. "You were mumbling something. Must have been dreaming."

My heart sinks, and I pull the cover over my head. "Dreaming?"

Tears are in the corners of my eyes as I realize Mo isn't here and will never be. My time with him is over, yet my brain can't seem to let him go. And now it seems to be getting worse.

I pull the sheet down and sit up. "I guess it's the medicine."

Wyn sits on the side of my bed and kisses the top of my hand. "How are you?"

I force myself not to pull away, to let him hold my hand for a second longer. "I'm as good as new. Maybe even better. Really." I lightly pull my hand back and move my long hair out from behind me so it doesn't look like it's a rejection of any kind.

He cocks his head. "You know, you scared me out there."

I look out the window to break his gaze. "I know. I'm sorry. If I'm being totally honest and vulnerable, I scared myself, too."

"An admission of weakness?"

I watch a bird sitting on the ledge, looking down, as if thinking about jumping. "No. Just the truth."

He rubs my arm lightly. "Thought I was going to lose you there in that cave."

At the mention of it, I try to lighten the mood or even change the subject. Last thing I want to do is talk about what happened in the cave.

"Ha. I'm too tough for that!"

Wyn laughs along with me. "That's probably true."

A few awkward moments linger between us. I study his face, realizing how disheveled he looks. Usually Wyn is dressed perfectly. Not the typical small-town fashion either. He makes a point to go to Asheville for his clothes, and usually he is perfectly pressed and clean-shaven. Today he looks tired, crumpled, and stubbly.

I point to his hair. "You're worried about me? Look at you."

He looks down at his wrinkled shirt and rubs his cheek with one hand, smiling. "Yeah, well, I've been here for two days."

I tease him and hold my nose. "No shower?"

He tilts his head. "Nope. No food either. Haven't been able to eat or sleep."

I immediately feel awful. "Oh, Wyn. You didn't have to stay. You need to take care of yourself."

"I know, but I didn't want to leave you." He pats the hard bed. "I wanted to be right here if – when – you woke up."

I hold his hand. "I haven't thanked you yet. For everything."

He finds my eyes and looks a bit sad.

I grip his hand harder. "Seriously, you saved me. I don't know what I would have done if you and Seth hadn't found me. If you hadn't been there to take care of me at my lowest. I would probably not be–"

He places his other hand over my lips. "Don't say that, G. You're here."

I put some space between us and lay back, acting tired. "Because of *you*."

He doesn't say anything for a minute, so I open one eye.

He grins. "I was pretty good, wasn't I?"

"You were great." I shiver once.

He immediately pulls the covers up higher and tucks it around my body. "So you think I could be a mountain man after all?"

I try to look serious. "No."

He drops open his mouth and acts surprised. "What do you mean? I can get me some Cole Haan boots, maybe a North Face jacket. I could look the part."

"Nah. It wouldn't suit you. Mud is not your color."

"Very funny." He tries to tickle me, but instead of laughing, I wince. He stops and jerks his hands back. "Oh gosh, I'm sorry."

"Ouch," I say, smiling weakly. "Trying to kill me, Wynford?"

He bites his lips. "On the contrary, Miss Independent. I'd like to keep you around for a long time."

He studies my face, and then his eyes move to my lips. I can't take it anymore. I feel like I'm being dishonest. I need to do what Tommy wishes he had done with me. Hit this head-on. It's my only chance at salvaging our friendship.

"Wyn, we need to talk."

"Uh-oh. Sounds serious." He stands and steps back a little as if my words will hurt him. "You don't have to say anything. We can talk about everything after you get out of this place."

I shake my head and pinch back tears. "No. We should talk now."

He shoves his hands in his pockets. "That can't be good."

I search my brain for the right words, but nothing seems right in this moment. "It's just... I..."

He puts up one hand and smiles wide. "Wait, I know what you're going to say. You love what happened between us in the cave, and you're madly in love with me. Right? Tell me that's what it is." His smile sags a little. "Please, tell me that's what it is."

I sigh loudly and break eye contact. I can't bear to see the look on his face.

"No such luck, I guess." He drops his head forward and stares at his shoes. Seeing that look on his face makes me feel horrible. A tear slips down my cheek.

"Wyn, you are such a wonderful guy. And to be honest, I'm not sure what went on between us in the cave. It's so foggy, I barely remember anything after falling down that hole."

He takes a step back as if I've kicked him in the chest. Then he uses the chair to steady himself before sitting down, already distancing himself. I wish I could go to him, but I'm not strong enough to climb out of the bed.

"Please come over here so we can talk. I care about you, Wyn. You're my best friend. These last few months have been horrible without you, and I've been so happy since we starting hanging out again. I missed you, and I need you in my life. You saved my life. I owe everything to you."

"But..." He finds my eyes with his. "There's got to be a big but. It's okay, I can take it. That's what friends are for. Right?"

"I'll be straight with you." I wring my hands together. "This is not about you. I'm just not over – everything – yet."

"Oh." He nods and drops his head into his hands. "You mean that Mo guy."

I can only nod as a teardrop rolls over my lip. "I'm so sorry."

He closes his eyes as if remembering something. "But what about the cave? You told me you loved me. You kissed me. What was that all about then?"

I don't have the heart to tell Wyn I was imagining Mo. That I was hallucinating about another guy while he was trying to show me how he felt about me after all this time.

"I guess I just wasn't all there. The hypothermia was stronger than I was."

He frowns. "So *kissing* is a side effect of hypothermia? Good to know."

I tip my head, making it pound. "Wyn, come on. Please don't. I'm sorry. I didn't know what I was doing. I've never had hypothermia."

"Well, if that's what it does, I hope you get it again." He gets up and drags the chair over to my bed. "It's okay. Really. I understand."

I narrow my eyes. "You do? You mean you're not mad?"

He winks. "Hey, what can I say? I copped a feel. How can I be mad?" I smack him upside the head, and he flinches. "Ow."

"Be serious."

"No, really. I appreciate you being honest. You can't help how you feel." He kisses my hand. "But neither can I."

"What?"

He stands up and leans over me, cups my face, and lightly pecks my lips. Then he pulls back and smiles. "Look. I know there's something between us, G. Always has been. I know you've been through a lot. And you know what? I can wait for you to deal with whatever you need to deal with."

"Wyn, I can't promise anything."

I press my temples as my head races in confusion. Should I tell Wyn I was thinking about Mo that whole time? That I'm not confused. Should I tell him I don't see a future for us?

Do I see a future for us?

He grabs his jacket. "I'm not asking you to. I just want you to know that I love you, and I'll wait for however long it takes for you to see how good we are together. I'm sorry, but I don't believe what happened in that cave between us wasn't real. There was no one else there, and you let down your guard. It was all real for me. Maybe you'll see that it was real for you, too. You said you loved me."

"I do. You're my best friend. You're all I have, really."

He shrugs. "Then that's enough for me. For now."

With that, Wyn kisses me on the forehead and leaves the room. He turns off the light on the way out.

"Sleep tight, G. I'll be here when you wake up."

I sit alone in the dark with my feelings all swirling around inside. I lay my head back against the pillow and stare at the ceiling. Confused and frustrated, I wonder how I seem to ruin everything I touch. Especially when my intentions are to help people. Why couldn't I tell Wyn the whole truth?

Then I wonder.

Is it because I'm not sure?

Maybe I'm wrong. Maybe I do care about Wyn more than I realize.

Maybe I'm tired of choosing a dead love over a possible living one.

# Survival Skill #17

*Take immediate action to ensure your physical safety and the safety of others. Remove yourself from the event in order to avoid further traumatic exposure.*

By the time Birdee and I get a hold of Mom, I'm released to go home.

The storm hit from here all the way to Asheville, doing more damage than anyone expected. Needless to say, Mom wasn't happy, but Birdee managed to convince her not to come home. I promised both of them I would quit, and Birdee vowed not to let me out of her sight ever again. For as long as we both shall live.

All I'm focusing on now is getting out of the hospital. Even though I'm still not feeling a hundred percent, after a few days in this place, I realize home will get me back to myself more than any place around. Just the thought of eating MoonPies in my own bed is enough to make me smile.

While Birdee is signing my release papers, I stuff the last of my things in the plastic bag they gave me. When Birdee opens the door to head off to the nurse's station to ask another question about my home care, Agent Sweeney walks in.

"Good morning. May I come in?"

Birdee frowns. "As usual, your timing is impeccable. Do you have like a beeper or something that informs you of the worst moment to show up?"

"Birdee!" I shout, totally embarrassed

He shakes his head. "It's okay. How are you?"

I sit on the chair to allow my legs to recover from standing so quickly so soon. "Well, Agent Sweeney, since I've been here a couple days with no visit, I hope you didn't come empty-handed."

He holds up a clump of greenery. I laugh and take the wilted stems. "Wow, you picked weeds for me? You shouldn't have."

He waves me off. "If you tell anyone, I'll deny it."

Birdee humphs her displeasure and heads for the door. "Don't you dare put any of your crazy ideas into that girl's hard head. I just finished cleaning them all out. You hear me, Sweeney? Or I'll have a bone to pick with you."

He takes off his hat. "Yes, ma'am." He waits until the door shuts and then pulls up a chair. "I take it she's mad?"

I can see Birdee spy through the side window in the door. He follows my eyes and waves to her with a big smile. She points two fingers at her eyes and then points them at Sweeney.

I interpret. "She's watching you."

He nods. "I got that part. Thanks." She quickly walks off as he faces me. "Guess she blames me for you being in the woods."

I crawl back onto the bed in my jeans and tuck the blanket around me, feeling chilly again. "She's just upset."

"No, she's pissed. And she has a right to be. It's my fault you were out there. I should have never let Porter talk me into anything." He hits his head with his palm. "Stupid to put any of you kids out there in the first place."

"You couldn't have known any of this would happen. We never have winter storms like this, and kids do research for organizations all the time. My cousin goes out in the ocean with The Dolphin Project to take pictures of dolphin fins. Even when it rains. That can't be less dangerous than this."

He looks down at his hat. "Still."

159

I notice my backpack on the opposite chair. "Can you hand me that? I need to show you something."

Agent Sweeney gets up and grabs the bag.

"Look in the front pocket."

He unzips the pouch and pulls out the green bandana. His eyes get big, and he looks at me. "Is this...? Where did you get it?"

I shake my head. "I don't know, and in the woods. Close to where I fell."

I go on to tell him what I saw. What I heard before we left. The footsteps. The whistling. And then about finding the bandana crushed in the snow.

Agent Sweeney rubs his face with one hand in disbelief. "Why didn't Wyn tell me?"

"He doesn't know."

He sits in a chair and sighs. "So I guess I was wrong. Al's back."

My stomach drops. "You think so? You don't think it could be a coincidence?"

He shakes his head and gets up to pace. "With dead wolves, bandanas, and whistling? No way. All signs point to Al."

"Yeah, doesn't look good. Before I fell, I found another wolf too. Im teh same area."

"Dead?"

"Nope. Alive. At least for a few minutes. He died when I was trying to help him." I shake my head. "I couldn't save him."

He reaches over and pats my arm. "Grace, I'm sorry. I can't imagine how hard that was. Especially after—"

"Finding Dad? Yeah, well, it seems to be a pattern lately."

I shake the wolf and Dad from my head. I can't focus on details, or I'll get sucked back into my depression.

Sweeney takes out his notebook and starts to jot things down. "Any clues to go on? Coordinates?"

I give him the location of the wolf and the bandana. "Sad thing is he looked just like the other one did. No blood. No sign of humans around anywhere. Appeared totally healthy."

"So then, Al's our only lead."

I pull the covers up to my chin as if I'm a kid trying to hide from the boogieman. "Why would he be back? It can't be for a sixteen-year-old. Maybe it has something to do with the documents Mo left me? Maybe they're his?"

"Maybe."

I ask him the same question I've been asking for months. Since the very day I handed those papers over to him. "What's on those papers anyway? Maybe that will help us."

"Us?" Sweeney walks over to the window and stares out at the falling snow. "You know I can't reveal that."

I hit the bed with my fists in frustration. "That's BS. After everything I've done, I deserve the truth about Al, about those papers–" I pause for a second. "And about Mo."

He swings around to face me. "You know what happened to Al and Mo. As far as the codes, I'll tell you what I think, but it can't leave this room. We still have an investigation going on."

"Go ahead."

"We think they're bank accounts and codes identifying people who are involved in something bigger than what happened with your father."

I wasn't expecting that. "You mean, more people could be involved?"

He crosses his arms. "Maybe. But I don't know for sure. It's just a hunch."

"So you think Al being back has something to do with that?"

"Either that or he's back for you."

I cross my arms and hug myself. "Well, just lay it out there."

He shrugs. "Why beat around the bush? You're smarter than that."

I swallow and look out the door for Birdee. She's still standing at the counter. She's going to flip out if she hears any of this.

"How can we find out if Al's involved in the wolf deaths?"

Agent Sweeney leans over the bed and keeps his voice low. "Listen, Grace, I'll let you in because you're a smart girl, and you've been involved from the beginning. And to be honest, I owe your dad for not doing more to help him when he needed me. But I need your word that you won't tell anyone."

My eyes get large and I nod quickly, anxious to hear what he's going to say. "I promise."

He glances at the door. "Even though Porter didn't think it was necessary, I went ahead and ordered an autopsy on the dead wolf you guys found a couple days ago. I hoped it would reveal some more information. If it wasn't natural causes, it might give us more insight. I'm waiting on those results, which might answer your question about Al. Meanwhile, you need to stay out of those woods and stay safe. Maybe I can put someone at your house."

"No. Birdee will panic." I sigh, knowing he's right. "I just need to quit this project before I get in too deep. This is too much for me."

"I agree."

A knock at the door brings the conversation to a halt. Katie pokes her head in. "Am I interrupting something?"

I smile and wave her in. She's carrying a huge bouquet of mixed roses and lilies. She puts the vase on the side table and comes to sit at the end of my bed.

I lean over and smell the flowers. "I feel like someone died."

She frowns. "Someone almost did."

I point to the arrangement and smile at Sweeney. "Now *that's* a bouquet."

Katie picks up Agent Sweeney's clump of grass. She looks up at him and makes a face. "Tell me you didn't. Surely the USFWS pays you better."

"You'd be surprised." He shrugs. "Besides, I like to be different. Nothing is better than nature's own."

"That is definitely *unique*." She looks at me and makes a crazy sign next to her ear.

I giggle at her gesture. "You're just figuring that out now?"

Agent Sweeney picks up a newspaper. "Don't talk about me like I'm not here."

"It's the thought that counts, right?" Katie touches my hand. "Grace. How are you?"

"I'm cool." Only Katie gets my really, really bad joke. "Nice one." She kicks off her cowboy boots and tucks her feet underneath her bottom. "You gave us quite a scare out there. But I hear if anyone can be stuck in the woods and make it, it's you. You are quite the trooper."

I smile. "I guess. But Wyn and Seth deserve all the credit. I wouldn't be here if it wasn't for them."

"Yes, well. You all did a great job, and I'm thankful you're okay." She studies Agent Sweeney and then addresses me. "I suppose this means you're off the team?"

My heart sinks when she says it, but I know it's for the best. "Yes."

Agent Sweeney stands. "I think we should shut down the whole operation."

She folds her hands in her lap. "And for once, I agree. Now I just need to get Porter to back down. He gets a little obsessed over these things. If the project stops, he loses funding."

I speak up before Sweeney does. "I did find another wolf carcass. Just before the whiteout. It looked to be the same as the one before."

Her eyebrows pull down. "Let me get Porter in here for this. He'll want to hear this."

She walks to the door in her bare feet and opens it. Seconds later, Porter follows her inside, holding his suspenders.

His voice booms, "Grace. Must say, it's good to see you. I'm sorry we split up. I really thought it would be safe enough since we were close."

Agent Sweeney frowns. "Not close enough though, huh?"

Porter flashes Sweeney a nasty look. "I can't control the weather. It was... unfortunate."

Sweeney raises his voice and stands. "Unfortunate? She's a teen, and she almost died. I told you it was too bad to go out in that weather."

"What a minute," Katie says. "I'll take some blame, too. I told Porter it was okay if the kids felt comfortable and if he went along. Guess I didn't make it clear I expected him to stay with all of them the whole time."

She folds her arms and her mouth is tense. "Porter, Grace here says she found another wolf dead out there. Do you know anything about it?"

He plays with his goatee. "Really? We didn't see anything." He faces me and takes out his small notepad. "Can you tell me more? How big? Any clues?"

"It was smaller than the one you and I found a few days ago. I couldn't tell if it was a male or female though."

He scratches his head. "Dang. I hope that wasn't the alpha female. It is so essential to the pack's survival out there. Did you by chance see the tag number?"

I think back. "Actually, now that you mention it, it didn't have a collar on."

He flips his pad and frowns. "That means it was one of the females. We lost one on the tracking system a day or two ago. I was hoping the collar was just broken." He faces Reynolds. "What do you want to do?"

Agent Sweeney pipes up. "Nothing. We're shutting down."

Katie gives him a look and comes at it differently. "I think we have enough data right now to pull these wolves back in. They're not safe out in the wild. I say we regroup and assess what we have."

Porter shakes his head. "This is very common in all releases. The most common causes of the wolves not making it are being shot or run over, which we haven't had – knock on wood." He drums his knuckles on the arm of the chair. "The others are disappearances due to collars not working and natural causes."

"I cannot authorize sending out any more volunteers. Especially kids," Katie says.

"Well I can." Porter raises his voice. "This is too important to stop because we had a couple wolves die and a bad snowstorm. This is important to the survival of the wolves going forward. They can't live in captivity forever!"

Katie stands and approaches Porter. "Look, I know you're disappointed. I am too. But we're putting kids in danger. I'm sorry."

Porter's face turns red. "So that's it?"

Katie nods. "I'm afraid so. We're shutting down. I'll call the Wolf Coalition members and schedule a meeting. They'll want to know why."

Porter storms out of the room.

Even though I think Katie made the right decision, I can't help but feel bad. The wolf project is being shut down because of me. Now, there will never be wolves in the wild. I hang my head.

Katie grips my shoulder. "Grace, don't go blaming yourself. This isn't your fault. These things happens all the time in conservation efforts. It's part of the job and part of the frustration. This is not the end of these wolves. It's just a delay. They'll be safer at the reserve anyway. It's nasty this year. Who knows, maybe we can try again some place else in the spring. I'll let you know if we do. Deal?"

She said exactly what I needed to hear.

I nod, and within the next few minutes, everyone leaves and my room is empty again.

I stand at the window and watch the mountains trying to hide among the low clouds.

I can't help but still wonder what's really going on out in those woods.

And now that the project is over, I'm afraid I'll never find out.

# Survival Skill #18

*Focusing on the basic needs — safety, health, eating, and sleeping — can help survivors cope with events that may be beyond anyone's control.*

Birdee calls out from the kitchen, "You hungry?"

Sitting on the couch, I tuck the blanket under my legs and balance the laptop on my thighs. "Depends on what you have in mind."

She comes out with a tray of MoonPies. "What do you think?"

"Ah. You read my mind." I smile. "I love being sick."

She places the tray on the coffee table. "Enjoy it while you can."

"I will. Had no idea you could pamper so well." I grab a double-decker mint treat and take a bite.

She sits in Dad's old chair. "It's just a temporary side effect of pure guilt."

I know she's kidding, but I stop eating for a second. "I'm sorry I scared you."

Birdee waves it off as she chooses a vanilla mini. "Let's just forget about it. I'm glad you're off that project. I'll sleep a little better tonight, and your mom will be happy to know you're home safe until she gets back."

"If you say so." I pop in the last bite and let the marshmallow ooze into my mouth. "Yum. I could eat these 24/7."

Birdee laughs. "You practically do. Good to see you're putting on a little weight."

My mouth drops open. "Excuse me. *That* is not a compliment."

"Well, that's how I meant it." She starts knitting with Petey perched on the chair behind her, and her glasses slide down to the tip of her nose. She looks like Dad when he used to read the newspaper form front to back.

I try to concentrate on the searches I'm doing and keep my mind off the past.

She pries. "Whatcha working on?"

"Just doing research for school. I thought if I turned in a paper on the Red Wolf Project, maybe Ms. Cox would feel sorry for me and count it toward my grade."

Birdee smiles at me over her specs. "I doubt it, but it's a good idea."

I write down a few random facts about wolves in my cameo notebook. I skim through some articles and news bulletins about the Red Wolf Project. Pictures of Katie Reynolds and Jerry Porter pop up.

I click on some of the links for Katie and realize she's had quite a posh life. Comes from a wealthy family in Tennessee. Her father, Craig Reynolds, was one of the top veterinarians in the nation, but died when she was a teen. No wonder I like her. We have so much in common beyond loving nature.

Her mother, Suzanne Reynolds-Smith, grew up in Nashville with her brother and parents. She lived there all her life and was the city councilwoman for two terms. She eventually remarried a high-ranking military guy who had only one son about ten years older than Katie.

I click around on the embedded links. It takes me to Katie's bio on her web site. I'm impressed. Didn't know she graduated with honors in business from Darden. Smart lady. She even won a national title in the Intercollegiate Pistol Championships. Evidently, a smart shooter too.

She's obviously one of those women who does it all. Someone I could see myself like in a few years.

I click back to the Red Wolf Project article and follow Jerry Porter's trail. He's lived in North Carolina his whole life. His father owned a farm out west that was sold off after he died. Porter went to NC State. Got a degree at the College of Veterinary Medicine and a master's in Forestry and Environmental Studies. He stayed on at NC State and served thirty years in the forestry department until his retirement a few years ago. I click on another link, and it takes me to an article, "Professor Resigns Over Misconduct Scandal."

Porter was accused of falsifying his credentials and his research. He was also accused with plagiarism and embezzlement and denied his pension. Though criminal charges were never brought, the article says he's been struggling financially ever since, acting as an independent guide and tracker to make ends meet. It shows a picture of his wife. I click on it and am sent out to another article, "Wife Dies in Wolf Attack."

My stomach sinks as I read the article about how Porter and his wife were working with the red wolves. One of the males attacked her when she entered the pin. I think back. That must've been the one red wolf attack he mentioned in the beginning. I don't see how he could like, let alone research, wolves after something like that. I wonder if Sweeney or Reynolds knows about this. I print out the article for later.

Next, I look up eBuild, the real estate company that is being affected by the wolves. I scan down the board of directors. The company has won tons of awards for building sustainable properties, so at least they seem environmentally conscious. I page down through their annual report last year scanning their financials, mergers, and partnerships. Digging some more, I find the parent company of eBuild is Cardinal, Inc., run by a Mandy Smith. She's CEO-at-large, whatever that means. When I click on Cardinal's properties, there's a list of about forty states where they own mountain or beach locations. Mandy Smith must be a rich lady. No wonder she's at large. She probably ran off to an exotic beach somewhere and is buying property from poor country folk.

Then I Google myself. Which is a huge mistake.

I see an article, "Grace or Curse? Local Teen Finds Endangered Wolf Dead." There are four pictures with the article. One is a bad picture of me, probably from middle school because I'm still wearing braces. There's a picture showing the black bears caged in the woods with a caption about bear-part trafficking. There's one of a dead red wolf, and finally, one of my dad smiling with Carl, Les and the man who I know as Mo's dad. They are standing in front of a pile of gear, obviously taken after some bust a few years ago. Besides Les, out of all the pictures, I'm pretty much the only person still alive.

My stomach sinks as I read the article, wondering if I am really a curse to everything in the area. The coverage will never end; and, unless I leave this place and start fresh, everything that's happened here will follow me forever.

No matter what, I'll never fit in.

I wonder how they got the story on the wolves. I didn't think Katie was making anything public just yet, and I know Sweeney is waiting on autopsy reports, so surely he wouldn't go to the press.

I toggle to the other window that is still open showing the picture of Jerry Porter standing next to a caged wolf that was probably just rescued. My eyes narrow. The only other person who could leak this story and who has something to gain is Porter.

And now that I know he has a motive in getting revenge for his wife, I have to tell Sweeney.

I quickly close all the windows, but not before taking one last look at my middle school picture. "Ugh. At least they could use a better photo."

When I glance up, Birdee is staring at me. "You're just torturing yourself."

I point to my screen. "So you knew about this?"

She nods. "Yup. Tossed it out with all my other garbage. Why do you read that negative crap anyway? It only hurts you."

"Maybe I deserve it."

"Don't you dare feel sorry for yourself. Your daddy raised you better than that."

I sigh. "Sorry."

She places her knitting needles in her lap. "Chicken, you don't deserve bad things because you stood up for what was right. I don't care who it involved or hurt. You weren't doing anything wrong."

I point to the computer. "According to the *Smoky Review*, 'Grace is cursed.'"

She waves her hand and starts knitting again. "You have to do what's right no matter what some stupid newspaper says. No matter what they think."

I smile. "Dad used to say that."

"He was a smart man." Birdee winks. "Raised by an even smarter woman."

I lie down on my side and cuddle the square knit pillow decorated in bears. Another one of Birdee's masterpieces. "You think I'll ever get past all this?"

"It doesn't matter what I think." She holds a little sweater up to Petey. "I do know one thing. You ain't responsible for the demise of this town. People just need someone to lash out at. We had some corrupt people; and unfortunately, they aren't here to take the heat. Bunch of cowards if you ask me. Dead or not."

"No matter what I do, I just can't win."

"What matters is that you play the game, and you don't let losers intimidate you. Besides, you can't even begin to win if you don't play."

I lay on my back with my hands behind my head. "I just want to make Dad proud. To make a difference like he did."

She nods. "Good. And you will when it's right. You're only sixteen. He was fifty-four. And trust me, when he was sixteen, he wasn't saving bears the way you did. I believe he was only saving ladies at the time." She chuckles to herself as if remembering something funny. "Give yourself time to save the world. It's hard to do when you've lived less than 6,000 days."

"Well, I guess I have some time to think about it. Without the wolf project, there's nothing to do but think until school starts up again."

"Why don't you try relaxing for once? Get out of your head and have some fun. Go on a date with Wyn."

When I open my mouth, she butts in. "And don't think I don't know about Mo. Your Mom told me everything, and it sounds like he was a total hottie."

I smile, feeling sad and happy all at once thinking of him. "He was. You would have liked him."

"Well, he saved your father, so he's high up on my list, bless his soul. How a kid so young could have the balls to stand up to those men. For your father and his. They don't make guys like that anymore."

I nod as tears fill my eyes. "That's what I'm afraid of." My throat tightens at the thought of never finding anyone like Mo. Of not ever seeing him again.

Birdee gets up and sits next to me. "Chicken, it's time to move past all this. The more you drag it along with you, the heavier it gets. Let it go. Hanging back with the dead keeps you from living." Tears stream down my face as I think of Dad and Mo. She wipes my eyes with a handkerchief. "I know it's hard. Believe me, I know. But the way I see it, we don't have a choice, so why fight it?"

I hug Birdee and blow my nose.

Petey flies over and lands on my lap. I sniff and stroke his head. "What do you think, Petey? What should I do?"

Petey bobs his head. "Quit your crying."

Birdee and I burst out laughing. She pulls off her glasses and thumps the little bird on the head. "Petey, that wasn't nice. Those dang R-rated movies are ruining this bird."

Petey cocks his head. "Oh, shut your mouth."

We both crack up, and I immediately feel much better. Nothing like a good laugh to lift your spirit. I put out my finger for him to climb on.

"Boy, you got him right where you want him," I say.

She smiles. "Petey says things we don't want to hear. But most of them are true."

He squawks. "The truth shall set you free."

And with that he flies back to his perch. But for once, Petey has a point.

I need to get out of this funk and fly again.

No matter how hard it is, maybe it's time I move on.

# Survival Skill #19

*Landmarks can be vital in determining where you are if you become lost or wind up stranded in unfamiliar surroundings.*

After sleeping a whole day, I finally have my strength back and go down for breakfast.

Even though I cried myself to sleep thinking about Mo and Dad and everything Birdee said, for the first time in months, I feel like I have newfound hope. Today is a new day.

But as soon as I see Birdee, the lightness that lifted me out of bed is replaced by the darkness of impending doom. She's sitting at the table staring at her coffee mug. I stop and immediately think of Mom.

"What's wrong?" I brace myself for something hard.

She looks up at me, her eyes red. "Agent Sweeney called this morning."

I sit. Whenever Birdee has that look, I've learned it's always best to not be on my feet. "And?"

She takes a sip of her coffee, and I think of Dad. It was always the first sound I'd hear in the mornings when coming down for breakfast. He'd be sitting where Birdee is, sipping coffee, and reading the paper.

She sighs. "Evidently, Porter took the other team out to do more research."

I lean forward. "What? But they shut the project down."

She nods. "I know. Evidently Porter did it on his own. No one knows why, but they found out this morning. The kids never came back last night."

I cover my mouth. "Oh my God. Was Wyn with them?"

She shakes her head. "No, he was with Skyler at the hospital."

"Oh." It's the only time I'm happy he was with Skyler. "Well, thank God." I sigh a huge breath of relief. "Do they think…?"

She answers before I finish my question. "They sent a search team out this morning and just found Madison and Big Mike. They're at the hospital recovering. But Porter and Seth are still missing."

I breathe the word, "Jesus." I close my eyes and rub my temples. "Are they still looking?"

She tries to swallow a piece of bread. "Yes, but I think they're thinking the worst."

I jump up and grab my coat, then I stop and lean against the wall as the blood rushes to my head.

Birdee stands. "Wait a minute, where do you think you're going?"

I sit down and wait for the dots to pass from my vision. "To the hospital. I need to see Madison and Big Mike."

She grabs her keys. "I'll drive."

☙

On the way to the hospital, Birdee and I sit quietly in the cab of her truck. The heater doesn't seem to be working because my breath comes out in huge white puffs. I pull the bottom of my hood over my mouth. The chill of yesterday returns, and I wonder if I'll ever be completely warm again.

175

I stare out the window at the snow melting. Poor Seth. I can't help but feel guilty. I wasn't very nice to him, and I certainly didn't make things easy for him. But while Wyn kept me alive, Seth saved my life.

An hour later after creeping down the slippery mountain going 10 miles per hour, Birdee finally pulls into the drop-off lane. I jump out and almost slip on the sidewalk. I grab the door to get my footing and then wave, "I'll see you inside."

As she pulls away, I run — or frankly, slide — into the hospital. The same pungent medical smell hits me when I push through the revolving door — bleach mixed with vinegar. I cover my burning nose. I hate places like this. Even though they save lives here, I'm always reminded of the ones who died. I've been here more than I'd like over the last few months. Besides for myself, I've been here with Tommy after the shooting, with Mom when she had her breakdown, and with Skyler for her foot. I can't seem to get away from this place.

Instead of waiting for the elevator, I walk the two flights of stairs. People in white coats pass by me, not even acknowledging my presence. At the top, I stop to catch my breath. My legs feel shaky, and my head's a bit foggy — all reminders that I could have died here, too. No matter how much I play it down, I'm lucky to be smelling anything at all.

I head for the nurse's desk and grab the corner to support myself. "Excuse me, but I'm here to see Madison Connell and Mike Davis."

The nurse who took care of me smiles. "When are you kids going to learn it's cold outside?"

I force out a sorry excuse for a grin. "Seriously."

She clicks on the keyboard and points down the hall. "They're in a shared room recovering. Room 304 A and B."

"Thanks." I walk down the hall, trying to keep my eyes forward.

I hate seeing people in their beds, sick and coughing. Some are even dying. The whole scene gives me the creeps. I glance up at the wrong time and catch sight of an old man scooting down the hall. His backside hangs out of his gown as someone helps him into the bathroom. You'd think they'd resort to zippers or Velcro. It would save everyone a lot of embarrassment.

When I get to Room 304, I peek in. A sheet hanging on rings separates the room in half. Madison is closest to the door, so I assume Big Mike is on the other side of the partition.

She opens her eyes and mumbles softly. "Grace."

It's hard to believe it was just a day ago I was in the same place — my legs and arms aching, the bulky heating pads lying on top of my chilled body warming my organs back to life. I pull over a chair and sit next to her. That's when I notice how red her eyes are from crying.

I point to the soggy meatloaf and green beans. "Don't worry. I cried over that meatloaf, too." She attempts a smile, but it falls short. I try again. "I can only assume you're getting the same royal treatment as me."

She sniffs and ignores my bad jokes. "Do you think he's dead?"

The question comes out of nowhere. "Seth? No way. He's too stubborn to be dead. He'll be fine, you'll see. He's probably hiding so we all worry and then he can come back to a big welcoming scene."

I don't tell her what I really think. That even the best outdoorsmen die in these mountains from hypothermia. The survivors are just lucky. Like me.

She shivers a little. "I hope so."

I tuck the blanket around her the way Wyn did for me. "What happened out there?"

Madison closes her eyes. "We found two more wolves dead. The same way. Coming back, Porter got turned around. It was awful. Somehow, Big Mike and I got separated from him and Seth. We hiked all night, never stopped once." Tears start streaming down her face. "I thought we were going to die."

I try not to cry. "I know how you felt. It's scary."

"I'm not going back out there. Ever. I don't know what I was thinking."

"It's okay to feel that way. It might change in time."

Her statement takes me back to the weeks after Dad died. The times I stood at the window, looking out at the wilderness I had once loved so much. How it had gone from a safe haven to a nightmare in such a short time. My haunted memories of holding Dad in my arms as he took his last breath, and the last time I saw Mo. Back then, it was all too much.

My breath catches in my throat, and I squeeze my eyes shut. When I open them, Madison is staring at me. "You okay?"

I nod. "Yeah, sorry. I was just thinking about something." I try to comfort her by sharing. "I was remembering saying the same thing to Mom after my dad died. I didn't think I'd ever go in those woods again. Look at me now."

She picks at the little tie on her gown. "I heard about that when I moved here. I'm sorry for your loss."

"Thanks. Me, too." I quickly change the subject. "Did Porter tell you Katie cancelled the project yesterday?"

She frowns and sits up straighter. "No. He didn't say a word about that. Just told us we were going back out. I was a bit surprised but figured he knew what he was doing. He's a tracker."

"Yeah, me too." I keep my suspicions to myself for now.

"What will happen to the wolves?"

I pat her arm. "Katie said they'll extract them and bring them back to the reserve. They'll be safe there until spring." The words sound good so for now I pretend to believe them.

She lays her head back. "Oh, good."

A deep cough comes from behind the curtain. "Can you guys keep it down? I'm trying to sleep." A big black hand pulls back the flimsy blue curtain. Big Mike is lying in a bed that's way too short for him. His feet are bandaged and hanging over the end, and one hand is wrapped in gauze. I know immediately why he's so bandaged up. Frostbite.

I wheel over in between them on the stool. "Hey, Big Mike. How are you?"

He lays his head back. "Hey, Grace. What are you doing here?"

"I heard what happened. Wanted to be sure you guys were okay." I shrug. "I guess I know how you feel."

He stares ahead. "Well, I'm alive if that's what you mean. But I may never play football again if my feet don't heal."

I try to cup his free hand, but his palm is twice the size of my whole hand. "That won't happen. You're too strong."

He turns his face toward me. "Let's hope so. I won't know for several weeks." He winces.

I can only imagine how bad his feet and hand must hurt. Dad always said frostbite was so painful.

I try to keep him positive. "You weren't out there too long. The chance of you losing anything is slim."

He stares at the ceiling again as his eyes water, like he's willing God to hold back his tears. "They found Seth yet?"

I look down. "Not that I know of." I look back up with confidence. "They will, though. It's just a matter of time. He's with Porter, so they should be fine."

"Stupid kid. Too stubborn for his own good. I told him to stay with us, but after we found those wolves, he went ahead for some reason. Porter went after him, and then everything went to hell."

My phone goes off. I read a text from Sweeney. *Porter found. He's alive and on way to hospital. No sign of Seth.*

My heart sinks. This is not good news. "They found Porter."

Madison starts to cry. "Thank God. Where's Seth?"

I just shake my head.

Her eyes grow wider. "But they were together the last time I saw them."

Big Mike nods. "They were arguing about something."

"Do you know what it was?"

"Nah. I assumed it was because Seth was being a tool bag and not following Porter's directions, but they both went off down the path. I saw Porter grab Seth by the shirt." He looked at Madison. "We waited for like thirty minutes, and they never came back. Porter had all the gear, so we got lost. Then it started to snow."

"The worst part was the wolves," Madison said. "They howled all night. We were afraid to stop and lay down." She smiled over at Big Mike. "If it wasn't for him, I wouldn't be here."

Big Mike coughs and looks embarrassed. "I did what anyone would do."

I smile. "Looks like there are a few heroes around here."

I pull out a map and lay the paper on Big Mike's bed. "So where were you guys? Do you remember where you saw Seth and Porter last?"

Big Mike studies the areas and eventually points to a spot on a marked trail. "It was about here. We saw a pack — a big one, too, like twenty of them — and we were following them. Then we found the dead ones close by."

I eye the spot. "Do you remember anything about the area that would stand out to rescuers?"

Madison calls out behind me. Her eyes are closed. "Waterfalls. Pretty ones, too. All iced over and glistening like some kind of sculpture."

"That's got to be the Chasteen Creek area in Smokemount."

Big Mike nods slowly. "Yeah, that sounds familiar."

I fold the map. "That's quite a hike. Especially in winter."

He eyes me. "You don't need to tell me."

"I bet." I stand. "Did you tell Agent Sweeney all this?"

Madison blurts out. "No. We haven't seen him. But Reynolds came by and was working on getting extra volunteers to help."

I glance out the window at the drifting snowflakes. Not too bad, but thick enough when you're in the woods. "You can never have too many people looking."

A voice pipes up behind me. "You're not thinking of doing anything stupid, are you?"

181

# Survival Skill #20

*There is a simple method of handling an emergency situation. Remember the acronym S.T.O.P.:*
*Sit — Think — Observe — Plan.*

When I spin around, Wyn is standing in the doorway, next to Skyler, who is leaning on crutches.

He studies me closely. "G, answer me."

I salute. "Sir, yes sir."

Madison and Big Mike laugh, but not Wyn. His face never changes.

"You still didn't answer my question." He peels himself away from Skyler's side and moves toward me. "You're not going to do what I think you're thinking of doing."

I act confused. "I lost you back at 'you're.'"

"Don't play dumb." He walks up and pokes my head. "I know you, and when you get something on the brain, there's no stopping you."

Madison jumps to my defense. "Wyn, Grace would never go up there after Seth. Alone. That would be suicide." She looks at me. "Would you?"

"Not for free." I smile at Wyn.

He narrows his eyes as Big Mike chuckles. "Not funny," Wyn says.

I grab my coat and point to Big Mike, who is still smiling. "Depends on who you ask. Right, Mike?"

Skyler hobbles over and tugs on Wyn's arm. "Let's go. I need to get home. My leg's starting to hurt." She looks at me with sad eyes like I've betrayed her or something and then quickly hobbles out without saying anything. I glance at Wyn, wondering if he told her anything about our time in the cave.

He points two fingers at one of his eyes. "Don't get any dumb ideas. I've got my eye on you." I immediately know Wyn and Birdee have been talking more than I realize. He's even picked up a phrase or two.

"Only one?" I do the same gesture. "Good to know."

I buzz past him into the hall and wait for the elevator. My legs can't take another flight of stairs.

Before the door opens, a hand touches my arm. "I mean it, G."

I spin around and face Wyn as the door dings behind me, telling me it's time to make an escape. "You're being paranoid."

"Am I? Then where are you going right now?"

"Birdee's waiting for me downstairs." I show him the text on my phone.

He seems satisfied. "Fine. I'll check on you later. And you'd better pick up."

I step inside the elevator car. "Deal."

He stops the doors with his hand and leans in. "By the way, you look beautiful." I must be shocked because he laughs and adds, "May want to close your mouth. You're catching flies."

I look at my reflection in the stainless steel doors and shake my head, trying not to smile. "You're crazy."

He steps back, and as the door closes between us, he calls out, "About you."

Maybe there's hope for us yet.

છ

At home, once Birdee heads to bed, I can't help but feel fidgety. I pace in front of the large window, watching the mountains peeking through the thin layers of clouds like they're hiding from me. The image of Seth out there in the freezing snow haunts me. I know how it feels out there at night, but I had Wyn. Someone who cares about me.

If it wasn't for Seth, I wouldn't be alive, sitting in this cozy house. I think of the last thing he said to me in the woods, about owing him my life since he saved me. At the time, he was kidding, but now, I wonder if it was a prophecy of some sort.

Someone knocks on the front door, sending my heart into a tizzy. When I flip on the porch light, Agent Sweeney is standing there.

I swing open the door and don't even greet him. "Did you find him?"

Agent Sweeney walks in and pats his coat with his hands to loosen the clinging snow. "No signs of him. And we have to call off the search for tonight. He's not at Bradley Fork."

I stare out at the looming mountains in the distance. The moon gives the horizon a grayish appearance, and tiny snowflakes tap the window, wanting to be inside.

I shut the door behind him. "You can't leave him out there all night. He'll freeze."

Sweeney looks haggard, like he's been up for two days. His eyes are surrounded by dark circles, and he looks ten years older just since yesterday. He clears his throat. "It's definitely not good news. I just wanted you to know. I left the search tent and thought I'd stop by on my way to see Seth's mom."

"Thanks." I nod and open the door again to let him leave, then something dawns on me. I follow him out the door and stand on the porch. The wind whips through me, reminding me of how cold I was on that mountain. "Did you say Bradley Fork?"

"Yeah."

I think for a second. "Big Mike said they were at Chasteen Creek. That's miles from Bradley."

Agent Sweeney stares at me, and then shakes his head. "Porter was adamant when we found him. It was Bradley Fork. He'd know more than Big Mike. He's a tracker."

I grip his jacket as tightness fills in my chest. "Oh my God. That's why you aren't finding any signs of Seth. Because of Porter!"

He frowns. "I'm not finding anything because it's snowing, and as you know, tracks get covered."

"No. It's because he told you to look in the wrong place."

"Now why would he do that?"

I think for a second. "Maybe he didn't want Seth to be found."

"Grace, please." Agent Sweeney pulls his hat on. "Porter is not a murderer. A little kooky, but not a killer of teen hikers."

I try to piece it all together. "Big Mike said they argued."

Agent Sweeney laughs. "Doesn't surprise me. Seth can be a pain in the ass." He puts a hand on my shoulder. "Do you know Porter never even went to the hospital? He wouldn't go. Instead, he went back in with a search team."

"Look, you even said you thought something was going on. What if Seth saw something and Porter's covering it up? Or worse, what if it's Al? It can't hurt to ask Porter again. Just to be sure he wasn't delirious or something when he gave you the location. Talk to Big Mike."

He nods. "I'll stop by the hospital on my way home. Now get inside. It's going to get nastier out here before it gets better."

All night I sit in my room staring at those mountains.

I look at the map where Big Mike pointed. Bradley Fork is two miles south of Chasteen Creek. If Porter is lying and Big Mike is right, they'll never find Seth.

Dead or alive.

I pace the living room all night, feeling the same way I felt when Dad was missing — on edge. Panic swells in my body, and the horror of leaving Seth out there alone clogs my head. It's that helplessness of not knowing, the feeling that I could do something to make a difference.

I stare at my coat and backpack. No. I can't go out there tonight. Not in this weather. I've learned my lesson on this one. It would be the dumbest decision since making it illegal to tear off mattress tags.

To distract my thoughts, I sit down and try to read *Hatchet*, but the story hits too close to home.

Seth is no Brian.

For the next few hours I lie on the couch and stare at the ceiling, wondering what to do. I think of how my mom felt when I was out in those woods; how Birdee felt when I was stuck in the cave. The thought of Seth trying to make it on his own is too much for me to bear. I owe him my life.

I can't just give up on him.

I won't.

As soon as the first crack of dawn arrives, I grab my stuff and head into the kitchen. Luckily, Birdee is not a morning person. Seth has been out there for over a day. There's still time. He could have made it through one or two nights, but the longer he's out there, the less his chances are of surviving.

I pause as I pack my gear. I have to go. I mean, I don't have a choice, right?

I pull up the weather on the computer. Sunny but cold. Only a ten percent chance of snow. Agent Sweeney said it would get worse before it got better. That means if we don't find Seth today, we might not find him until spring.

I know the way. It's not too far. I can get in and out before sunset.

I bite my fingernails as I map out the fastest route, the best way to get to Chasteen Creek and back before sundown. I shove the map in the bag with my knife, then I sneak into Dad's office and grab the key off the top of the cabinet. Unlocking the desk drawer, I reach in the very back, wondering if Mom put what I'm seeking back in the desk after they found it in the woods.

My hand touches something cold. I slide out the 9MM and grab a handful of bullets from the middle drawer. My hand shakes as I tuck the gun and ammo into the side pocket of my bag. I might be going out alone, but this time, if Al is out there, I'm prepared.

I sneak outside and roll out the snowmobile, pushing it down the hill. I can get in pretty close on this and walk the rest of the way. Then, when I find him, we can get out quick.

At the tree line, I sit on the seat and stare into the woods. This is it. Decision time. Once Birdee gets up, my chance is over. I rehash everything. It's light out, and the weather looks clearer than it's been all week. I have protection and transportation. I put on my helmet and start the engine.

I'm going.

Birdee practically said it herself.

Not doing anything is worse than doing the wrong thing.

# Survival Skill #21

*Making it in the wild depends on your ability to operate under stress, your adaptability and flexibility, and your determination to survive.*

𝖖 race down the path toward Chasteen Creek.

I'm trying to get as far as I can before the woods get too deep and the snow gets too dangerous to ride. I park my snowmobile on the edge of some trees and log the coordinates, just in case it gets snowed over. Checking my compass and my map, I start to hike the rest of the way. I know these woods like the back of my hand, but in the winter, the trails and landmarks look very different, if they're even visible at all. This time, I'm not taking any chances.

A thick blanket of snow covers the world, making it look new and untouched, pure and untainted. I stretch out my gloved hand and let the snowflakes rest on their journey to the ground. They linger for a few seconds before disappearing into the warmth of my mitten. The thousands that land safely tiptoe along the ground without making a sound. Tiny icicles cling to the trees and glitter in the morning sun like little prisms of light. The smell of wet wood fills the air as it basks in the sun, hoping to dry before nightfall.

I'm actually proud of myself. I took the precautions needed and made a plan. Dad would be proud of me, too. I held back my impulse and did things right this time. Some would question if I should be doing this at all, but not Dad. I think he would approve.

I walk along the path. Green shrubs reach up through the thick wall of white, trying to break out of its heavy hold. A noise catches my attention. I stop and listen as a faint whimpering sound fills the air like someone's crying. I start to run.

It has to be Seth. Thank God!

As I jog around the bend, I spot flashes of movement through the white and green backdrop. Before I can hide, a pack of wolves walks out of the woods and crosses the path a few yards ahead of me. I practically skid to a stop and freeze.

It's the first time I've seen any alive, and I'm immediately enamored with them. The larger ones stop as the younger ones skitter around their feet, wrestling and rolling. Their coats are a blend of tawny cinnamon mixed with gray and black.

I would go around them, but I don't want to scare them off. I definitely don't want to get attacked either. Wolves are much more protective when pups are around, and after reading about Porter's wife, I'm not going to risk it. I decide to wait until they pass.

Slowly, I slowly lower myself to the ground and slip the pad of paper out of my bag's mesh pocket. I frantically start to take down the data we've been looking for this whole week. Five males, three females, and two pups. I jot down what each member is doing. Sniffing. Standing guard. Rallying the pups. Everything they do gets logged. No matter how small.

I note their behavior as they cross the path and scamper into the woods. How the mom corrals the pups. How the alpha keeps an eye on the woods. How the other males play around until the alpha makes a move, and then they all follow. It's amazing stuff I'll probably never see again.

In this moment, I am so happy. To finally see a wolf alive and well. The way they should be. To see them interact in the wild is awesome, especially considering the animals are on the verge of extinction. Not many people get to see or will ever see what I'm experiencing.

This is what Dad loved most about being a ranger. Saving animals. Making a difference in their world by keeping the forests safe from poachers. Being one of nature's keepers.

In this brief encounter, I realize why I can't seem to stay away from the woods. Danger or not, this is and always has been my home. And even though I've kept my distance, when I'm here, I feel closer to Dad. I make a decision. There's no way I can let what's happened scare me away from this place where I belong.

I shift a little and immediately the alpha freezes and stares in my direction. I sit still but watch him closely, wondering if he's the one I scared off the other day. His head is larger than the others', and his body's much thicker. The light breeze trails through his long, reddish-brown fur as if waving at nature. His ears perk up, and his mouth opens a little, showing his tongue. His eyes are surrounded by black, making it look like he's wearing a small mask. He looks so regal in that moment.

He must decide I'm not a threat, because he doesn't move any closer. I assume he's used to people watching him if he's from the reserve. But it still doesn't explain why he seemed so intent on attacking Skyler and me. He seems totally different now. Something must have spooked him that day.

But what?

My breath catches in my throat, and a tear comes to my eyes as I stare into his golden ones. It's one of those moments in life that comes and goes in an instant.

It's a moment I'll never forget.

CB

As quickly as they came, the pack heads off into the woods.

Their den must be close because wolves usually don't stray far from home when they have pups. I note the location in my book and look back at where we've been searching previously. Porter's tracking collars don't seem to be very accurate.

I wait until they are out of site before I leave. I get my bearings and head up the trail another mile to Chasteen Creek. I can hear the sizzle of the river when I get close, and I step out of the trees and look down at the water moving fast from the melting ice and snow. The mossy embankments are covered in a fine dust of flurries. Sheets of ice cover the rocks and icicles hang down from the roots of trees along the embankment.

I stick to the trail that runs along the river and come to a sign piled up with snow. I wipe off the wood post and follow the path north. Less than a mile to go until I reach the falls. I pray Big Mike was right. It's Seth's only chance.

Normally in the summer, this trail is not as remote, but in the winter, it's a tough climb. The trek gets steeper and becomes harder to walk. My hiking boots slip as the path turns into an icy slope. The creek remains to my left as I climb the hill, holding onto roots and branches for support. Luckily, the weather is holding off for me. It's actually nice — sunny and cold with clear blue skies above. If I want to make it back before dark, I still have a couple hours left before I need to head home.

When I reach the top of the falls, I glance around looking for prints of any kind, human or animal. Problem is, I have no idea where Seth could still be. If he wandered around, which is very likely knowing him, he might be anywhere. I lean over the falls and look down to the bottom.

Halfway down the other side, I spot something. I inch my way around the edge, careful not to slip. The thought of falling thirty feet into shallow, icy water makes me dizzy. As I make my way to the other side, I see legs jutting out from under a large oak. I'm overcome with joy and can't help but shout as I run down the other side.

"Seth! Seth!"

I sit on my butt and carefully maneuver my way down the embankment and slippery rocks to the ledge he's sitting on. I can't get there fast enough and jump the last two feet.

"Thank God I found you! I guess we're even now." I inch my way over to him, but he's still obscured from my full view by a large tree. "Who's the hero now?"

I come around the tree and there sits Seth. Eyes closed, against a tree.

"Seth?" I nudge him with my toe and cover my mouth.

If he weren't frozen, I swear, he'd look like he was resting along the river shore, simply enjoying the view.

But he's dead.

I kneel down in the spot where I'm standing, feeling nauseous, and lower my head.

I'm too late.

Again.

# Survival Skill #22

*Wolf conflicts with humans are rare,*
*but if you encounter a wolf, stop,*
*stand tall, and do not run.*

I make my way to the other side of the tree and throw up everything in my stomach.

Then I kneel at the river's edge and start to cry.

It's my fault.

I should've pushed Agent Sweeney harder last night. I should have never let him stop that search. Though from the looks of it, there's nothing I could have done to save Seth. He died sometime yesterday or early yesterday evening — quietly in his sleep.

I throw a rock into the river hard. Why is death all around me? If it's not animals, it's people. If it's not people, it's a whole town. I glance back at Seth. His eyes are closed as if he's asleep. He's not gross or disgusting, just a pale blue statue of who he once was. A shell.

I hope he died in peace. But I know firsthand how painful hypothermia can be, and I've heard death from it can be even worse. Unless he was lucky enough to just fall asleep before it hit.

I mark the trail and tree with orange tape and log the coordinates. At least Agent Sweeney can do a body recovery. Then I pick up my bag and start the long hike home.

As I trudge along the path, my legs feel like lead. Heavy. Winter birds chirp, breaking up the thoughts racing through my head. How will I tell Ms. Burrows about Seth? I've known his family since elementary school. Seth was always a pain, but I think it was just because he wanted attention. His dad was in the military and rarely ever home.

Not having a dad can mess with you. I know.

My chest fills with sorrow for Seth's mother. He was an only child and all she had. I remember what my mom went through last summer. At this very moment, Ms. Burrows has no idea what is about to happen, no idea her life is about to shatter into tiny pieces. Right now, she's probably sitting at home, full of hope, and praying Seth will return soon. Like I did for months. With every phone call, she's wishing. With every news update, she's hoping. And once again, I'm the one who's going to crash someone's already fragile world. What if she blames me for Seth's death the way Skyler blames me for Carl's?

Maybe the *Smoky Review* is right. I'm cursed.

Off to one side, I spot something stuck in the snow. It's a piece of plastic with a sharp end, like it was part of a syringe. I pick up the foreign piece and study it, wondering if I should take it back. I quickly tuck the trash into my bag just as a foreign noise draws me out of my thoughts.

It's the shriek of a bird, but something about the sound makes me stop in my tracks. Something familiar. I stop and listen, trying to identify it.

The bird sounds off again. It takes me a millisecond to realize what it is — a Carolina parakeet. I think about Birdee, and then it hits me. It's the bird's distress call, the one we played on my computer.

Instinctively, I step behind a tree and scan the woods. Maybe it's a bear or a wolf. I listen and hear scuffling. Sounds too big to be a wolf and too quiet to be a bear.

The warning call sounds off again, and a little blue and yellow bird zips by me.

I squint and dart my eyes toward every movement. Any branch. Any bush.

Then I see something.

A dark shape that resembles a figure. I can't make out the face, but can see he's camouflaged well. It takes me a second to process who it could be.

Al.

I look around. Where do I go? What do I do? I don't know if I can outrun him, but I can try. Without hesitating any longer, I bolt off down the path and cut into the thick woods. Heavy footsteps are in pursuit, thumping along the underbrush. My breath comes in sharp rasps as I charge through the woods. The rhythm of my pace takes over in my head as I move. Fast. Arms at my side, I breathe steady — in, out.

Al cannot catch me in these woods again.

Luckily on this higher path, the snow is broken and sparse along the ground. My hiking boots get good traction as I propel myself up the hill. My pack is strapped on well and doesn't weigh me down, and I know the way out. It's just a matter of making it to the snowmobile in time.

I hear deep grunts far back behind me, telling me Al's struggling to catch up. I don't even want to turn around. I just need to concentrate on getting out of here alive. I was dumb to come back. Naïve in thinking he was gone. His face fills my head. His sneer. His dark eyes. His knife at my throat. The way he attacked Mo, and the way he killed Carl and Dad.

In cold-blood, without blinking an eye.

I can't let him corner me again. I won't. Because this time he'll be sure I don't make it out alive.

As I run, I crash through anything in my way. Limbs, bushes, logs. Nothing stops me or slows me down. I keep my eyes forward on the path. I don't have long to go.

My brain races in panic. Is he gaining on me? Is he right behind me?

I veer off the main trail and sprint straight up the hill. The snowmobile is only about a mile away. Thank goodness it took me longer to get in then it does to hike out.

My legs dig into the mountainside as I push my way uphill. My calves burn and my chest grabs at the air, struggling to take in a proper breath. Tears sting my eyes as everything pumps through me. The next ten minutes are the longest of my life. Every minute I keep waiting for a hand to reach out and grab me.

My lungs are screaming and my vision is dotted. My body is not strong enough to keep pushing, but I have no choice if I want to live.

I give it everything I have until I finally make it to the top of the ridge. Without so much as even pausing to catch a breath, I push through the thick tree line. Snow dumps on my head and into my eyes, but I don't miss a beat.

When I finally reach my snowmobile, I fumble for the key in my pocket. It slips through my fingers and plops into the snow. I reach down and grab it and shove it into the hole. When I turn the key, I pull on the start cord like a lawn mower, but nothing happens.

"Come on!" I shriek.

Behind me, I hear crashing through the woods. Al is still in pursuit. Keeping my eyes forward, I turn the key again. *Come on! Please!* The worst-case scenario plays out in my head. Al's going to come charging out of the woods and grab me off my snowmobile. He's going to throw me to the ground, and I'll never see my mother again.

Then it dawns on me: I forgot to pop up the kill switch. I jerk the red button and turn the key. This time, I double-check the cord is attached, and I flip the choke button to help. I pull on the cord a couple times and finally the engine sputters to life. I jump on and speed out of the woods with branches slapping me in the face, scratching my cheeks. Snow dumps on my head and shoulders, but I don't even bother to wipe it away. My only thought is, *Get away now!*

I don't breathe or look back until I hit the main path home. Somewhere along the way, I remember I have a gun and a knife, but a hand-to-hand combat with a man twice my size was probably a good thing to avoid.

I stop about a half mile from my house, where I finally have the nerve to glance back. The trees stare back but no one is following me. I exhale. I did it. I'm safe and I found Seth.

Al has not won.

I race the mobile up the rest of the hill, park it on the side of the house, and run in, slamming the door behind me.

Birdee is waiting with her hands on her hips. "Where the hell did you go?"

I try to answer, but my body is shutting down. I bend over and put my hands on my knees.

She comes over. "Are you okay?"

I nod and take in a few breaths. "Yes. I just went for a ride."

She narrows her eyes. "For a ride, huh? Maybe I should be more specific. Who did you go with and where?"

"No one." I look into her eyes and see behind her anger is fear. I force out the words. "I... went... alone."

Petey squawks and then answers first. "Stupid girl."

I yell back at him. "Shut up, Petey."

It's only after I holler that I realize I'm arguing with a parrot, who's now bobbing his head and saying, "Petey dance," as he whistles the "Macarena".

"Alone?" Birdee repeats. She takes her straw hat off and tosses it onto the table. "So Wyn was right."

"Wyn?"

"He called and said he thought you were up to something. He was worried you would go off alone and try to find Seth. Tell me you didn't do that."

I grab a glass and fill it at the sink, cursing Wyn under my breath for worrying Birdee. As I guzzle it down, I stare out the kitchen window at the swaying trees, half-expecting Al to come charging through the woods. I wonder if he knows where I live. With the Internet, I'm sure he can find me.

Birdee speaks to me again. "Grace? Tell me you weren't that dumb to go looking for Seth."

"They were looking in the wrong spot. I hiked up to where Big Mike said he was. Just to be sure." I spin around with tears in my eyes. "I found him."

Birdee's face perks up briefly. "Oh my gosh."

She reaches out to hug me, but I pull away and shake my head.

"No, Birdee. I was too late."

She cups her mouth with both hands for a second and then gasps out two words. "I'm sorry."

She wraps her arms around me and pulls me close, and we both cry in the kitchen together for a few minutes. I pull back and wipe my face with a stinky dishtowel.

"I need to call Agent Sweeney with the coordinates before the weather turns worse so they can go get… him."

She nods as her eyes start to water again. "Poor Sally. She's going to be devastated. I don't know how she'll get through this with Chet still stationed overseas."

I try not to think of Sally Burrows, or I'm afraid I'll crumble. I grab the phone to dial Sweeney, but my hand is shaking. Instead, I just stare out the window as if time is standing still for just a second.

Birdee speaks up behind me, pulling me from my daze. "This isn't your fault, Grace. You know that, right?"

I swallow the doubt. "I guess."

She walks over and holds my shoulder. "You did all you could."

"It wasn't enough." Just like before with my dad, nothing I did mattered.

"It was more than anyone else did." She squeezes me and kisses my head. "I need to go see Sally. Someone needs to be with her when she finds out. When I get back, we'll have some tea and talk." She kisses me goodbye as I pick up the phone.

My fingers finally cooperate and dial Agent Sweeney, who picks up on the first ring. "Hello?"

I can't seem to respond, so he answers again. "Hello?"

My voice doesn't come out how I intended. "I found Seth."

"What?"

I project more. "I found him."

For a second, neither of us says anything. Then Agent Sweeney's voice breaks through the silence. "Is he..."

My voice comes out in a whimper. "He didn't make it."

Agent Sweeney lets out a long sigh before he mumbles, "Where is he?"

I give him the coordinates and the details of how I found him. Agent Sweeney listens quietly. "That was a dumb thing you did up there," he says.

"I know. But I needed to find him. I knew Big Mike was telling the truth. Porter, on the other hand, I'm not so sure."

"Thanks, Grace. I'll take it from here."

I prod him. "Are you going to arrest Porter?"

"For what?"

"For lying. I think he's involved."

Agent Sweeney sighs. "Well, I think a lot of things, but that pesky thing called *evidence* always gets in the way."

Since I met Agent Sweeney, he's always listened to me. I was his key witness, so now that one sentence hits me hard.

He sounds just like Carl. The doubt in his voice. The frustration. I try to push it away, but it bothers me that he questions me for the first time since I've known him.

"I found a piece of a needle by Seth. What if he was drugged?"

"The less paranoid reason would be that he died of hypothermia."

I think for a second. "But what if he didn't? What if Porter killed him."

Agent Sweeney sits on the other end of the line and doesn't answer.

I sigh. I can't help but feel like I did a few months ago when I was trying to convince Carl my dad was still alive. I hold my breath, praying Agent Sweeney believes me, trusts my judgment after everything we've been through. I can hear his breath through the phone.

"Okay. I'll look into it. But you have to keep this to yourself. You hear me?"

I pretend to fasten a button over my bottom lip even though he can't see me. "I won't say a word."

"Fine. I'll call you. I need to follow up with the family and do a recovery. If you need anything, you know where I am. Until then, watch your back."

I realize after we hang up I forget to tell him about seeing Al in the woods, but I can't take any chances staying here.

I pick up the phone and call Katie.

"Grace, are you okay?"

I start to cry. "I don't really want to be alone. Can I come to your place until Birdee gets back?"

# Survival Skill #23

*Asking for help in a life-or-death situation is not a sign of weakness.*

T he ride to Katie's office is long.

The road is deserted most of the way, and the air is cold. And my heart is heavy. If Agent Sweeney isn't going to do anything about Porter, I know who will.

I pull into the circular driveway. The building is nondescript — a long, tan structure with brown shutters and very few windows. A state flag clicks against a pole outside. Conservationists have it as bad as rangers. No wonder they hate to stay in their offices.

By the time I make it up the steps, she is already at the door. Her hair is pulled up in a cute ponytail, and she's dressed in jeans and a long-sleeve fleece. She yanks open the wooden door.

"Grace. Get inside before you freeze."

Shaking my hair, I walk in and slip off my jacket, hanging it on the old hatrack. "Thanks."

She motions me down the hall and into her office. "Go sit. I already have some water boiling."

I can't help but notice her face is flushed like she's either been outside or crying. She's probably upset about Seth, too. I sit in the distressed leather chair with gold buttons. Only a few are missing. The way I can tell it's her office is by the shooting plaques and pictures of her on the walls.

Katie walks up and hands me a steaming cup filled with hot cocoa and little marshmallows. I smile as she takes a sip.

"What's so funny?" she asks.

I poke a tiny marshmallow down in the hot liquid. It bobs back up to the surface, not ready to go under. "I didn't expect you to be a cocoa kinda lady. You seem like you'd be more of a tea person."

"Me? No." She wrinkles her nose. "I guess s'mores are out of the question for a quaint snack?"

"No argument from me." I smile and take a sip.

Her grin drops as she sits in a comfy leather chair. "Tell me what's going on."

I lean over and place my cup on her desk. "You know I found Seth, right?"

She looks at the cup and hands me a coaster, which I slide under the steaming mug. "Yes. Agent Sweeney called me right after he talked to you. What in God's name happened?"

I tell her about talking to Big Mike, and what he said about Chasteen Creek. "When I found out Agent Sweeney had called off the search for the night, I couldn't just sit around and wait. After all, Seth saved my life. I owed it to him to find him. I left early this morning as soon as the sun came up."

"Not very smart, considering."

I stop mid-sip, a little surprised. "Considering what?"

"Oh, Grace, come on. You're not the only one who snoops around here. I know all about what happened to you and your dad. The town."

I drop my head. "Oh."

I hear her take another sip. "I don't think it's smart for you to go up in these woods — especially this time of year — alone." Before I can protest, she holds up her hand. "Even though I hear you are quite the woods-lady, it's just not good survival skills. But I'm sure you know that."

I think of what Dad would say. "Yes. It's just sometimes…"

She cuts me off and smiles, her piercing blue eyes holding mine. "Sometimes you think you have to get things done, and you don't care what it costs. Because it's the right thing to do. And you'll risk your life for those you care about."

I stare at her, surprised she knows me so well in such a short time. Finally someone who gets me.

I nod slowly. "Yes. Exactly."

"I get it. I was like that, too. Well, I still am. I just hide behind the word 'adult,' so I can get away with it without a lecture." She winks.

I grin. "Must be nice."

"I want you to know I appreciate your spunk, and I'm the last one to dish out a lecture. They've been looking for Seth for more than a day, and you found him in less than one." Her eyes squint and she takes another sip. "Though this is not the outcome I prayed for last night. His poor mother."

Seth's frozen face fills my mind. I stare down at the last marshmallow clinging to the side of my cup as it slowly melts. As if it's afraid to go under the surface, never to come up for air again.

"It was too cold," I say.

"Well, it's partly my responsibility. I started this project, and I'm the one who recommended Porter."

"That's actually why I'm here. I think Porter might be involved in this."

She leans forward, concentrating on what I'm saying. "Go on."

"He was the one who took the team out after the project was cancelled. And the last time Big Mike and Madison saw Seth, they said he was arguing with Porter. Not to mention, Porter has been there every time we've found a wolf dead."

She tucks her legs underneath her butt in the chair. "But that doesn't mean anything. He's the guide. Of course he would be there."

I think back to my conversation with Agent Sweeney. "He told the police the wrong area to look for Seth."

"Why would he do that? Did you find anything else that points to him?"

I tell her about the syringe, even though Agent Sweeney asked me not to. "He knows about this kind of thing, right?"

She does not look happy. "Well. This adds a whole new level."

I ramble on, happy to have someone on my side for once. "I don't think he wanted Seth to be found. Maybe Seth caught him doing something."

Katie sits and stares at the ceiling. "This is all very interesting. But considering your past, I'm wondering if this Al guy is back and setting up Porter for the fall."

I hang my head. So she thinks all of this is happening because of me. I fess up. "You might be right. I think I saw him in the woods."

She looks horrified as I tell her the story. "Well, maybe he's the one doing all this to get back at you. Don't get me wrong; I'm not saying it's your fault. How could I? From what I read, he's a madman."

I shake my head. "I understand the wolves but why would he kill Seth? He had nothing to do with anything."

"Because Seth saved you."

I lean back in the chair and pull my knees up. "But how would he know?"

"Seth always loved attention." She lifts a paper.

A picture of Seth is on the front, and he's smiling, holding his arms up like he's a champion of some kind. The headline reads, "Our Hometown Hero." I can't help but smile at his face, but then I get sad all over again.

Katie leans back in her chair and looks out the window. "Porter may be a kook, but this Al guy is crazy."

Maybe she's right. Maybe I'm pointing a finger at Porter to avoid dealing with Al. Because if it is Al, that means once again, a death is my fault. If Al wasn't after me, the wolves and Seth would still be alive. Katie comes around and sits in the matching chair next to me.

"Grace, I'll tell you what I'll do. You're a smart girl, and I know you pretty much took down that poaching ring on your own. So I trust your judgment. I'll call Sweeney and see if he and I can talk to Porter together. Deal?"

I sigh a breath of relief. Finally someone who gets me *and* trusts me. She's the first person who hasn't treated me like a child.

"I'll be right back," she says. "Make yourself at home."

She opens the cupboard and pulls out a box of MoonPies. "Here's a little something to keep you busy." I stare at the assortment as she pats my shoulder. "A little Birdee told me you liked them."

I grab a small chocolate one. "That old bird was right."

She laughs as she leaves the room and calls out to me from the hall. "Don't worry. I didn't count them."

I bite into the treat, and I chase it down with another swig of hot cocoa. The last lonely marshmallow slides into my mouth, and I put it out of its misery. Nothing like a sugar rush to get me going.

I stand and walk around the room, scanning the pictures on the wall. Off to one side, Katie has a hanging display that pays tribute to her father. I see an old picture of them hugging, both wearing white coats and holding a baby deer. Both his veterinarian diplomas and a rifle hang on the wall. I lean in and see his initials carved into a brass patch on the stock.

Looks like Katie loved her dad as much as I loved mine. Another thing we have in common. As I walk around the room, Katie returns.

"I called Agent Sweeney. He's on his way to the hospital to talk to Porter."

"He is?"

"Looks like maybe he believes you after all." She pats my arm. "I don't blame him. You have good instincts. I like that in a girl."

I exhale again in relief that this thing might be almost over. "I thought he was over at Sally's."

She nods. "He just left Sally with your grandmother."

I smile. "Don't let Birdee hear you call her that. I've been forbidden to ever mention that word in her presence. Speaking of which I better get home. If she finds out I'm out again, she'll probably tie me to a chair."

Katie walks me to the door and hands me a MoonPie to go. "Thank you for finding Seth and for telling me about Porter."

"Anytime."

"I'll let you know if I find out anything. To return the favor."

Before I leave, I reach into my pocket. "Can you give this to Sweeney when you see him? I don't really want to hold on to it if it means something. I have a bad habit of losing things. Important things."

She takes a tissue out of her pocket and takes the syringe from my hand. "Of course."

"Maybe he can test it or something."

She smiles. "You did good today. Better than expected."

She closes the door behind me, and I walk to the snowmobile. Snowflakes are still drifting across the darkening sky. For the first time in a long time, I drive away with a feeling of hope.

Agent Sweeney and Katie both believe me. I found Seth, and no matter how sad that is, at least his mother knows what happened to him and where he is.

Plus, Porter is being questioned about his involvement in some fishy things.

Even though Al is still out there somewhere, maybe this means I've turned a corner. Maybe things have changed from the summer. Maybe things are turning for the better. Maybe I can come back from everything that's happened.

Anything is possible.

# Survival Skill #24

*Never engage or participate in any online discussions*
*that make you uncomfortable*
*or are otherwise negative in nature.*

Ꝗ pick up the note Birdee left on the counter when I was on the phone earlier.

*Be back soon. Taking Sally Burrows dinner. Left some for you. We'll talk when I get back.* I look inside the fridge and grab the plate of barbeque chicken salad and bread and sit down at the table to eat. My head is racing as I replay the events of the day. So much has happened in so little time. It's amazing how things can be totally different at night from how they were just that very morning.

I swallow hard to force the bread down my throat. Poor Seth. I throw the sandwich down on the paper plate and push it away. It doesn't seem fair to eat after the person who saved my life is dead. It seems disrespectful in some way.

I can't help but wonder what Seth and Porter were arguing about, and what was in the needle I found. Was it all related or just some sick coincidence? I'm relieved Katie and Agent Sweeney are investigating it more. Maybe they can get something out of Porter that will tell us what happened. Part of me doesn't want it to be Porter, but the other part doesn't want it to be Al either. If Al is involved, the wolf deaths and Seth all tie back to me. And for once, I don't want to be involved anymore.

Not knowing what happened is probably the worst part. The wondering. The waiting. After a while, it starts to get to you. I need something to get my mind off this thing until I hear from Katie. Then I remember something.

In the aftermath of Seth's death, I completely forgot about seeing the wolves. I push back my chair and send it tumbling to the linoleum. I jog into the living room and pull out my notes from the observation. I reread them and smile. Maybe Seth's death can actually help do something good.

I jump on the computer and  log in to the database we've been using to enter anything about the red wolf project. Not that there's been much. As I'm waiting, a few spam windows pop up. Annoyed, I close them out and read some articles about the project.

I sit back and sigh, still staring at the article on the screen about the four wolves we found dead in different locations. The picture shows a large dead wolf lying in the snow as if he was just asleep.

Who would do this? And why would anyone kill these gorgeous creatures? It doesn't make sense. I use Google to do a few random searches about the fur trade and wolf pelts being sold. Mostly the fur trade involves timber wolves, not red wolves. I stumble on a Breaking News article in *The Charlotte Observer.*

Two decades after a grand experiment began to restore the nearly extinct red wolves to their North Carolina homeland, the wolves are dying again.

In the 2010 release, six wolves were shot despite the federal law protecting them, reducing the pack number from 20 to 14. The shootings underscore the depth of age-old animosity toward wolves. While conservationists celebrate their return, hunters and landowners often see wolves as mountain vermin.

Now with another effort led by the state and the U.S. Fish and Wildlife Service, more deaths are putting the wolves in danger. This time, the cause appears to be natural. But one thing is clear, the red wolf is no longer safe in the North Carolina wild and should be kept at the reserve to keep numbers from declining any further.

eBuild is scheduled to appeal their work permits in light of the project cancellation.

These animals can't get a break, I think. If eBuild has their way, they'll be breaking ground within a week. I shake my head and log into the database and enter the information from my wolf sighting today. Just as I'm finishing, a message pops up on my screen.

*I see you...*

I quickly type back *jerk*, and as I'm about to shut down, a single word appears in very large font:

*...Grace*

I think of Al and grab my phone. I see Wyn has called, and I quickly call him back. I spy out the windowpane on the front door and spot a dark shadow slinking up the driveway along the tree line.

I snatch my coat and backpack off the hat rack. Slowly, I back down the hallway. Maybe Katie is right. This is all happening because Al is crazy and obsessed with getting me back.

Why am I sitting around waiting for him to get me?

I quietly slip out the back door. As soon as I spot someone hiding along side the house, I race toward the woods. Behind me, the footsteps get faster and louder. A branch slaps me in the face and causes me to trip over a log or root. I jump back up just as someone grabs hold of my ankle.

In that split second, my brain tries to register who it could be. Only one name comes to mind.

Al.

I try to scream, but the cold air constricts my lungs. As I'm being dragged backward, I grasp at anything — roots, branches, bushes — to keep from being pulled away from the safety of the forest.

For a few seconds, I flail around, expending all my energy. Then I stop and quickly rein in my wild emotions. Being held stomach-down on the ground is the worst possible fighting position, especially for a girl. I have to get control of the situation.

I quickly flip over onto my back and flail my legs, hoping to kick the crap out of the person's kneecap or get a direct shot to the groin. My attacker pounces on top of me, knocking out my breath. A hand covers my mouth, blocking air from entering or escaping.

I fight back, but my body is still weak from the long hike, not to mention still recovering from hypothermia. I'm not nearly as strong as I need to be. A fake-out is my only hope. I close my eyes and go completely limp, releasing any tension in my body.

Someone shakes me and calls out my name. At first I think I'm hearing things. Dreaming. Maybe another nightmare. I slowly open my eyes and gasp. A hand slaps over my mouth before I can scream, and a smile crosses the familiar face.

A lovely accent cradles the words I've longed to hear, "Hello, Blossom."

Mo keeps his hand on my mouth. "Look, I know this is… strange, but you can't scream."

My eyes bulge, and I nod slowly.

His accent seems thicker than I remember. "Someone is watching you. If you scream, we'll have a whole other set of issues."

Tears spring into my eyes. Is this for real? Maybe I fell and hit my head. Maybe I'm asleep and don't know it. I look up into Mo's big brown MoonPie eyes. Maybe I am getting a second chance.

I nod and he slides his hand off my mouth slowly. As soon as I'm free, I scoot away until my back is against a tree. The wet snow seeps through my pants, but I don't dare move. I'm afraid the beautiful picture in front of me will disappear. Again.

My mouth is dry as I try to speak. "Is this a joke?"

Mo smiles that ever so wonderful smile, the one I've been praying to see again. The one that eases any fear I feel. The one I've dreamt about for the last three months. "If it is, that bloke's got a sick sense of humor."

Hearing his voice and seeing his smile stuns me. So many feelings pass through me in that moment — anger, fear, love, gratitude. I reach out and lightly touch his face. My fingers barely trail across his cheek as if he might suddenly dissolve into thin air without a trace. He clutches my hand hard and kisses it.

"Grace, I've missed you so much."

I don't have a verbal response yet. I have no clue what to say to someone who comes back from the dead. *You look great? Welcome back?* I pause for a second before jumping into his arms. I don't even try to hold back as I cry into his shoulder, sobbing quietly so no one hears me. All the pain from the last few days comes surging out. It's the first time I don't feel like I've lost everything. All his familiar features, smells, and my old feelings are back. Like they ever really left.

He hugs me tightly and whispers in my ear. "I'm so sorry."

I just nod into his coat and sniff a few times, praying I don't snot on his outerwear. Not a nice welcome basket. I still don't say a word — even though I will demand answers and apologies for days to come — all I know in this moment is Mo is still alive, and I am no longer alone.

Deep down, I already know the answers to most of my questions anyway. In my gut, I know Mo's been working for Agent Sweeney. Sweeney himself is not a great liar. But after months of his denying it, I started to believe him. And I know there must be a dang good reason why Mo's been hiding out, pretending to be dead, these last few months.

These long months without him.

I sob into his jacket and try to muffle the sound so no one hears. I try to get a grip, but all the emotions I've bottled up — the ones I've tried to forget, the ones that have torn at my heart, the guilt I've been feeling — they all come out. I can't stop them.

Mo just holds me and whispers. "Shh, Blossom. I'm here now. It's okay."

I pull away and stare into his eyes. He wipes the tears off my face with his thumbs.

I poke him. "Are you for real?" I start to laugh as happiness consumes me. "Seriously?"

"Afraid so." He winces. "You're going to hit me, aren't you?"

I shake my head. "There will be time for that later."

His eyes glance down at my lips. "Good. Then maybe this will keep you quiet."

He cups my face and gives me a small peck on the cheek. His lips graze my jawbone until they find mine. I grab the back of his head and smash our mouths together. I pull him down into the snow and kiss him like I've dreamed of kissing him for the last few months.

He pairs his lips with mine and hangs there awhile. We share the same breath, and he slowly slides his tongue into my mouth. I welcome him, and soon we're both breathing heavily. My whole body is doing somersaults inside as the feeling I'd almost forgotten returns.

His kiss is the only warmth my body knows as my back presses into the wet snow. And I know in that moment, Mo is thinking of nothing else. I can feel it. His entire soul seems to be concentrated solely on our lips touching. It's unlike anything we've ever shared before.

The guy I love is back. He's not dead. And he still loves me.

A sound pulls us out of our kiss.

He places his hands over my mouth and keeps his body over mine, protecting me. He glances through the trees and points at my house. A man dressed all in dark colors is heading up the porch stairs.

"What do we do?" I whisper. "What if Birdee comes back?"

Mo helps me to my feet. "Go. I'll distract him."

# Survival Skill #25

*Watch out for flashbacks, hallucinations, and paranoia. They are all symptoms of survivor's guilt and can be damaging.*

ꟼ grab his wrist hard. "You are out of your bloody mind. I am not leaving your side ever again."

He smiles. "Right. That's fair. Stay here for a second." I tighten my grip. He reassures me with those eyes of his. "I'll be right back. You can watch."

He sneaks off and sweeps around the side of the house. The man jiggles the doorknob and peers in the kitchen window. I pray Birdee doesn't come home soon. If anything happens to her – especially because of me – I'll never be able to get over it. That I'm sure of.

Mo must throw something, because just as the guy is about to push on the door, a clanking sound comes from the front drive. The man pulls out his gun and heads the opposite way to the front of the house.

Mo slides back through the woods and holds out his hand. "Coming?"

"Where?"

"Let's just get to the car. I need to call someone."

Instead of arguing, I concentrate on the warmth of Mo's hand and follow him obediently through the woods. If I don't let go, it means he can't disappear.

Every now and then, I look back to see if the man is following us. "Who is that man?"

"I don't know." Mo says without turning around. I almost can't hear him.

I skip over a fallen tree. "Was it Al?"

He shrugs as he tugs me behind him. "I don't think so."

If Sweeney and Kate are at the hospital with Porter, who else could it be? When we reach the top of the ridge, a black Jeep is hidden on the side of the road.

"Whose car is that?" I ask.

Mo narrows his eyes. "What? You don't trust me?"

I narrow mine back. "Dad said to never trust a guy. I'm pretty sure a dead guy still qualifies."

His eyes look sad when I mention Dad. Then he nods. "Smart man." Mo opens the door for me and waits until I'm in before walking to the driver's side. He slides in and starts the car.

I gawk at him as he climbs in the seat. "You drive?"

He turns on the seat warmers and blasts the air, waiting for the heat to kick in. "That surprise you?"

I shrug and realize there's still so much I don't know about him. "I just never saw you drive before. That's all."

He keeps his lights off and swerves onto the forest road. "I'm a brilliant driver as long as I stay on the right side of the road. Kinda forget it's opposite here sometimes."

He pulls out a cell phone and presses some buttons. He winks at me as he listens to the ringing.

Eventually, he says, "Hey. Yeah. I got her. Where should I go?" He glances at me and pats my leg. "Got it. We'll meet you there."

He hangs up and stares at the road. I keep my eyes on him, afraid he'll disappear if I look away.

"So? Who was that?"

"Look, Grace, I know this is all... very weird."

I cut him off. "Weird? A dead guy shows up after months, kisses me, and whisks me up into the mountains in a new Jeep without telling me where we're going... Why would you think that?"

He smiles. "Same ole Grace. Love it. That was Agent Sweeney. He wants me to take you to Katie Reynolds' place until he meets us there."

I lay my head against the seat. It suddenly feels full and congested with information. "Sweeney. Imagine that. I knew he was lying this whole time."

"He had no choice."

I turn my head to face him, leaving it against the headrest. "How did he know you were coming for me?"

Mo sighs. "I'll be straight with you. You deserve it. I've been assigned to watch you for the last few months. He called me after you called him about Seth. He was worried something might happen. A gut feeling really. He went to recover Seth and talk to Porter."

I snap my head up. "You know about all that?"

He nods as I focus on the road. The blurry headlights illuminate the road. Snowflakes brush across the windshield, trying to get out of the way.

"I was there," he says.

I think about what that means for a minute. "You? You were the person in the woods chasing me?"

"Yes."

I smack his arm and frown. "Mo! I thought you were Al! You scared the crap out of me. You're lucky I didn't shoot you. I had a gun, you know."

He doesn't flinch. "I tried to call out to you, but you took off so fast. Sweeney was miffed I lost you. Made me look like a wanker in front of my boss."

"Sorry."

He leans over and kisses me with the side of his mouth. "I'm the one who should be apologizing, Blossom. Besides, I forgive you."

I playfully push him away. "*You* forgive *me*? Ha!"

We both sit in silence for a few minutes. I stare at the side of his face and take in the features I never thought I would see again. The ones I love so much. The strong jaw, the dark eyes, the puffy lips.

"I thought you were dead."

Mo grips my hand and squeezes. "I know. Crumbs, I'm so sorry I hurt you." He glances over at me and wipes the bangs off my face. "But I'll never leave you again."

My voice comes out soft, like a little girl. "Promise?"

He nods once. "Abso-bloody-lutely."

I mumble. "I've heard that before."

As the car winds around the bend, snow slaps against the windshield. My eyes focus on the wipers, sliding back and forth smearing the window. I don't know whether to be happy or mad. The last few months have been hell without Mo, and he was alive the whole time? But then again, I'm so thankful he is. This is a second chance most people don't get. A chance I've prayed for every night.

I curl up in the front seat and watch him drive, his eyes fixed on the road. Except for the stubble on his face and his hair being slightly longer, he looks just as wonderful as I remember. The features of his face have been etched into my brain for the last several months — the smile lines around his eyes, the sunspot on his right cheek, the way he talks.

It seems like forever ago when I last saw him in the poachers' camp. When he took a bullet for my dad. When he promised to catch up to me. I remember sitting in the cave after Dad slipped away, waiting. Hoping and praying I hadn't lost everything.

Yet now that I see him, it seems like just yesterday. And the feelings of that day come rushing back to me. I try to sift through them and focus on the happiness I feel now that Mo is back, yet I can't help but feel wounded once again by the sorrow of watching my dad die.

Without noticing me, he runs one hand through his hair and pulls at the top. I remember that gesture well. He's nervous and knowing Mo is nervous makes me uneasy. I reach over and squeeze his hand, which makes me feel better. I never thought I would feel his touch again. His skin is warm from the heat.

He glances over and winks. "Nice night for a drive."

"Maybe. If a maniac wasn't trying to kill me."

I watch the flurries dancing in the car's headlights and suddenly feel sick. I try to imagine what it would be like just driving with Mo, laughing and talking like we used to do in the woods, with no threat behind us. I can't even fathom what that would feel like. To be normal.

"Don't worry," he says. "You're safe with me."

I hug my legs, now propped on the dashboard. "Famous last words."

Mo turns into a long driveway that winds and ends in front of a huge house. A luxurious, cabin–style house, not the rustic kind. The fancy, "looks like a cabin so we feel like we're rural" kind of house.

"This is Katie's house?" I say. "Wow."

I remembered the articles and how wealthy her family was. It must be nice to have money like this, and yet she still focuses on the environment. Admirable. I'm not sure I would do the same. I lean forward and look out the window as we circle in front.

Mo throws the Jeep into park. "Definitely not your average fixer-upper."

Before I can climb out, he jogs around the side of the car and opens my door. I raise my eyebrows.

"My, aren't we just the perfect gentleman."

"I'm English. What do you expect?" He grabs my hand, and we walk up to the house together.

As soon as I'm on the porch, I smell something sweet. I look down. "Cedar decking."

"Is that good?"

"Expensive."

Mo punches a code into the keypad and pushes open the door. I stand and wait. "Am I supposed to carry you or something?"

I laugh and smack his arm. "What? That's only if someone is married."

"Right." He leads me into the house and flips on the lights. "Agent Sweeney said we could make ourselves at home."

I look at all the books lining the walls. "Only no home of mine ever looked like this."

He lets go of my hand and walks around the room, flipping on a few lamps. He whistles once the light comes on. "Definitely fancy."

I study the rows of books along the wall — everything from medical books to fiction to animal books to fiction, from the classics to current bestsellers. I pull out a first edition of *Hatchet* and smile.
"She's rich and smart."

Mo studies a picture hanging on the wall as if we are in the Biltmore in Asheville. "Loves art, too," he says.

I touch one of the chairs. "She is really serious when she says she keeps the environment in mind. These chairs are bamboo. I know because my dad tried to get my mom to buy one for his office. He didn't feel right using leather."

Mo sits down and bounces a little. "As much as I love talking about the woodsy décor, I think we should talk. I owe you an explanation."

I plop down next to him. "Yeah, you do. Your cute accent and dreamy ways can only get you by for so long."

His smile drops, and his expression changes into a serious one. He touches my face.

"God, it's so good to be able to talk to you finally. I can only imagine how hard this has been on you. Thinking I was gone. And I'm so sorry I wasn't there for you. Especially after your Dad."

My chest tightens when he says that. The truth is, it's been unbearable without Mo because I've had to hide all my feelings.

"I saw you at the memorial service," he says.

My memory scans the room that day. "You were there?" I shake my head. "No, I would have noticed."

"Sweeney let me watch from the balcony. You looked so empty and sad. I wanted so much to hold you. I knew how much you were hurting, and knowing it was partly because of me was awful."

He runs his hands through his hair. "I tried to get Sweeney to let me see you. Just once. But he felt it was too dangerous. He suspected Al would definitely come back if he knew I was alive, considering how much I know about his operation. I didn't want you to get caught in the crossfire."

"Gee, thanks." I process his words for a few seconds. "I thought you only knew my dad. How long have you been working with Sweeney?"

"After my dad died, I vowed at his funeral to find his killer and bring him to justice. I found his papers, stashed them, and started hanging around gun shows like I told you, looking for some of the ring members. Dad's notes said they wore green bandanas.

"One day at a gun show, I befriended Al and Billy. They invited me to go shooting the next day, but before I could leave, Sweeney approached me. He told me about the USFWS, and how they were tracking a poaching ring. They felt it was involved in my dad's death."

221

I watch Mo breathe. I never thought I would see his chest rise and fall again. I place my hand on his heart and feel it beating. This is real.

"So he let you join him?" I ask. "Just like that?"

"I think at the time I was their only connection. Their only way in. Joe — your dad — was with Sweeney that day." He pauses, "They told me they needed someone on the inside. Someone the ring would never suspect. I offered. It was all I wanted to do."

"Weren't you a little young?"

He shrugs. "None of us cared. I had nothing to go back to. Mom and Dad were both dead."

"So what happened that day in the woods?"

He lays his head back on the sofa. "When you left me on the hill, I was in bad shape. I'd been shot in the ribs. I watched you and your dad go down the trail until I knew you were out of sight. I never saw Al follow you, so I thought you were safe. I hid for a bit until Sweeney showed up with some men and took out all the guys. When the chaos was over, he covered me with a sheet and loaded me on a gurney and wheeled me out."

I think back to that day in the woods, the man in a suit pushing a gurney up the hill. "I saw that," I say.

"You don't know how hard it was for me to lie under that sheet and hear you crying. By that time, I knew Joe had died, and Tommy was in bad shape, too." He shakes his head as if remembering all that happened. "When you called out, Agent Sweeney told me to lie still. Then I could see you standing over me. I remember holding my breath, thinking, 'She's gonna pull back this damn sheet and kick my bum.'"

I laugh out loud. "I would have."

Mo turns his knees toward me and holds both my hands. "I watched you from the back of that van, and when you crumbled into your mom's arms..." Tears form in his eyes. "It almost killed me. Jesus, I've hated myself every day for what I did to you. What I left you to deal with. Alone."

He swallows, and I notice his chin quiver slightly. "I understand if you never want to speak to me again."

I cup his face and wipe a tear from his cheek. "Are you crazy? Mo Cameron, I'm not letting you out of my sight. I know you did what you had to do. We've both made mistakes. I don't hate you. I consider this my second chance, and trust me, I've been praying for one. I'm taking this with both hands."

He smiles slightly and twists a piece of my hair around his finger. "Be careful what you pray for."

"In that cave, one of the last things my dad said was how good of a guy you are. I know you took care of him at that camp the best you could. You're the one who kept him alive the whole time. You're the only reason I even got to hold him again. Even if it was just to say goodbye. And if he says you're good, that's enough for me. We can start over."

"Brilliant." He rises to his feet and holds out his hand. "Hello, I'm Mo."

I giggle. "I remember that day in the woods, and you were much more scared than that."

He looks at me and keeps his arm extended.

I play along and put my hand in his. "Grace."

Mo pulls me to my feet and kisses my knuckles. "The pleasure is all mine, Miss Grace." He leans in and stops. "Surely you're not going to let me kiss you right after we just met? We're strangers, remember?"

I clutch his jacket and yank him closer. "I'll make an exception just this once."

Mo leans in and we kiss lightly. And with that kiss, our hourglass of time is flipped.

And we start over.

# Survival Skill #26

*In any survival situation, you can't let your guard down. Stay alert to your surroundings until you know you are safe. This helps to avoid other problems.*

Mo and I melt into each other.

I'm not sure how much time passes, but in those moments, we make up for what we lost, hugging and laughing and talking and kissing. I almost don't hear the floorboards creak until someone speaks.

"Well, I guess you're safe."

Mo jumps to his feet and pushes me behind him, shielding me. "Oy! Who are you?"

I peek around Mo's side and see Wyn standing there with a sad look on his face. "Wyn? Jesus. What are you doing here?"

I step out next to Mo, who clutches my hand tightly.

Wyn glances at our joined hands and then looks at me. "You said you were coming over when you called from the house." His face turns pink as if he's either angry or embarrassed. "So, of course, when you didn't show, I got worried."

I smack my hands to my head. "Oh, God, Wyn. I'm so sorry. I totally forgot."

"I see that." He keeps talking as if my apology meant nothing. "Anyway, first I called Birdee."

"At home?"

"On her cell. She was still at the Burrows' house."

I breathe a sigh of relief, thinking anyone who was stalking the house is probably gone by now after realizing no one is home. Wyn walks to the window and looks out, but I can tell he's eyeing Mo's reflection in the glass.

"When she didn't know where you were, I called Agent Sweeney. He said you were up here. Now I see why he told me not to come. But I thought you were alone. I didn't mean to intrude, though I can't say I'm not happy about breaking up this little party."

I ignore his jab and give him a hug. "I'm so sorry I worried you."

When I touch him, his body is stiff at first, but he quickly relaxes.

"I got some nasty IMs and saw some guy sneaking around my house," I explain. "I went out the back, and Mo found me. I totally forgot about…"

"About me?" Wyn glares at Mo. "Hmm, *that* never happens."

Mo walks forward and sticks out his hand in a friendly gesture. He smiles that perfect smile that would surely win me over again instantly. "I should probably introduce myself. I'm Mo Cameron. It's nice to finally meet you. Grace has talked a lot about you."

"Funny." Wyn stares at Mo's hand without reciprocating. "Only thing I heard about you was that you were dead."

Obviously the dashing smile doesn't work on Wyn the way it does on me. I give Wyn a dirty look, and my voice comes out in a scolding tone. "Wyn."

Mo comes to his defense. "It's okay. I deserve that. I'm sure this is all very confusing."

Wyn looks down at me. "Guess that part wasn't true after all."

I push him away a little. "Wait a minute. Don't assume I've been lying to you. I thought Mo was dead, too, this whole time. I'm just as surprised as you are."

I glance back at Mo who is standing tall, looking regal without knowing it.

Wyn moves around me. "Didn't look that surprised."

Guilty as charged. I cover my mouth as if that will conceal any kiss Wyn witnessed when he walked in. He walks over to a chair and sits with one leg up over his other knee.

"So unless we're in a zombie apocalypse, you going to tell me what's going on?"

I glance over at Mo, who jumps in before I can say anything. "Sure. I work with Agent Sweeney. We pretended I was dead to make sure Al didn't come back for Grace. Sweeney thinks someone is out to get her. We just don't know who exactly. It's either Porter or Al. He asked me to bring her here and watch her. Keep her safe."

Wyn nods and leans forward. He places both index fingers on his mouth as if he's thinking. "Interesting. So you're keeping her safe with your lips?"

I shriek. "Wyn!"

He glances at me. "What? It's a valid question. I didn't know lip-locking was a new, undercover security technique. Especially since this dude left the front door unlocked so pretty much anyone could walk right in. Seems he needs a *little* more training." Wyn holds his fingers up an inch apart when he says "little."

I rub my head. "Wyn, please."

He sits back in the chair and bounces his foot. "Please, what? Understand? This? I don't know if I can."

I face Mo. "Can you let us talk for a second?"

Mo glances at Wyn and then kisses my forehead. "Sure, Blossom. I'll have a look around. Make sure the house is secure."

Wyn calls after him. "That'd be a first."

I wait until Mo is out of earshot before sitting across from Wyn. "Look. I know you're a little hurt."

He scoffs. "Hurt? You make it sound like I just got a paper cut."

"Okay. A lot hurt."

Wyn rubs the crease between his eyes. "We kiss in the woods. I pretty much save your life. Then you call to talk and pull a no-show. The whole time, I'm worried sick about you, afraid something has happened, that you're hurt. Meanwhile, you're up here mugging with some dead guy, who, let's face it, could be a soap opera star because he's just that handsome. That kind of hurt?"

"Stop."

He shakes his head. "I think it's fair to say 'hurt' is not the word I would use. More like 'devastated.'"

I sigh. Somehow I've managed to push Wyn away again — when I didn't mean to. Again. I soften my voice and reach over to grab his hand.

"Wyn, we talked about this. That moment in the woods. I was out of it. I didn't mean for it to happen."

He looks at the ceiling. "Oh, so I forced you to kiss me like that?"

"I'm not saying that." I still can't tell him I was thinking of Mo. It's just too cruel. I shake my head. "Let me finish. I'm not saying anything was your fault. I'm just saying it wasn't the real me. I was delirious and hallucinating. Both are serious side effects of Stage Three hypothermia."

"Um. You're not helping my ego, and I don't need a medical lesson."

I kneel in front of him. "I love you, Wyn. You're my best friend, and you're a huge, important piece in my life. One of the biggest, I would say. The last few months without you have been almost unbearable." I look up and try to grab his eyes with mine. "I'm sorry I can't love you the way you want me to. But I don't want to lose you."

Wyn's face softens, and he touches my face. "Grace, that day in the woods was the happiest and scariest day of my life. I thought we'd finally broken through all the walls we'd built up. That we had gotten back to where we were before your Dad went missing. I thought you were going to die, and I realized I couldn't be without you. I love you."

Tears spring into my eyes. "Please. Please. Be my friend. Please don't push me away. Don't make me choose." My voice starts to shake. "I've lost so many people close to me. So have you. We both can lean on this friendship. We can start over."

"I don't want to start over. I want to move ahead." His eyes tear up.

I bite my lip, not wanting to hurt him any more than I have, but needing to be totally honest, to be sure I don't lead him on in any way.

"You asked me to always be honest with you, and I promised I would." I pause, trying to form the words, afraid it might be the last sentence I say to him before he pulls away. "Wyn, I love him. I do. The last few months without Dad, thinking Mo was dead, have been horrible. Seeing Mo today was the first time in a long time, I've been truly happy. It gave me hope that all this darkness might have a small light at the end. For me. Please don't let Mo come between us. Not now. Not after everything."

He shakes his head and pulls his hands away. "He already has."

"Wyn, please."

He stares at me for a minute. "I don't know if I can do this. Watch you two together. It's not that I want to hurt you. I just don't know if I have it in me. To watch the girl I love be happy with someone else."

My voice is barely a whisper, and I hang my head. "I understand."

He lifts my chin with his hand, and his eyes are sad. "But I'll try. I promised I wouldn't turn my back on you again, and I plan to keep my promise."

He kisses my forehead and leaves his lips there for a few seconds too long.

I hug him hard. "Thank you."

He sits back and takes a deep breath. "Doesn't mean I have to like it." He motions to Mo, who is in the other room checking the window locks. "Or him for that matter."

I nod once and smile. "Deal."

"Besides, I know my history. The English and Americans don't like each other."

I smile. "First of all, you hate history. Secondly, that was in the 1700s."

"Welcome to your future." He eyes Mo in the other room. "Doesn't mean I can't take jabs at him either."

Mo speaks up from the doorway. "Right. I can take it."

Wyn's face turns red again, and he stands. "Listen, man. I didn't mean to bust your–"

Mo walks over and pats Wyn on the back. "Sure you did. And I totally understand. Grace does that to men. Makes them crazy. I get it. Trust me." He holds out his hand. "Truce?"

Wyn reluctantly takes it and looks at me before standing up straight to make himself taller. "For now. But just know, you hurt her or turn your back for once second, I'm gonna be there."

Mo does one more shake and nods. "Sounds fair to me."

Wyn snaps his fingers. "In a nanosecond."

"I got it." Mo raises his eyebrows.

I watch them bicker. "Hello, I'm in the room, you know. I get to make my own choices. So if we can leave Testosterone City, we–"

Before I can finish my sentence, the lights cut out.

# Survival Skill #27

*When facing danger, it is critical that your group stays together.*
*Power travels in numbers.*

$\mathcal{M}$o pushes me down and ducks next to me. He places one finger to his lips.

Wyn looks down at us. "Didn't know they played Duck-Duck-Goose in England."

Mo frowns and puts his finger to his mouth.

Wyn kneels next to me. "Is he afraid of the dark?"

Mo hisses. "Shut up."

I whisper, "Maybe it's Sweeney?"

Mo shakes his head and keeps his voice low. "He wouldn't tinker with the lights."

"Maybe it's just a fuse," Wyn says. "It is winter, and the lights have been out in—"

"Does he always chatter on this much?"

I nod as Wyn frowns.

Mo pops his head up and looks outside. "Let's hope he's right. I'll check it out. I saw the fuse box in the kitchen." He grips Wyn's shoulder. "Watch her. Do not leave her side."

Wyn smirks and hugs me. "Thought you'd never ask."

Mo leaves the room in a crouch.

I take a huge breath and exhale when he's out of sight. I can't help a little panic whenever he leaves my side. It's like he's never coming back. "Maybe I should to go with him."

Wyn sits next to me on the floor and rubs my back. "I'm sure he'll be fine. He's a big boy."

I try to act confident even though fear is surging deep inside me. To be honest, it would be much better to have never gotten Mo back than to get him back only to somehow lose him all over again. I don't think my heart could take it twice. I breathe in and out quietly and mentally talk myself down off the ledge. *Everything is fine. Mo is fine.*

The next few minutes go by so slow. Like time is crawling at a sloth's pace. My legs start to cramp, so I shift on the floor. I keep checking my watch. I can sense Wyn watching me, but he doesn't say anything.

Finally Mo comes back. "Fuses seem fine. It's outside."

I study his face, which is pinched tight. Worry lines create deep trenches across his forehead. "What does that mean?" I ask.

Mo raises his eyebrow to Wyn and then strokes my hair. "That someone is here."

Wyn interrupts. "Or the power went out. Let's not scare her completely if we don't have to."

"Rather have her scared and alert than have her drop her guard."

Wyn rolls his eyes. "Spoken like a true hero."

I sit back against the couch and start to breath heavy. All the feelings from hiding in the woods, being chased, the constant fear are swirling inside me. They all come rushing back. My breath quickens. "Oh, God."

Wyn smirks. "Let's hope it's not. Unless he's here for Mo. Then I can't say I would object."

I flash him a dirty look and face Mo. "What can we do?"

Mo pulls out his cell phone and punches in some numbers. "Let's just make sure that on some odd planet, it's not Sweeney."

The phone rings. When Sweeney picks up, Mo puts it on speaker. Sweeney sounds groggy, tired. "Hey. I'm still about thirty minutes away. The weather is awful. Power lines down—"

Mo butts in. "I think we have a visitor."

Sweeney sounds perturbed. "Why? I told him to stay put."

Wyn practically cowers in the corner like he's hiding from the phone.

Mo looks frustrated at having to explain. "He's here, but I'm talking someone else. I'm fairly sure they just cut the lights."

Sweeney pauses, and I think I hear him hit the steering wheel. "Stay in the house. I bet it's Porter trying to scare someone."

I lean over and speak into the phone. "Wait. I thought you were with him at the hospital."

"So did I. Evidently, he checked out about an hour before Reynolds and I got there."

I'm confused so I'm silent for a second. "But why would Porter want to hurt me?"

Agent Sweeney pauses. "I don't know for sure he's trying to. I just know he's acting strange. I'll be there as soon as I can. Watch your back and stay inside."

I swallow hard. "Okay. See you soon. Oh, and hurry."

Mo hangs up the phone, and I stare out the window, taking it all in. Porter must have killed those wolves. He must have been tracking them and getting to them before we did. Seth found out, and Porter killed him. But why? Because of his wife's attack twenty years ago? And where do the bandanas come in? Are Porter and Al working together?

Wyn snaps at Mo behind me. "So what now? We just hang out here? Like monkeys in a tree?" His voice is strong and forceful. Sharp. Cutting.

Mo answers calmly, not feeding into Wyn's attitude. "What would you have me do?"

Wyn peers out the window. "Maybe we should check it out."

I snap out of my daze and spin around. My voice is the loud one this time. "*That* has to be the dumbest thing I've ever heard. Yeah, let's tromp outside in the dark when we think Porter might be out there."

Mo massages his temples. "Or Al. We can't rule him out yet."

Wyn narrows his eyes. "I don't hear any brilliant ideas coming from you."

Mo studies Wyn's face. "Maybe he's right."

I sit up. "What? No! We do like Agent Sweeney said and wait."

"For what?" Wyn says. "For all we know it's a power outage. Happens all the time. Suddenly, it's a conspiracy?"

"Wyn, remember the cave?"

He looks sad and mumbles. "I'll never forget it."

I smack his arm. "Stop. I mean the person walking outside."

He shrugs. "We don't know who that was. Could have been a rescuer. A hiker. Could have been Porter for all we know."

I nod once, thinking of the bandana. "Maybe. But it was someone who was intent on being quiet. Until we know for sure who is out there or that it's nothing, we stay inside."

I grip Mo's arm. "Right?"

His face wrinkles, and he makes a noise. "Cor blimey. How can I resist that beautiful face?"

He kisses my hand as Wyn turns away.

Mo stops when he notices Wyn in the corner, avoiding looking. "Listen, I'm just going to check the rest of the house. Upstairs and downstairs to make sure we're as snug as bugs in rugs."

"So you're not going outside?"

Mo smiles and runs his finger down my cheek. "Not if you tell me not to. I've put you through enough."

I hug him and look at Wyn over his shoulder.

Wyn rolls his eyes. "I feel like I'm listening to one of those bad soap operas my mom records."

I do what every mature girl does. I stick out my tongue.

Wyn mumbles, "Oh, that's mature."

Mo hovers in for a kiss. He stops himself. "We need some candles and flashlights."

I stand, needing something to do before I go nuts. "I'll do that. They must be around here somewhere."

Wyn leans against the chair. "I'll stay with you."

Mo appears reluctant this time, like he doesn't want to leave me with Wyn.

I lean over and peck Mo on the lips for reassurance. "It's okay. Go. I can handle him." I tilt my head toward Wyn and smile.

"I know you can." Mo kisses my nose and leaves the room without so much as another glance at his rival.

Once he's gone, I put my hands on my hips. "You're not making this easy."

Wyn stands and sifts through a drawer. "Not my job, and certainly not in the agreement."

"Yeah, but do you have to make us all miserable?"

He just shrugs. "Why should I let the Brit take over? They tried that in the past, and it didn't work. Why should I surrender now? My forefathers died for me."

I walk around the room, looking for candles. "Oh, please. You don't give a rat's butt about your *forefathers*." I sit down at Reynolds' desk and start looking through drawers. "You know you're being completely childish and unfair, right?"

Wyn grabs a candle off the bookshelf and mumbles. "Life isn't fair. Trust me, I know."

I sit back in the chair and sigh. Wyn is starting to get on my nerves. Big time. Being hurt is one thing, whining about it is a whole other. And it's so not attractive on him. "Can we play this drama out later? For now, we need to work together. Something serious could be going on, but you're too busy pouting to help."

"Fine." Wyn picks up a picture and looks at it. "But this whole thing doesn't make sense. Why would Porter go all nutso like this?"

He shows me the press photo of Agent Sweeney, Porter, and Reynolds. Reynolds is holding a conservation award.

"Nice." I keep sifting through the desk for matches. No point in telling him about Porter's wife. I need to keep Wyn focused. "Maybe he's mad at the university. They did accuse him of some awful things."

He squints his eyes. "Maybe."

"Sucks that Katie will be affected. I think she was really hoping to make a difference."

I lean in and stare at the certificate on the wall claiming she is quite the pistol-shooter. The only way I can even tell is because the moonlight is streaming in through the window.

"I never would have expected her to be some kind of marksman," I say. "She seems so—"

"Sexy." Wyn interjects.

I look at him, shocked. "I was going to say feminine." I sift through papers looking for matches.

"Like you would know." He chuckles under his breath at his own joke.

I throw a crumpled up paper at his head. "Oh, thanks. You really are going to make me pay, huh?"

He winks. "I'll milk it for as long as I can."

I slide my hand into a drawer. "And if you know me so well, you know that won't be much longer." I touch a cold handle. "Bingo."

I pull out a flashlight, but along with it comes a stack of papers. They fall out and spread across the ground. "Oh crap." I gather up the papers. It looks like Katie's collecting articles and documents on Cardinal, Inc. "Ha. Looks like Katie's next victim is Mandy Smith."

Wyn calls out from across the room. "Who's that?"

"CEO of Cardinal, Inc. Evidently they own eBuild. The company that's trying to build up here. Serves them right. Let them rape some other town."

"It's not like this one is doing so hot. We could probably use some tourism and development."

Thinking of our poor, sinking town economy, I stack the papers neatly back in the drawer alongside Katie's loan documents for the cabin. My eyes find the price tag.

"Hey, you don't even want to know how much this cabin is."

He darts over. "Tell me." He grabs the documents and whistles as I look over his shoulder. "Whoa. If I had that kind of money, I sure would not be working as a conservationist, I tell you that."

"Maybe she wants to make a difference. Maybe she's not about money."

He shrugs. "Maybe."

I can't help but scan all the information before looking away, feeling guilty for snooping.

I snatch the papers. "We shouldn't be doing this."

"You started it." He heads over to the fireplace and lights the few candles he's found. The room lights up with a dim glow. "Wish my forefathers left me enough jack for a place like this."

I put the papers back in the folder and hit him over the head with it. "Would you stop with the ancestor talk? It's getting old."

I take out the flashlight and look at my watch. "Mo should have been back by now."

# Survival Skill #28

*When faced with an uncertain situation, listen to your gut. Often your unconscious brain will detect something before you are consciously aware of it.*

I swing my flashlight toward the hallway. "Wonder what's taking Mo so long."

Wyn mumbles. "Who cares?"

I ignore him and walk to the doorway, calling softly, "Mo?"

No answer.

I stand in the hallway and look around. I have no clue what is where in here, since I've only been hanging out in the den since I got here.

"You think he's okay?"

Wyn scuffles behind me, placing candles around the room. "Well, I know he's not *dead*."

"Ha-ha." I move down the hallway. "Maybe I should look for him."

Wyn comes to the den entrance and hangs from the door molding. "He's probably upstairs. This place is a mansion."

I open the door to the basement and whisper, "Mo?"

When I don't get an answer, I walk down a few steps. Wyn is at my side in a heartbeat. "He told us to stay here."

I take another step and hold the flashlight out in front of me. "Last time he told me that, I never saw him again. Well, alive anyway. Until now, I mean."

Wyn shakes his head. "Geez, this whole situation is so messed up. How do you find this kind of stuff to get into? You're just a simple girl from a simple town."

"It's complicated." I take another step. "You coming?"

"Do I have a freakin' choice?" Wyn follows next to me. "Just remember if I die, I'm going to come back, too. But instead of a dead lover-boy, I'm gonna haunt your skinny butt."

"You already do." I take a step, and he squeezes next to me. "Can you not follow?"

"Why can't you follow?"

We make our way down the stairs at the same time, our shoulders pressing into each other. I try to flip on the light without even thinking. The click echoes in the dark, reminding me the power is still out. My flashlight starts to dim. "Gah! Figures. Murphy's Law."

I hit the tube against my hand, trying to knock some light back into. It beams bright and then flickers out.

Wyn whispers, "Great. Now we gotta climb back up in the dark."

"Just give me a second," I whisper and slap the flashlight against my thigh. It pops on and shines right into a face.

I scream and drop the light.

Wyn screams next to me, and I hear him thump down the steps as he falls.

Mo calls out in the dark, "Crumbs. You guys scared the bejesus out of me."

I bend over and pick up the fading flashlight. "Me? What about you? Why didn't you answer?" I shine the light around, looking for Wyn. He's lying a few steps down. "Wyn? Are you okay?"

He curses at my feet. "I think I hurt my leg."

I shine the light on him and go to inspect it closer. "It's just a sprain."

He frowns. "Just a sprain? Guess I have to *die* and resurrect to get any attention around here."

"Oh stop being a baby." I scowl up at Mo. "Why didn't you say anything? You had me worried."

His face shows concern. "I didn't mean to, I was trying to be quiet."

Without saying anything, he grabs Wyn's arm and swings it around his neck. I can't help but smile, knowing how much Wyn hates that Mo is carrying him up the stairs. At the top, we sneak back into the living room and turn off the flashlights. Wyn grunts as Mo lays him on the couch.

Then Mo lowers his voice. "There's definitely someone out there."

My hands are still trembling. "Do you know who it is?"

"No, but my Jeep's tires were flat, and I saw fresh footsteps around the cabin."

Wyn rubs his leg. "Maybe they were mine."

I think for a second and put my hands on my hips, frowning at Mo. "Wait. You went outside?"

Mo wrinkles his face. "Yes."

I hit him. "Why in the world would you do that? You could've been hurt."

He pulls a gun out of the back of his pants. "I wanted to be sure I could protect you."

Wyn groans. "You left your gun in the car too? This is like something out of a bad movie."

Mo's jaw flexes. I can tell he's getting frustrated with Wyn's jabs and constant comments, but before he can say anything, I face Wyn.

"Shut up. We need to work together, and the peanut gallery is not helping."

Wyn mumbles. "Just saying it wasn't smart."

Mo cracks under the pressure. "Look, I know it was daft of me, but I solved the problem. So on your bike."

Wyn laughs. "On your *bike*? Oh, gee, you got me there." He looks at me. "And you think that's sexy?"

"I'm not doing this with you. You can either help us, or shut up about it." I bite my lip. "I don't think you realize what's going on here."

"Yeah. I do. Porter is whacked and Sweeney is about to arrest him."

Mo puts his gun on the side table. "Only we don't know if it's Porter at all."

I gasp and my legs collapse beneath me as the obvious hits me. "Oh, God. It's Al." I start rubbing my hands together. "He's going to kill me. I know it."

"Way to go, knight in shining armor," Wyn says. "Send the damsel in distress into complete hysteria."

Mo kneels down next to me. "I'm sorry. I was just being honest."

Wyn mumbles. "There's a first." He points to the front window. "You sure this place is locked up tight?" When Mo nods, he reassures me. "There's no way Al is getting in here."

I hug my knees and start to rock. "If he can find a way out of the ropes I knotted, he can get in here. Easily."

Wyn's eyes narrow. "Yeah, come to think of it. How did he get out of that?" He stares right at Mo.

Mo looks surprised. "Don't look at me. I wasn't even near him. Sweeney got me the hell out of those woods before anyone could see me."

Wyn doesn't look convinced. "Well, someone must have set him free."

I keep staring at the ground. "Maybe I didn't tie them good enough. I wasn't in the best state of mind."

Wyn reaches over and cups my hand. "If you say you tied it, I know you did a dang good job."

Mo notices Wyn's hand on mine, then he looks at me. I pull my hand away. I can tell by Mo's face, he's on the edge, and Wyn's pushing him too far.

I pat Mo's knee. "Let's just focus. What do we do?"

"We hope Sweeney gets to us before anyone else."

# Survival Skill #29

*Watch out for impulsive reactions, irrational behavior, and poorly thought-out decisions easily caused by frustration and anger.*

A few minutes later, a crunching sound comes from outside.

Mo grabs his gun and heads out of the room. I race after him, leaving Wyn lying on the couch mumbling. Part of me feels bad. I know Wyn is moody because of me. He's never mad or down, yet somehow I've pushed him to a breaking point. I hate that I've done it. He's my best friend. But I love Mo, and I can't let Wyn think otherwise. It wouldn't be fair.

Mo stands at the window. "I think it's Sweeney."

My body relaxes. "Thank God."

He runs one hand through his hair. "Let's not get too cocky. We don't know what's going on yet."

Agent Sweeney's ranger truck pulls up the circular driveway and stops. He gets out of the driver's side and walks toward us cautiously, gun drawn.

Mo unlocks the front door. "I'd better go out and cover him. Just in case." We walk out onto the porch. "You stay here." But before Mo can take another step, a gunshot rings out.

Agent Sweeney barely has time to raise his gun when he's hit. He yells and spins around before collapsing to the ground.

I hear myself scream out as Mo tears down the steps toward him.

All I can do is stand there. My feet are stuck to the wooden floor as flashes of being back in the woods cloud my vision. Screams, gunshots, chaos. Tommy going down. Carl raising his gun. Mo getting hit. Al charging and shooting Dad. The chaos forces me to check out.

I don't hear anything except Mo's voice. "Grace! Get inside!"

I shake my head to snap out of my daze and turn, running back indoors. Once I'm safe inside, I slam the door and lock it behind me. Wyn hobbles out of the living room.

"What the hell?"

I shriek. "Call 911!"

He shakes his head. "Can't. The phones are out, and Mo has the cell phone."

I knock my head on the glass and eye the ranger truck. "Sweeney's radio! Maybe I can get to it?"

Wyn limps up behind me. "Over my dead body you're going out there. I know how these kinds of situations pan out. And so do you."

I press my face against the cold glass. What do I do? The panic and fear inside me have taken over, and I don't know if I could get outside if I wanted to. My legs don't seem to be working. I watch as Mo drags Sweeney behind the car just as another shot rings out. He hits the deck, and I can't tell if he's been shot or not.

This cannot be happening again.

I hear another shot ring out. In that split second, I make a decision. I'm not sitting here and letting Mo get hurt again in any way. I scream his name and grab the handle to open the door, but Wyn blocks it with his body.

"No! We have to wait. You can't go out there."

I growl at him. "Get out of my way. I don't want to hurt you." I shove Wyn aside, which sends him stumbling backward on his bad ankle. I don't stop to see if he's okay. I can't. Mo and Sweeney are all I can think about. I throw open the door and run in a crouched position onto the porch.

"Grace! No!" Mo screams at me.

He's cradling Sweeney with one hand and waving me back with the other. In that moment, I'm conflicted. Go to Mo and help, or slink back inside with my tail between my legs and let people die?

I already know how that second option pans out.

I hid with Dad in the cave and look where it got me. He still died as I sat there and watched.

I ignore Mo's demands and run to the porch steps as a bullet whizzes past my head. I'm so stunned I forget to hit the deck. Instead, I look over and spot a shadowy figure walking on the edge of the dark woods. An arm is stretched out, and a gun is pointed right at me.

Mo screams, "Watch out!"

He jumps up and leaves Sweeney lying behind the car. He bolts toward me just as a loud bang explodes.

Before I can move or duck or dive, a bullet clips my shoulder. As I'm falling, everything slows down. I see Mo running toward me. His face is distorted in rage, but he's running so slowly, it's like he'll never reach me in time. I slam onto the deck and land on my back. My head hits the pole, and stars twinkle in my eyesight. I writhe in pain as fire shoots across my shoulder and down my arm.

"No! No!" Mo yells like a madman.

I lie on my side with my eyes wide open, suddenly feeling nothing. I watch as Mo squats down in a stance and open fires on the dark figure in the trees. My head is so foggy, I can't count how many bullets it sends. One? Two? The figure drops with a loud thud and doesn't move.

Mo calls out to Sweeney. "He's down."

Wyn appears at my side. He lifts my head and props me on his leg. "Jesus, G. I told you not to go outside."

"Stay with her." Mo stands above me with his gun drawn.

I grimace, forcing out words. "You have to tie something around my arm."

Wyn takes off his button-down, leaving him in nothing but a t-shirt, and wraps my arm as I keep my eyes on Mo. It's like I'm afraid if I look away for one second, he'll disappear and I'll never see him again.

Mo slowly moves down the steps and methodically approaches the gunman, never dropping his weapon. He suddenly seems so much older to me. He's seen his father die, and he isn't afraid to use a gun on someone. How circumstances in life force us to grow older is crazy.

He uses his foot to kick the shadow's gun away and then kneels next to him. Mo stays alert as he reaches over and checks the figure's pulse. He lowers his gun and looks at me then shakes his head.

I let my head fall back against the deck and close my eyes.

Thank God, Al is dead.

And I didn't even have to see his face.

# Survival Skill #30

*When our fight or flight system is activated, everything in our environment can be perceived as a possible threat.*

Everything speeds back up again, and before I know it, Mo practically trips up the steps and crumbles at my side. "Bloody hell! Grace, let me see."

Wyn moves back and lets him take over.

Mo moves my bloody hand and checks my shoulder. Tears spring into his eyes. "You're going to be okay."

I hate seeing Mo so upset. Over me. "Isn't that what they say to people who are about to die?"

He frowns. "That's not funny. You're lucky the bullet just grazed you."

"My first gunshot and it's not even real?" I clench my teeth in pain.

He shakes his head and strokes my face. "You're crazy. Why did you do that? I told you to stay back."

I breathe hard and buckle in agony. "I listened to you last time, and I lost you."

"You are so frustrating." He kisses my forehead. "What am I going to do with you?"

I try to smile through the pain throbbing in my shoulder and down my arm. "You can't get rid of me. I just took a bullet for you."

I immediately think of the oath I made to Seth that I never got a chance to keep and go silent.

Mo looks up at Wyn who's leaning against the door. "Can you get me a towel?"

Wyn salutes and doesn't hide the fact that he's annoyed. He limps back inside. "Yes, sir."

Sweeney's not moving when I look in his direction. It's like someone has pressed replay, only this time instead of Tommy, it's Sweeney.

I whisper to Mo. "Is... is he alive?"

Mo shakes his head. "He was, but I'm not sure how bad it is. Everything happened too fast."

"Go check. I'm fine."

He stands just as Wyn limps back out of the house and throws the towel at his head. It hits Mo in the back.

Wyn snaps. "You always *protect* her this well?"

Mo doesn't respond. He simply moves toward the steps, his eyes on Sweeney.

"Wyn, stop," I say, trying to head off his pending fit.

He pokes Mo in the back. "Hey, look at *me*. I'm serious. Ever since you met her, bad things have happened, and she always gets hurt one way or another. You're not good for her."

Mo faces Wyn. "Back off."

Wyn pokes him again. "I won't. *You* back off."

Mo locks his jaw and gets in Wyn's face. "Don't be mistaken. I've put up with your crap for *her*. I wouldn't give a monkey's uncle about you. Touch me again, and I can't promise I'll be a gentleman any longer."

He lets go of Wyn and turns his back to walk down the steps, but Wyn charges him from behind.

I force myself to sit up "Stop it! Wyn!"

At that last minute, Mo moves one step to the side, and Wyn goes down on his bad ankle.

Wyn charges again. This time plowing into Mo's stomach.

Mo grabs him, teeth gritted together and eyes dark.

I start to cry. Not only from the serious pain screaming through my body, but also from the total breakdown happening before my eyes between the two guys I love most. All because of me. My voice shakes and I even spit a little when I talk.

"Mo… please don't."

Mo stops and glances over at me. His eyes soften when he sees how upset I am, and he tosses Wyn aside like he's a doll. He kneels next to me and holds my face. "I'm sorry."

I nod. "Just go to Sweeney. He needs you. Please."

Wyn groans on the porch beside me.

When Mo walks away, I reach over and hit his arm. "What the hell are you doing?"

"Defending you." He sits up and moves closer.

I cock my head and look up at him with tears in my eyes "No, you're *hurting* me. This is not helping. At all. In case you haven't noticed, Sweeney is down. Someone is dead. And I've been shot in the arm. So excuse me if your ego needs to take a backseat."

I move a little and grunt from the pain that shoots through my body.

He sighs and wipes off his pants. "This isn't about my ego." He checks the bind on my arm and adjusts it.

I watch his face as he studies my wound. "Then what is it?"

"I'm better for you than he is."

I sigh and hold his hand. "That's not for you to say. It's my decision. We already talked about this and we agreed—"

"You talked. I listened. And I don't know if I agree with anything anymore."

Before I can answer him, Mo comes up the driveway holding a bloody towel. He scowls at Wyn. "If you're man enough to pick a fight, then you're man enough to help me bring Sweeney inside."

Relief relaxes my body some. "He's okay?"

Mo nods and smiles. "Well, he's *alive*. Sweeney's too stubborn to die, but I need to stop the bleeding and get him some help." He looks back over his shoulder at the other man still lying in the gravel. "I'm going to radio this in."

I look over at the figure still lying on the ground. "You sure he's dead?"

"Yes."

I lay my head back against the wall. "Thank God. I'll never have to worry about Al again."

Mo is silent for a minute. "It wasn't Al."

I check his eyes to see if this is a joke or if he's mistaken, but Mo's face is hard and serious.

I whisper, "What?"

"It's not Al. It's Porter."

I don't know if I'm devastated it isn't Al or happy it's Porter. What I do know is I was right this whole time in thinking Porter was responsible for Seth's death.

I scan the woods. But if Porter's here, that means Al's still out there.

Somewhere.

# Survival Skill #31

*Take note of details when in a stressful situation.*
*Later, they may form a different picture.*

ℐnside, Agent Sweeney is placed in the chair, and I'm seated on the couch.

Candles still light the house, and a fire roars in the fireplace with its orange flames popping and sizzling. Sweeney coughs and holds his bandaged side.

"Man. What a crappy day," he says.

Mo checks my arm for the twentieth time in five minutes.

I watch him tend to my wound, thankful he's still here. "You don't have to watch me. I'm fine."

He mumbles as he works, "I'll decide that."

When he touches the cloth, I wince, and he leans over and kisses my forehead. "Sorry, Blossom." He ties a cloth around my arm. "Lucky for you, the bullet didn't go in."

"Hm. Lucky for me."

Wyn sighs and shakes his head. "There's a dead guy in the driveway. Guess he's not too *lucky*."

Mo keeps his eyes on me. "Seriously, it could have been much worse."

I sit up more with Mo's help and focus on Sweeney. His head is rested on the back of the chair and his eyes are closed.

"Sweeney, you okay?"

He raises his eyebrows without looking. "Never been better. My fault, though. I shouldn't have been so careless. I didn't think Porter would go to such extremes."

I think about the wolves and Seth. I'm almost positive he was responsible for both somehow.

"Why would he do this? It just doesn't seem like him." Wyn says.

"I found out Porter's wife died. A red wolf killed her."

Mo shakes his head. "So he goes crazy 40 years later and kills everybody? Something doesn't fit."

Sweeney sighs and explains to the group what I already know. "Well, I suspected something was going on." Sweeney repositions himself and winces. "Anyway, something showed up on the autopsy."

I sit up straighter, waiting for more. "I knew it! What did you find out?"

"They found sodium thiopental."

"Bloody hell." Mo shakes his head as if he's processing the information.

I have no clue what they're talking about, but Wyn asks the question before I can. "What is that?"

Mo answers for Sweeney. "A drug used in euthanizing animals."

The information swirls in my head. "So those wolves didn't die of natural causes. They were *killed*?"

Sweeney coughs before answering. "Put to sleep. Yes."

Wyn probes more. "How would Porter get access to that kind of stuff?"

Sweeney looks up at the shadows dancing along the ceiling tiles. "Because he was in biology at NC State. He probably knew people."

My mind searches through files of information. "Wait. The university hates him. He was banned from there for some unethical stuff. How would he have access?"

Wyn shrugs. "He probably knew someone."

Sweeney nods. "And I guess he found out I was checking and panicked."

"But how would he find out? And why come after me?"

Sweeney puts the pieces together neatly. "Easy, you found Seth. And you told Katie. She was obviously calling around looking for him. He probably assumed you told her something that incriminated him."

I shake my head. "She wouldn't leave messages. She's not stupid. And you said by the time you and Reynolds went to the hospital he was gone. No, he found out some other way."

Mo looks from me to Sweeney. "Maybe he's been watching Grace closer than we realized."

It dawns on me that Reynolds is not here. "Where is Katie, by the way?"

"She was still working when I left her," Sweeney says. "Trying to track down Porter. I think she felt responsible and wanted to find out where he had gone. I tried to call and tell her we had him here, but some of the phone lines are still down."

Before I can ask, Wyn speaks. "But why would Porter work to protect the wolves only to kill them? Sounds like a lot of work. Why not just sneak out and pick them off. No one would have found them."

Agent Sweeney looks back at him. "I don't know that yet. I was hoping to question him. I assume there was a reason."

"I told you, it's his wife's death." I say, and everyone stares at me. "Maybe he still wanted to get justice somehow. In some sick way." Then something pops into my head. "Did you test the syringe to see if it matched?"

"What do you mean?"

"I gave the syringe I found to Katie to take to you."

Agent Sweeney shakes his head. "No. She must have forgotten. We were so busy trying to find Porter. I only saw her for a few minutes. I'll get it from her in the morning when I see her."

I fold my arms in frustration.

"Wait, I need to catch up." Wyn rubs his forehead and faces me. "You found Seth? And a syringe?"

Sweeney answers for me. "Grace went out looking and located Seth's body. She found a syringe close to where he was sitting. We're not sure it means anything, though."

Wyn rubs his temples. "So now we think Porter *killed* Seth? Seriously? Isn't that a bit extreme? An animal is one thing, but—"

"Killing an animal for no reason is just as horrible as a hurting a person," I say, almost getting a whiplash looking at him. "One leads to the other if you get desperate enough."

He holds up both hands. "Easy, Jane. Tarzan no argue."

"Look, we don't know anything about Seth yet," Sweeney sighs. "But right now, anything is possible." He eyes me. "Let's hope not because you're right. That would take this thing to a whole new level."

Sweeney tries to stand, but he teeters.

Mo helps him back down into a chair. "I called this in a while ago," Mo says. "The USFWS should be here by now."

"I tried calling Birdee too. The lines are down everywhere."

"The weather's getting worse," Sweeney says, closing his eyes. His face is as pale as a china doll's. "We may have to wait it out until morning."

Then he pushes forward in the seat. "Before it gets too bad out there, walk me to Porter. I'd like to take a look around before anyone else gets here. See if we can get some clues as to what the hell is going on. Maybe he has something on him that'll give us some insight into this whole mess."

Mo squints. "You sure you're up for it? There's not much to see."

He stands. "Never know what you can find."

I force myself to ask what I've been trying to forget. "But what about Al?"

"Now that we know it's Porter, I doubt Al's around," Sweeney says. "We would have gotten some response from him by now."

I breathe a sigh of relief.

Sweeney cups my shoulder. "He's still out there somewhere, just not here tonight." Mo faces Wyn. "This time keep her inside. No matter what."

Wyn glances at me. "Won't let her out of my sight."

"That's what I'm afraid of." Mo hands me his gun. "Keep this just in case."

"Hey! Why does she get the gun?" Wyn says.

I smirk at him. "Because I know how to use it. You think I'd let *you* hold a gun? You couldn't even make it up the stairs without an injury."

He gives me a dirty look. "That's because it was dark."

"Still is, and I don't want to get shot again."

Mo can't help but laugh on the way out. "I'll be right out front. Shouldn't take long."

Ten minutes later, Wyn is already snoring on the couch.

I shake my head. "Some bodyguard."

I stand and walk to the back window. The lawn is covered in a blanket of snow as if Mother Nature has swaddled the earth for a cozy night. There's not one blemish in the white sheet. The moon looks down on me, and the blackness of the forest is dotted with white polka dots of snow hanging off the sagging branches.

The snowflakes make the world a little blurrier than usual, reminding me of a Van Gogh painting we studied in art class last year. As I watch the peaceful world drifting to sleep outside, I suddenly feel claustrophobic, like I need fresh air. The events of the day have made my brain fuzzy, and I glance at the back door. If Sweeney and Mo think it's safe to check out Porter, I wonder if I could just pop outside and breathe for a second.

"Wyn, I'm going outside. Is that okay?" I glance back at him, and he's now lying on his back with his mouth open.

He snorts his response.

I smile. "I take that as a yes."

I open the back door, and a rush of cold air pierces through my body. I grab my jacket off the rack and slip into it, pulling up the hood. As soon as I step onto the back steps, I smile.

Snowflakes drop from the sky like glimmering sparkles in the moonlight. They land on my jacket and disappear into thin air like magic. The white trees are stiff, frozen like statues. The snow has been perfectly laid down by nature, no imperfections or blemishes except for its own markings.

I take one step into the thick snow and sink a few inches. The crunch under my foot is one I can never get sick of. I take another step and look back at my footprints blemishing the white carpet. One small step toward a fresh beginning.

I smile as I walk along the back of the house, letting the frigid air swirl into my lungs. I follow the white cotton puffs of my breath as they float away into the night sky. The air is quiet. Still. Peaceful. For the first time since Dad died, I feel like me again. A new me with a new normal. The person I used to be is coming back, and my world feels safe again.

Porter is dead, and even though Al is still out there, I have hope that my luck is changing. I can't help but wonder what the wolves are doing tonight.

In the distance, one howls as if on cue. I smile, wondering if Bandit and his family have moved to another den for the night to snuggle with their young and wait out the nasty storm.

I look up at the puffy clouds forming in the sky. I should do the same. Last thing I need is to be stuck out here again. I turn and head back to the house, following my tracks along the makeshift path to avoid ruining any other space. As I approach the deck, I see something tied to the post, flapping in the light breeze.

I take a couple steps forward and freeze.

A green bandana.

# Survival Skill #32

*As with many attack moves, recognizing the move that's about to happen is a big part of defensive strategy.*

Panic rushes through my body in a wave.

My legs won't move, and my feet are plastered in the snow as if cement has been poured around my ankles. I hear footsteps behind me, but I keep my eyes forward. I'm afraid to turn around, fearful of who I will see. As long as I'm facing this way, my world is still peaceful and quiet. The winter wonderland I love so much is still mine.

I grip the bandana and inspect it.

"Hello, Grace."

I spin around and face Katie. Then I smile and grab my chest. "Jeez, you scared me!"

She smiles and cocks her head. "Did I? I'm sorry."

"No, it's okay. I'm glad it's you. Trust me." I eye the forest and stuff the bandana into my pocket.

Her voice is stern and curt like she's stressed. Then again, aren't we all? "I've been looking for you," she says. "You need to come with me."

"Why? What's happened? Is Birdee okay?"

She smiles and takes a few steps away from the house, looking back over her shoulder. "She's fine. But Agent Sweeney and Mo think Al is back. They want me to get you out of here. Now."

I look around. "Where are they?"

Katie points to the woods. "They went off to track him. Found some footprints. Guess you found something too." She points to the green cloth hanging out of my pocket. "Scared?"

"Yes." I panic that Mo has left me again and scan the woods, looking for movement.

She touches my shoulder. "Don't worry, they'll be fine. They're good at what they do. You just have to trust them."

I glance up at the window. The lights are back on in the house. "Okay. Let me tell Wyn where I'm going so he doesn't freak out again."

She keeps her voice down. "I tried to, but he's still sleeping."

"Ha. Slacker."

Katie walks ahead of me, and I follow her closely, constantly checking over my shoulder, half-expecting Al to come charging up any minute and snatch me from behind. I should have stayed inside. No matter how many things I try to think through, I tend to make the dumbest decisions sometimes. I curse myself. Dumb. Dumb.

"You know, you're a very smart girl," Katie calls out over her shoulder.

I watch the back of her head as she glides through the snow. "Really? Why do you say that?"

She keeps talking, but I struggle to hear because she's facing away from me.

"I don't think I gave you enough credit in the beginning. Now I'm wishing I would have paid more attention. It would have been better for business."

I stop in my tracks. "What do you mean?"

Katie faces me and looks a little surprised. "You mean you haven't figured it out? Really?" She looks amused. "I thought you had for sure."

Suddenly my heart races. Something is wrong. I take a step back. "I think I should go back."

As I spin around to leave, Katie grabs my sore arm and squeezes tight. "Not this time, Grace."

"Ow!" I almost collapse in pain, but I manage to stay on my feet. I look into her eyes. They've darkened in the dim light, and her mouth is drooping into a sneer.

That's when I notice the green bandana hanging out of her pocket and the gun in her hand. And the fact that she's dressed in all black.

"You aren't here to save me." Fear fills my body like water being poured into a glass. "You're here to kill me. This is all connected to you, isn't it?"

She raises her eyebrows. "Keep going. You can piece this together. You're smart."

Sentences run through my head. Articles I've read. Slowly, the important facts bob to the surface.

"You're behind the wolf killings, not Porter."

She laughs. "See. I have faith in you. Porter was a necessary sacrifice. I needed someone to do the work for me, and he was the only one I could pay off."

My legs start to tremble and my wound throbs. I think about all I know and realize it was there the whole time.

"You know vet medicine. Your dad was a vet, and you worked for him. I saw the picture. You've been helping euthanize those poor wolves. But why?"

She pokes the gun into my side. "You can talk, but you need to keep moving. We don't have much time."

She pushes me forward so hard I almost trip in the thick snow. My breath quickens. Why would a beautiful and powerful woman like Katie Reynolds sabotage a conservation program of which she's the head? Then it hits me.

"You have a lot to lose, don't you?" I stop and feel the gun bump into my back. I muster up the nerve to turn and face her. The gun is now pointed directly at my chest. "*Mandy*."

She frowns. "How did you know that?"

I clutch my head as the information all falls into place. "Oh my God. You own Cardinal, Inc. Katie Amanda Reynolds, or should I say CEO-at-large Mandy Smith. You've been going by Katie Reynolds because that was your dad's name. But your mom remarried, changed her name, and you were adopted by your stepdad. So your name changed, too."

She pushes me again. "Shut up and keep walking."

I stumble backward. "You're pretending to support conservation and the red wolf program, but the whole time you've been sabotaging it. Then eBuild can start developing again." I point to the forest we're walking through. "This is prime real estate."

Her voice is hard. "A few wolves aren't worth millions. Not to me."

"So this is about money?"

"Isn't everything?"

I turn and start walking again, but I move a bit slower, letting her get closer to me, waiting for her to get within range of my back kick.

"So what now?" I say. "You think someone won't figure this out? I did. Sweeney will find me."

"He'll find you dead. And he'll think Al got to you. That's what they'll all think — that Al is back. They'll never think I did it. I'll get rid of you and slip back to work with an alibi. And by the time they find you, your body will be cold, and Al will be gone."

I think over everything. "That's why you didn't give the syringe to Sweeney."

She kicks my heel. "That was where Porter went wrong. The fool. If he'd done what I asked and not gotten careless, everyone would have suspected Seth died of hypothermia. You weren't supposed to be out there anyway. No one was going to find Seth until spring. Until you had to continue butting in. You never know when to stop."

I laugh. "Guess you don't know me as well as you think."

"True. I will give you that." Katie huffs in frustration. "I never expected you to volunteer after all the things your family went through. That was where I went wrong. But then I thought you wouldn't last a day after you found that wolf."

"I don't scare off easily."

She pushes me again. Hard.

I fall forward in the snow and land on both arms. I scream out in pain as my right arm turns to fire.

Katie grabs my hood and yanks me to my feet. Tears are streaming down my face now.

I stand and face her, teeth gritted. "I told Sweeney about the syringe. He knows you have it. He'll come for it, and he'll know you're lying if you say you don't have it."

She holds up a syringe. "You mean this one? Or the fake one in my office I'll give him in the morning when he comes to tell me of your unfortunate death."

I clutch my arm. It's wet and warm. My fall started the bleeding again.

"So Al was never here? This whole time you've been pretending?" I hunch over a little in pain.

"Perfect, isn't it? Al is long gone from this place. He'll never be found. But I had no idea how well it would work. I didn't realize the power he had over everyone around here."

With that stupid comment, I swing my leg up and clip Reynolds right under the chin. She is so taken off guard, the gun pops out of her hand, and she falls backward on the ground. I bend over to grab the weapon, but she charges at me, practically growling. She tackles me to the ground, and I yelp in pain. But before she can pin me, I flip her off and struggle to my feet. Even though my legs are wobbling and my stance is far less than steady, at least I'm up. I shake away the stars in my vision.

"I won't let you get away with this," I say.

She swings and punches me in the jaw. I stumble backward as she hisses at me.

"You don't have a choice. You think I'm going to let some brat teenager bring me down? Do you realize how hard I've worked?"

She punches me in the stomach, and I double over, almost hurling into the snow.

"Do you know how long it's taken me to get the respect I deserve? To get all of this?" She waves to her house.

At that moment, I side kick her in the ribs. She grunts this time and stumbles, falling to one knee.

I smile. "Do you realize what I've been through? Do you think I'm going to lose my dad and fight off some madman poacher, bring down a family friend, and then let a bratty, rich woman beat me down?"

I punch her in the stomach and grab her arm, twisting it up behind her. She elbows me in the gut, and I release her, putting my hands on my knees and coughing. I lunge and grip around her neck, but she's slightly taller than me and is able to flip me onto my back. The air shoots out of my lungs, and I gasp for breath.

Her face appears above me, and she points a gun in my face. "I win. Now get up."

I writhe in the freezing cold snow, unable to stand. She tosses the green bandana onto my chest as I continue gasping for air.

"To be honest, you should have died with your daddy. But this time, it all ends for you, Grace. I'll go back, and they'll mourn you. The wolf project will be cancelled, and eBuild will develop these mountains the way my company has always planned. And I will be even richer than before. Best part is I will get away with it all."

A gun cocks behind us. "Over my dead body."

# Survival Skill #33

*Never underestimate the size of an opponent.*
*Everyone is capable of strength, speed, skill, and the*
*will to defend themselves.*

𝒬 smile and look back.

Birdee is standing a few feet away, wearing her Wellies and a straw hat while holding a rifle. She fires one shot into the air and breaks the silence of the forest. The woods awaken and sound off a natural warning. Birds scatter and squawk in different directions as the shot reverberates through the trees.

Birdee walks toward us. "Put the gun down and get away from her."

I smile up at Katie. "I'm not the only person you underestimated. Guess someone else knows your plan now, too. What now? Your Al story won't hold up anymore unless you kill both of us."

"That can be arranged. What's one more?" Katie points the gun at Birdee and slowly backs up. "I'm not going down without a fight."

Birdee takes a step forward. "And you ain't going. So it looks like it's a duel to the death."

I force myself to my feet and hobble over to Birdee.

She glances at me quickly, then back at Katie. "Go get Sweeney."

I watch Katie, who's eyeing Birdee and me as if waiting for one of us to make a wrong move.

"I'm not leaving you out here," I say.

Birdee grits her teeth but keeps her eyes on Katie. "Don't argue, I said... go."

Even though my whole body is rejecting any movement, I muster up all my strength to sprint up the hill, afraid of hearing a shot ring out behind me. Pain jolts through my arm, and my stomach throbs. I scream Mo's name at the top of my lungs. As I reach the house, he comes tearing outside with Sweeney hobbling behind.

Mo looks panic stricken. "Bloody hell! Grace!"

I collapse into him. My head is woozy and my vision is blurry. I point down the hill but can't catch my breath. Sweeney glances around with his gun raised, protecting Mo and me.

"We heard a shot," he says.

Mo touches the bruises forming on my face. "What happened?"

I force out words. "Katie attacked me. Birdee's with her." I gasp for oxygen as Sweeney races down the hill. I push Mo away. "Go! Sweeney's hurt. He can't handle Reynolds. She's crazy!"

He looks torn. "I promised I wouldn't leave you."

I'm sobbing now. Gasps and tears punctuate my words and broken sentences. "Please, Mo. I can't lose Birdee too."

Mo yells. "Wyn!"

Wyn bolts onto the deck and points after Sweeney. "Go! I got her." He hops down the stairs and limps toward me.

"Be sure this time." Mo kisses me and darts off into the dark woods without even saying goodbye.

I try to push up so I can go with him, but my body gives out. Just as Wyn reaches my side, another shot goes off. I scream and bury my head in his jacket, wailing.

He strokes my hair. "It's fine, G. I promise."

I shake my head and cry, feeling like I've just lost everything for the second time.

He whispers in my ear as he rocks me. "It'll be okay."

I mumble, "How do you know?"

"Because this time, no matter what happens, I'm here."

I sniff and pull back, nodding. "What about Mo?"

He holds me tight. "Doesn't matter. You're my friend, and I love you. I'm not going to let you down again."

I hug him tight. "Promise?"

He pulls back my face and kisses my forehead. "Scout's honor."

I sit there on the snow with my eyes still on the woods, scanning the trees. Waiting for anything to tell me what happened. Waiting for Birdee and Mo to come walking out of the woods.

Together.

Alive.

But the minutes pass slowly, and no one shows.

I'm afraid my world has just collapsed.

Again.

# Survival Skill #34

*Sometimes, because of emotional stress, we may expect dangers or threats that might not really exist.*

ℐt seems like forever until Sweeney walks out of the woods.

Followed by Mo.

I wait and watch the tree line. Praying. Hoping. Waiting for Birdee.

But she doesn't show.

Mo and Sweeney approach me, and their faces are long. Neither can look me in the eye.

I search them for the truth, but I can't even force out the question forming in my mind, *is Birdee dead?* I start to cry, and Wyn holds me tight.

Before they say anything, Birdee's straw hat bobs out of the trees. She has her rifle slung over her shoulder like she's in some kind of Western movie. I rip out of Wyn's arms and push through the pain to my feet, stumbling down the hill. I throw myself on her, laughing and crying at the same time.

"Birdee! Thank God you're alive."

She catches me and drops her gun. "Shoot, I might be old, but I ain't gonna let some crooked lady take me down. No, siree. She thinks I was bluffing. I showed her. No one messes with my family."

Squeezing her, I can't stop laughing and crying. "You shot her?"

"Didn't have the pleasure. Dang lady shot herself. Took the easy way out, if you ask me." She pulls me back and looks

268

at my face before noticing my shoulder. "Jesus, Chicken, you look like crap. Let's get you inside and out of this weather. Make you some tea."

"Sounds good."

She helps me up the hill until we reach Mo.

He smiles at Birdee. "I'll take it from here, Ms. Birdee."

Birdee nods and grins. "I bet you will, young whippersnapper."

Mo scoops me up, and I wrap my arms around his neck and look over his shoulder at my grandmother. She points to his butt and gives me the thumbs up. I try not to giggle and give her a dirty look as she walks with a limping Agent Sweeney and a hobbling Wyn.

I bury my face in Mo's neck. His familiar scent of musk surrounds me, and I clutch on to him the way a monkey clings to its mother as he carries me inside the warm house. I don't realize how cold I am until I'm finally sitting in front of the fire, feeling my body start to thaw.

"What happened out there?" Mo asks.

I tell everyone about Katie and Cardinal, Inc., and her real name. I tell them how she was having Porter euthanize the wolves so the Relocation Program would be cancelled and she could build again.

"She was paying Porter to do her dirty work. He was just as bad as she was," I say.

"Maybe not." Mo looks at Sweeney. "Explain what happened to Porter."

"What do you mean?" I ask.

Sweeney checks his side and grimaces. "Porter never fired a shot. Someone else was shooting at us."

My head hurts. "How can that be?"

"He had a revolver, but all six bullets were in it. Katie was shooting and setting him up."

Sweeney holds up the syringe and a bullet casing. "We'll confirm everything once I send these to the lab. I bet the bullet that killed Porter was Katie's."

I shrug. "It doesn't matter. I know what happened. Katie was paying off Porter to kill the wolves to stop the project. Seth must have seen Porter do something, so Porter left him out there. The whole time Katie was trying to scare me off by having me think it was Al. Porter got careless and dropped the syringe, so she had to go to Plan B. She didn't want that tested and linked back to her."

When I take a breath, everyone is staring at me.

Birdee smiles. "Wait, who are the agents in this room?"

Mo laughs and Sweeney sits down. "It's a shame. I liked her, too. She seemed like a talented lady."

I scoff. "Yeah, talented in guns, euthanasia, and manipulation."

I see something flash in Sweeney's face that tells me they might have had more than just a working relationship. He catches my eye, but I don't say anything. He's probably confused enough.

Wyn says, "I can't believe she's dead."

Sweeney nods. "Trust me. She's dead. I checked. People have a way of coming back around here." He looks at Mo when his phone beeps, and he stares at it for a minute.

His expression changes a few times — shock, confusion, anger — until he looks at me. Then a look of fear washes over him.

I sit up. "What is it? Did something happen?"

"That was headquarters."

Mo leans forward. "Yeah, and?"

Sweeney reads his phone again as if he's making sure he read what he thinks he read. "I can't believe it. I must say I did not see this one coming."

Wyn urges him. "Well, don't keep us in suspense! This is better than reading Hardy Boys."

Sweeney stares at me. "I did a background check on Mandy Smith. I don't know how to say this, but... Katie was Al's stepsister."

My mouth drops open. "What?"

Mo runs his hands through his hair. "Are you sure?"

Sweeney nods. "Her stepfather — the man her mom remarried — was Al's father. Evidently, they were very close. Guess that's where Smith comes in."

I drop my head into my hands. "So that's what she meant. She said Al wasn't here, and he was long gone. That must mean they've been in touch."

Sweeney nods. "It seems she's been depositing large sums into a bank account overseas ever since the week after your dad died."

Mo stands and paces. "Does that mean Katie was involved in the bear-poaching ring, too?"

My head swirls, and I feel the room tip. "She was responsible for my dad's death?"

Sweeney looks at me. "I'm not sure. But whether or not she was, now Al's going to think you're responsible for hers."

Birdee looks frightened and grips my hand. "Are you saying Al is going to come back for Grace?"

"No." Sweeney eyes Mo and me. "But until we find him, Grace is in still in danger."

# Epilogue

*No matter how prepared you are, nothing is controllable.*

Nothing should be caged.

Whether or not it's in danger, every living thing deserves to be free. Reserve or not, it just feels wrong. I watch the mama wolf lick her new cub, her reddish fur flickering in the light breeze.

"I could watch them all day," I say.

Mo throws a log on the small fire he's built outside the Relocation Center's fence.

"Seems like that's how long we've been sitting here, because my bum is starting to go numb," he says.

I sigh and lean my back against the fence. "Sorry. I just feel bad they're back at the center again. It would have been nice to know wolves were still roaming these mountains. It's like just as they were free, they got barred up again. It's not fair."

"The center said they'd release them again in the spring. It's a rough winter anyway. They'll get a second chance when it warms up."

I smile. "Just like we did."

He winks. "Exactly."

The wolves bound around together in the snow, biting, wrestling.

"Strange how when things seem over, something beautiful comes along," I say.

Mo drapes the blanket around my shoulders and kisses my cheek. "I was just thinking that."

He sits down on the log next to me.

I smile at him. "Thank you."

He tilts his head and stares at me intently. "For what, Blossom? The compliment? The fire? Or for keeping you warm?"

"For taking care of me. For not leaving me." I pause and curl into him. "For putting up with me. But more importantly, for coming back."

He shrugs. "It's just the assignment."

I eye him. "A 24/7 assignment?"

"If the *client* wishes."

I grin. "Oh, she does. If he does exactly what she says."

He nods in a regal way. "Ha, yes. I figured. That is quite the task... and my pleasure." He twists a piece of my long dark hair around his finger like a corkscrew. "I'm sorry I wasted all that time. That I wasn't here with you."

"You did what you had to do." I lean my forehead against his. "Just don't do it again."

He throws his head back and laughs. "That is a deal, Blossom."

We stare at each other for a few minutes. He slowly traces his finger down the side of my face, along my jawbone, down my nose. Then he lightly touches my lips. He curls his finger under my chin and pulls me forward into him. My body automatically leans as if Mo's programmed me to go to him.

He stops and lets his mouth hover over mine. "I love you, Grace."

I smile, and my heart skips along in my chest. "I love you, too."

He presses his lips into mine, and we melt together. He pulls me onto his lap, and I straddle him. I can hear his breathing intensify as our kisses grow deeper and our tongues entwine. My belly churns a little with excitement. I would love to go to the next level with Mo. I've never felt about anyone the way I feel about him. I just want to open myself up and let him investigate every nook and cranny.

His warm tongue slides across my cold lips. I hear him tell me he loves me again. He grabs my waist and hips as we hold each other. Eventually he pulls back.

"You drive me crazy," he says.

I play-slap him. "I'm not sure that's a good thing."

He kisses my neck. "I mean in a good way."

I lift my head and look at the sky as he kisses my neck. Little white flakes sprinkle along his dark hair, reminding me of the Sno-Caps dad and I used to buy at the drive-in movie. I stick out my tongue to catch them. Mo reaches up with his mouth and covers mine.

I bite his lip playfully. "We have to go. It's getting colder."

He groans a little and kisses me at the same time he talks. "Hm. I didn't notice. Feels hot to me."

I pull back. "Seriously. Birdee's gonna come looking for me if we don't get home."

That gets him. His eyes widen, and he practically throws me off his lap. "Sure don't want that. I saw what happened last time she came. Ms. Gunslinger."

I jump up and grab the blanket as he snuffs out the fire. "You sure you're up for meeting my mom? This is going to be a long story."

"Abso-bloody-lutely." Mo grabs my hand and runs me to his Jeep.

"If she likes you, you might get invited to Christmas dinner."

"I'll be on my best behavior. Use my English charm."

"Worked on me. I'd say you're a shoo-in." I smile. I'm actually starting to look forward to the holidays a little.

Having Mo around will make things different. At this point different is good.

He opens my door and then runs around to the driver's side, hopping in and rubbing his gloves together. He leans over and puckers up, closing his eyes. "Just one more, and I'll be set for at least another hour."

"You are bad." I put both mittens on his face and kiss him a couple of times on his nose, cheek, and lips.

I sit back in my seat as he hovers there with his eyes still closed. "Just drive, Romeo."

He shakes his head as if he was dazed. "Yes, ma'am."

"Try to stay on the right side of the road."

He smiles as he starts the Jeep. "Wait. My right or yours?"

"You know what I mean, English boy."

As he drives down the road, I stare out the window. Gloomy clouds fill the sky, telling me more storms are coming before things clear up. Colored Christmas lights dot the grayish horizon as everyone prepares for the holiday.

My mood changes as fast as the weather. I sigh and review everything that's happened over the last year. This time last year, I was helping Dad cut down a tree for the holidays and sneaking tastes of Mom's pies. And carving a bird figurine for Birdee.

What a difference a year makes.

Mo's hand cups my knee. "You got quiet all of a sudden."

"Just a bad feeling, that's all."

His phone beeps, but he ignores it. "Wanna talk about it?"

"Nothing to talk about. Just same ole stuff."

He puts his hand by my face and moves my hair back. "I'm sorry."

I grab his hand and hold it tight. "Only good thing that came from all this… is you."

"Ditto, Blossom." His phone beeps again. "I better get this." He pulls over to check his text messages. His face changes and he looks at me.

"Who is it?" I ask.

"Sweeney."

I smile and put my head against the headrest. "Another mission impossible?"

Mo faces me. "Not exactly."

I watch the lines on his face deepen, and he runs both hands through his hair. "Did someone die?"

It's sad that's my standard question these days.

Mo's face softens, and he faces me with his seatbelt still on. "Crumbs. No, of course not."

I get him to look into my eyes. "Then what?"

"Al was spotted."

I did not see that coming. My whole body tenses as if I've turned to stone. I swallow and hold back what I really feel. "That's good, right? Now we know where he is."

He shakes his head and cups my hand. "No. They lost him. But…"

"But what?"

"He knows about Katie's death." Mo furrows his eyebrows. "Sweeney thinks he's headed this way."

I stammer. "When?"

He puts both hands back on the steering wheel. "I don't know, but I have to take you to Sweeney."

He shifts the Jeep into drive and merges back onto the deserted road. The rest of the way to the USFWS station, Mo stays eerily quiet. I lean against the window and watch the street reflectors pass the wheels.

"Mo?"

"Hmm."

"What do you think this means?"

He looks at me out of the corner of his eye, but keeps his face forward. "I'm not sure."

I sit sideways so I'm facing him. "But what do you *think*?"

He sighs. "I think Sweeney wants to send you somewhere. Away from here."

I shake my head. "I'm not leaving my family. My home. You. Because of Al. I'm not running any more."

He grips my hand and zooms down the road. "Let's just wait and see what happens, Blossom."

I focus on the horizon that has quickly grown dark as night. Tears fill my eyes. It seems as soon as I find a sliver of happiness, clouds roll in and cover it with massive storms.

Maybe after all this my life will never be easy again.

Never peaceful. Never normal.

From here on in, I have a feeling it will be even more uncontrollable.

Unless, somehow, I get to Al before he gets to me.

# *THE END*

Dear Reader,

When I started this series, I had no idea if it would ever see the light of day. I needed to continue publishing books in the *Nature of Grace* series with the hope of making a difference in this world.

*Uncontrollable* touches on the plight of the red wolf. These animals once roamed freely, but are now on the verge of being extinct with the majority being kept in captivity. The idea came to me when I read an article about the gray wolves being released in Colorado. However, no matter how many they released, the numbers in Colorado remained low. I always wondered if people were silently killing the wolves for unknown reasons.

*Uncontrollable* is my way of shedding a ray of light on a problem we don't know much about. The plight of the red wolf is very real. They have a hard time living in the wild, yet I can't imagine a world where they always have to live in captivity.

With this book, I hope to create awareness around their story and struggles.

Just as in *Untraceable*, this book is still thrilling and mysterious with a strong girl character, two hot boys, and some great kissing. :) But in the end, my purpose is to inform.

I hope you like reading *Uncontrollable* as much as the first. If you find yourself bothered or angry with some of the abuse to wolves in this book, please see my "Call to Action" section so you can find your own way of making a difference.

I would love to hear from you anytime! You can email me at shelli@srjohannes.com or visit me online at srjohannes.com.

Best,
*Shelli*

# Call to Action!

You can make a difference!

Here are some quick and easy actions you can take from your own home.

## To find out more about the red wolves in *Uncontrollable*:

1. Find out more about the <u>Red Wolf Recovery Program</u>
2. Learn about the <u>Red Wolf Re-establishment Program</u> at Alligator River National Refuge.
3. To <u>sign a petition</u> to bring back the red wolves or to <u>save them from extinction</u>
4. Learn about the <u>timeline</u> of the red wolf

## To help the black bears in *Untraceable*:

1) Sign <u>my petition on Change.org</u> to close the bear pits in Cherokee, North Carolina.
2) Find out how the game show host, <u>Bob Barker</u>, has been working to <u>close the bear pits</u>.
3) Help <u>Peta</u> in their work to close Cherokee bear pits.
4) Join organizations that are helping to stop the illegal trade and poaching of the black bear such as <u>WSA</u>.
5) Find out more from WWF about <u>bear illegal trading</u> and the <u>bile trade</u> in Asia.
6) Find out about some campaigns to stop illegal <u>wildlife trade</u>.

# Shout Outs!

First, I'd like to thank all the wonderful bloggers for always supporting me and for everything they do for books every day.

To all the teachers, librarians, and booksellers for supporting an indie book.

Thank you to all The Bookanistas, The Hopefuls, and SCBWI for finding a way to support me.

To the Indelibles, for helping me down this path. For your undying support, awesome advice, and brilliant debates.

To Jennifer Jabaley, Kate Tilton, Graeme Stone, Kimberly Derting for reading my book(s) and offering constructive feedback.

To Vania, once again, for her creativity and bringing this book to life with her beautiful photos.

To Megan Miranda, Katie Anderson, and Jessica DeHart, for the advice, daily chats, and laughs.

A special and heartfelt thanks to Kimberly Derting for always believing in me and being there when I needed to brainstorm, vent, or celebrate.

To my assistant/intern Kate, for always taking my calls, picking up my slack, and staying so positive in the midst of my "crazy" times.

To my family, thank you for cheering me on by pawning off my book to every friend and foe you have ever had. ☺ Every sale helps!

A special thanks to my lovely mom for being my best friend and biggest fan and for always reading my stuff whenever I ask.

To my sweet dog Charley for lying quietly at my feet while I work.

To my babies, Madelyn and Gray, I thank God every day for you because you make me a better person.

To Ali, my everything, for always dropping everything and staying up late just as many nights as I do to help me with all the extras only you can do best. But most of all, for loving me – no matter what.

Most importantly, to all my awesome readers/fans, I am so grateful you spent the time and money to give my book a chance. Thank you for all your letters!

And last, but certainly not least, to the Big Man in the Sky, for always guiding me down the right path even if (when) I resisted.

Made in the USA
Lexington, KY
14 June 2014